A moment to escape

Sido hadn't dared move since the count had left. Yann found her still sitting on the floor, her head in her hands. She looked up at him.

"Where have you been? Count Kalliovski was here."

"It took longer than I thought. We'll be gone in a minute." He went straight to the bed and pulled back the covers. "Wake up," he said gently, shaking Têtu back into life as he helped him to his feet. He was pleased to see that the dwarf's eyes were purple-black once more and his skin no longer pale.

"Where am I?" said Têtu, who for a moment thought that he must have woken from a bad dream. Yann said something to him in a language Sido had never heard before. Têtu gulped as the memory of what had happened came back to him.

Yann turned back to look at Sido, sitting crumpled and abandoned on the floor, and for a moment he had an over-whelming desire to take her with them, to save her from being one of the headless ones.

There was a knock at the door. Sido scrambled to her feet. Quickly Yann and the dwarf disappeared behind the screen and through the panel, sliding it back into place just as the count entered, followed by a footman carrying a tray with Sido's supper.

OTHER BOOKS YOU MAY ENJOY

the red necklace

A Story of the French Revolution

Sally Gardner

speak

An Imprint of Penguin Group (USA) Inc.

SPEAK

Published by the Penguin Group

Penguin Group (USA) Inc., 345 Hudson Street, New York, New York 10014, U.S.A.

Penguin Group (Canada), 90 Eglinton Avenue East, Suite 700, Toronto, Ontario, Canada M4P 2Y3
(a division of Pearson Penguin Canada Inc.)

Penguin Books Ltd, 80 Strand, London WC2R 0RL, England

Penguin Ireland, 25 St Stephen's Green, Dublin 2, Ireland (a division of Penguin Books Ltd)

Penguin Group (Australia), 250 Camberwell Road, Camberwell, Victoria 3124, Australia
(a division of Pearson Australia Group Pty Ltd)

Penguin Books India Pvt Ltd, 11 Community Centre, Panchsheel Park, New Delhi - 110 017, India

Penguin Group (NZ), 67 Apollo Drive, Rosedale, North Shore 0632, New Zealand
(a division of Pearson New Zealand Ltd.)

Penguin Books (South Africa) (Pty) Ltd, 24 Sturdee Avenue, Rosebank, Johannesburg 2196, South Africa

Registered Offices: Penguin Books Ltd, 80 Strand, London WC2R 0RL, England

First published in Great Britain by Orion Children's Books, 2007
First published in the United States of America by Dial Books, a member of Penguin Group (USA) Inc., 2008
Published by Speak, an imprint of Penguin Group (USA) Inc., 2009

3 5 7 9 10 8 6 4 2

Copyright © Sally Gardner, 2007
All rights reserved

THE LIBRARY OF CONGRESS HAS CATALOGED THE DIAL BOOKS EDITION AS FOLLOWS:
Gardner, Sally.
The red necklace : a story of the French Revolution / Sally Gardner.
p. cm.
Summary: In the late eighteenth century, Sido, the twelve-year-old daughter of a self-indulgent marquis,
and Yann, a fourteen-year-old Gypsy orphan raised to perform in a magic show,
face a common enemy at the start of the French Revolution.
ISBN: 978-0-8037-3100-4 (hc)
1. France—History—Revolution, 1789–1799—Juvenile fiction.
[1. France—History—Revolution, 1789–1799—Fiction. 2. Social classes—Fiction. 3. Romanies—Fiction.
4. Orphans—Fiction. 5. Magic tricks—Fiction. 6. Adventure and adventurers—Fiction.] I. Title.
PZ7.G179335Red 2008 [Fic]—dc22 2007039813

Speak ISBN 978-0-14-241488-0

Printed in the United States of America

Designed by Kimi Weart
Text set in Centaur

To *Weavel*

my darling brother Stephen, the first person
I ever told my stories to.

This is for you. I hope you enjoy it.

With all my love

Turtle

This is Paris; here the winds of change are blowing, whispering their discontent into the very hearts of her citizens. A Paris waiting for the first slow turn of a wheel that will bring with it a revolution the like of which Europe has never known. In the coming year the people will be called upon to play their part in the tearing down of the Bastille, in the destruction of the old regime, in the stopping of the clocks.

This is where the devil goes walking, looking with interest in at the window of Dr. Guillotin, who works night and day to perfect his humane killing machine, sharpening his angled blade on the innocent necks of sheep. Little does the earnest doctor know that his new design will be center stage, a bloody altarpiece in the drama that is about to unfold.

But wait, not so fast. King Louis XVI and his queen, Marie

Antoinette, are still outside Paris, at Versailles. This is the winter of 1789, one of the worst in living memory. Jack Frost has dug his fingers deep into the heart of this frozen city, so that it looks almost unrecognizable under its thick blanket of snow.

All still appears as it should be. All has yet to break . . .

chapter one

$\mathscr{H}$ere, then, is where our story starts, in a run-down theater on the rue du Temple, with a boy called Yann Margoza, who was born with a gift for knowing what people were thinking, and an uncanny ability to throw his voice.

Yann had a sharp, intelligent face, olive skin, a mop of jet-black hair, and eyes dark as midnight, with two stars shining in them. He was a solitary boy who enjoyed nothing better than being left alone to explore whatever city or town he was in, until it felt to him like a second skin.

For the past few months the theater had been home to Yann and his friend and mentor, the dwarf Têtu.

Têtu acted as assistant to his old friend Topolain the magician, and together they traveled all over France, performing. Without ever appearing on stage, he could move objects at will like a sorcerer, while Topolain fronted the show and did tricks of his own. Yann was fourteen now, and still didn't understand how Têtu did it, even though he had helped behind the scenes since he was small.

Têtu's age was anyone's guess and, as he would say, no one's business. He compensated for his small size and his strange high-pitched voice with a fierce intelligence. Nothing missed his canny eye, nobody made a fool of him. He could speak many languages, but would not say where he came from.

It had been Têtu's idea to invest their savings in the making of the wooden Pierrot.

The clown was built to designs carefully worked out by Têtu; it had a white-painted face and glass eyes, and was dressed in a baggy blue top and trousers.

Topolain had not been sure that he wanted to perform with a doll.

"A doll!" exclaimed Têtu, throwing his arms up in disgust. "This is no doll! This is an automaton! It will make our fortunes. I tell you, no one will be able to fathom its secret, and you, my dear friend, will never tell."

Topolain rose to the challenge. The result had been a sensation. Monsieur Aulard, manager of the Theater du Temple, had taken them on and for the past four months they had played to full houses. Monsieur Aulard couldn't remember a show being sold out like this before. In these dark times, it struck him as nothing short of a miracle.

The Pierrot had caught people's imaginations. There were many different opinions going around the neighborhood cafés of the Marais as to what strange alchemy had created it. Some thought that it was controlled by magic. More practical minds wondered if it was clockwork, or if there was someone hidden inside. This theory was soon dismissed, as every night Topolain would invite a member of the audience up on stage to look for himself. All who saw it were agreed that it was made from solid wood. Even if it had been hollow, there was no space inside for anyone to hide.

Yet not only could the Pierrot walk and talk, it could also, as Topolain told the astonished audience every night, see into the heart of every man and woman there, and know their darkest secrets. It understood their plight even better than the King of France.

For the grand finale, Topolain would perform the trick he was best known for—the magic bullet. He would ask a member of the audience to come up on stage and fire a pistol at him. To much rolling of drums, he would catch the bullet in his hand, proclaiming that he had drunk from the cup of everlasting life. After seeing what he could do with the automaton, the audience did not doubt him. Maybe such a great magician as this could indeed trick the Grim Reaper.

Every evening after the final curtain had fallen and the applause had died away, Yann would wait in the wings until the theater was empty. His job then was to remove the small table on which had been placed the pistol and the bullet.

Tonight the stage felt bitterly cold. Yann heard a noise as a blast of wind howled its mournful way into the stalls, and peered out into the darkened auditorium. It was eerily deserted, yet he could have sworn he heard someone whispering in the shadows.

"Hello?" he called out.

"You all right?" asked Didier the caretaker, walking onto the stage. He was a giant of a man with a deep, gravelly voice and a vacant moonlike face. He had worked so long at the theater that he had become part of the building.

"I thought I heard someone in the stalls," said Yann.

Didier stood by the edge of the proscenium arch and glared menacingly into the gloom. He reminded Yann of a statue that had come to life and wasn't on quite the same scale as the rest of humanity.

"There's no one there. More than likely it's a rat. Don't worry, I'll get the blighter."

He disappeared into the wings, humming as he went, leaving Yann alone. Yann felt strangely uneasy. The sooner he was gone from here the better, he thought to himself.

There! The whispering was louder this time.

"Who's there?" shouted Yann. "Show yourself."

Then he heard a woman's soft voice, whispering to him in Romany, the language he and Têtu spoke privately together. He nearly jumped out of his skin, for it felt as if she were standing right next to him. He could see no one, yet he could almost feel her breath like a gentle breeze upon his neck.

She was saying, "The devil's own is on your trail. Run like the wind."

Topolain's dressing room was at the end of the corridor on the first floor. They had been moved down to what Monsieur Aulard grandly called a dressing room for superior actors. It was as shabby as all the other dressing rooms, but it was a little larger and had the decided privilege of having a fireplace. The log basket was all but empty and the fire near defeated by the cold. The room was lit with tallow candles that let drifts of black smoke rise from the wick, turning the ceiling dark brown in color.

Topolain was sitting looking at his painted face in a mirror. He was a stout man with doughy features.

"How did you know the shoemaker had a snuffbox in his pocket, Yann?" he asked.

Yann shrugged. "I could hear his thoughts loud and clear," he said.

Têtu, who was kneeling on the floor carefully packing away the wooden Pierrot, listened and smiled, knowing that Yann's abilities were still unpredictable. Sometimes, without being aware of it, he could read people's minds; sometimes he could even see into the future.

Yann went over to where Têtu was kneeling.

"I need to talk to you."

Topolain put his head to one side and listened. Someone was coming up the stairs. "Shhh."

A pair of heavy boots could be heard on the bare wooden boards, coming toward the dressing room. There was a rap at the door. Topolain jumped up in surprise, spilling his wine onto the calico cloth on the dressing table so that it turned dark red.

A huge man stood imposingly in the doorway, his smart black tailored coat emphasizing his bulk and standing out against the shabbiness of his surroundings. Yet it was his face, not his garments, that caught Yann's attention. It was covered in scars like the map of a city you would never wish to visit. His left eye was the color of rancid milk. The pupil, dead and black, could be seen beneath its curdled surface. His other eye was bloodshot. He was a terrifying apparition.

The man handed Topolain a card. The magician took it, careful to wipe the sweat from his hands before he did so. As he read the name Count Kalliovski, he felt a quiver of excitement. He knew that Count Kalliovski was one of the wealthiest men in Paris, and that he was famed for having the finest collection of automata in Europe.

"This is an honor indeed," said Topolain.

"I am steward to Count Kalliovski. I am known as Milkeye," said the man. Milkeye held out a leather purse before him as one might hold a bone out to a dog.

"My master wants you to entertain his friends tonight at the château of the Marquis de Villeduval. If Count Kalliovski is pleased with your performance"—here he jangled the purse—"this will be your reward. The carriage is waiting. We would ask for haste."

Yann knew exactly what Topolain was going to say next.

"I shall be delighted. I shall be with you just as fast as I can get myself and my assistants together."

"Haste," Milkeye repeated sharply. "I don't want our horses freezing to death out there. They are valuable."

The door closed behind him with a thud, so that the thin walls shook.

As soon as they were alone, Topolain lifted Têtu off his feet and danced him around the room.

"This is what we have been dreaming of! With this invitation the doors of grand society will be open to us. We will each have a new wig, the finest silk waistcoats from Lyon, and rings the size of gulls' eggs!"

He looked at his reflection in the mirror, added a touch of rouge to his cheeks, and picked up his hat and the box that contained the pistol.

"Are we ready to amaze, astound, and bewilder?"

"Wait, wait!" pleaded Yann. He pulled Têtu aside and said quietly, "When I went to clear up this evening I heard a voice speaking Romany, saying, 'The devil's own is on your trail. Run like the wind.'"

"What are you whispering about?" asked Topolain. "Come on, we'll be late."

Yann said desperately, "Please, let's not go. I have a bad feeling."

"Not so fast, Topolain," said Têtu. "The boy may be right."

"Come on, the two of you!" said Topolain. "This is our destiny calling. Greatness lies ahead of us! I've waited a lifetime for this. Stop worrying. Tonight we will be princes."

Yann and Têtu knew that it was useless to say more. They carried the long box with the Pierrot in it down the steep stairs, Yann trying to chase away the image of a coffin from his mind.

At the bottom, fixed to the wall, was what looked like a sentry box. In it sat old Madame Manou, whose task it was to guard the stage door.

"Well," she said, leaning out and seeing that they had the Pierrot with them, "so you're going off in that grand carriage, are you? I suppose it belongs to some fine aristocrat who has more money than sense. Dragging you off on a night like this when all good men should be making for their beds!"

"Tell Monsieur Aulard where we're going," said Têtu, and he handed her the card that Milkeye had given Topolain.

All Topolain was thinking was that maybe the king and queen would be there. The thought was like a fur coat against the cold, which wrapped itself around him as he walked out into the bitter night, Yann's and Têtu's anxieties forgotten.

The carriage, lacquered beetle-black, with six fine white horses, stood waiting, shiny bright against the gray of the old snow, which was now being gently covered by a fresh muslin layer of snowflakes. This carriage looked to Yann as if it had been sent from another world.

Each of them was given foot and hand warmers and a fur rug for the journey ahead. Topolain lay back enveloped in the red velvet upholstery, with its perfume of expensive sandalwood.

"This is the life, eh?" he said, smiling at Têtu. He looked up at the ceiling. "Oh to be rich, to have the open sky painted inside your carriage!"

Effortlessly the coach made its way down the rue du Temple and past the Conciergerie, and crossed the Pont Neuf. Yann looked along the frozen river Seine out toward the spires of Notre Dame outlined against a blue-black sky. He loved this city with its tall lopsided houses, stained with the grime of centuries, stitched together by narrow alleyways.

The thoroughfares were not paved: They were nothing more than open sewers clogged with manure, blood, and guts. There was a constant clamor, the clang of the blacksmith's anvil, the shouts of the street criers, the confusion of beasts as they were led to slaughter. Yet in amongst this rabbit warren of streets stood the great houses, the pearls of Paris, whose pomp and grandeur were a constant reminder of the absolute power, the absolute wealth of the king.

The inhabitants, for the most part, were crammed into small apartments with no sanitation. Here sunlight was always a stranger. Candles were needed to see anything at all. For that the tallow factories belched out their stinking dragon's breath that hung tonight and every night in a menacing cloud above the smoking chimneys. It was not hard to imagine that the devil himself might take up residence here, or that in this filth of poverty and hunger grew the seeds of revolution.

On they went, out toward St. Germain, along the rue de Sèvres, where the houses began to give way to snowy woods that looked as if they had been covered in a delicate lace.

Topolain had fallen asleep, his mouth open, a dribble of saliva running down his chin. Têtu had his eyes closed as well. Only Yann was wide-awake. The farther away from Paris they went, the more apprehensive he became. Try as he might, he could not shake off a deep sense of foreboding. He wished he had never heard the whispering voice.

"The devil's own is on your trail."

chapter two

$\mathcal{T}$he Marquis de Villeduval's debts were alarming. He took no notice of his financial advisers, who told him that he was on the verge of bankruptcy. He believed there would always be money. It was his birthright. He had been born with expensive tastes and the privileges of nobility. What matter if funds were low? He would simply raise the rents on his estate. This time next year all his problems would be over. In the meantime he would just have to borrow more from Count Kalliovski, who never blinked an eye at the outrageous sums the marquis requested.

This was how he had financed the building of his newest property, a small château halfway between Paris and Versailles, which allowed him easy access to the court and the capital. When he tired of both, he was to be found at the château on the family estate in Normandy. All that he owned was effortlessly perfect; his taste was superb, the bills always shocking.

That evening the marquis was holding a supper party to thank Count Kalliovski for his continuing generosity. The guest list included the great and the good of French society—dukes, princes, counts, cardinals, and bishops. Like the marquis, they all had good reason to be grateful to the count.

But why such generosity? What was there to be gained from it? Count Kalliovski was extremely rich, that was true, a well-traveled, cultivated, and entertaining man. His little black book contained most of the important names and addresses in French society. He was often to be seen out hunting with the king's party, and was rumored to have helped the queen with one of her more embarrassing gambling debts. In return for his constant generosity, he simply asked for those tiny little secrets, the kind of thing you wouldn't even say in the confessional box. All you had to do was whisper them to him and absolution was guaranteed, the money given. He kept his friends like pampered lapdogs. They never suspected that the hand that fed them had also bought their souls.

Many rumors circulated about Kalliovski, which he encouraged. When asked his age he would say he was as old as Charlemagne. When asked about his great black wolfhound, Balthazar, he would say that he had never been without the dog. One thing, though, was certain: Many were his mistresses and no one was his wife.

The secret of his success lay in the absence of emotion. Over the years he had learned how to empty himself of sentiment, to keep himself free of passion. Love he considered to be a blind spot on the map of the soul.

He had an iron-clad heart. His motto was one that should have warned all who knew him of his true nature, but a greedy man only sees the purse of gold before him. Count Kalliovski's motto was simple: Have no mercy, show no mercy.

For the marquis's part, he was in awe of the count, fascinated by him. If he was honest with himself, something he avoided at all costs, he was more than a little jealous of him. Tonight, though, he wanted to impress the count. Nothing had been spared to make the celebration a success. Only the finest ingredients were to be used for the banquet. The country might well be starving, but here in his kitchens there was food enough to waste.

He had even gone to the trouble of having his daughter brought home from her convent to satisfy a whim of the count's, who had asked to see her. Why, he could not imagine. He thought little of his only child, and might well have forgotten all about her if it hadn't been for Kalliovski's request. For the marquis considered Sido to be a mark of imperfection upon his otherwise perfect existence.

The marquis's splendid new château stood testament to his secretive nature and his sophisticated taste. Each of its many salons was different. Some were painted with scenes of the Elysian Fields, where nymphs picnicked with the gods. In others, there were gilded rococo mirrors that reflected the many crystal chandeliers. On the first floor all the salons opened up into one another through double doors with marble columns. The effect was a giddy vista of rooms, each one more opulent than the last, and each complemented by sumptuous arrangements of flowers, their colors matching the decoration, all grown in the marquis's hothouses. It might be winter outside, but here the marquis could create spring with narcissi, mimosa, tulips, and lilacs, lit by a thousand candles.

But behind the grand façade of smokescreens and mirrors lay what no eye saw, the narrow, dark, poky corridors that formed the unseen and unsightly varicose veins of the house. They were for the servants' use only. The marquis liked to fancy that an invisible hand served him. And so his army of footmen and maids performed their tasks quietly in felted slippers, like mice behind the skirting boards.

On the day of the party, the Mother Superior told Sido that she was wanted at her father's new château near Paris.

It had been two years since she had last seen him, and for a moment she wondered if he had been taken ill. Her memory of her father was of a cold, unloving man who had little time for his daughter. Sido had grown into a shy, awkward-looking girl who walked with a limp, an unforgivable impediment that reflected badly on the great name of Villeduval. She had lost her mother when she was only three, and for most of her twelve years she had been brought up away from her father at the convent. The marquis had handed her over to the Mother Superior at the tender age of five, with instructions to teach the girl to be less clumsy and to walk without limping, if such a thing were possible.

Her surprise at finding that she was going to the château just for a supper party filled her with excitement and trepidation. As the coach drove away, and the convent doors closed behind her, she hoped passionately that she would never have to see the place again, that this might be the start of a new life where her father would love her at last.

Sido's happiness soon vanished as the coach made its way along the country roads. Peering out of the frosty carriage window, she could hardly recognize the landscape they were driving through. In the thin, blue, watery light, figures seemed to rise out of the snow like ghosts, given shape only by the rags they were wearing. They trudged silently along the side of the road with grim determination. Faces stared at her, registering no hope, all resigned to their fate. Old men, young men, women carrying babies, grandmothers, small weary children, all were ill-equipped for the bitter winter weather as they slowly and painfully made their way toward Paris.

Sido stared at this terrible vision. She knocked on the roof of the carriage, her words sounding hollow and useless. "We should stop and help," she called to Bernard, her father's coachman.

The coach kept on moving.

"Please," Sido called again. "We must help them."

"The whole of France needs help," came the answer. "If we stop for these, there are a hundred more ahead. Best not to look, mademoiselle." But how was it possible to turn your eyes away from such a sea of sadness?

This was the first time that Sido had seen the château. The carriage made its way up a drive bordered by trees. The road was being swept clear of snow by men who stopped to let the coach pass, doffing their hats, the bitter cold making their breath look like dragon smoke. Others were up in the snow-laden branches of the trees, hanging little lanterns that were to be lit later that evening.

Her father's new château looked like a fairy-tale castle, complete with towers and turrets, floating free of the formal gardens that surrounded it.

The coach went around to the servants' entrance, where it came to a halt. The marquis's valet came out to greet her.

"How are you, Luc?" asked Sido, pleased to see a face she recognized.

"Well, mademoiselle." Then, feeling some explanation was due, he went on, "I have been instructed to take you up the back way to your chamber. The marquis does not wish to be disturbed."

Sido followed the valet up a set of cold stone stairs and through a plain wooden door into a long dark corridor. Luc lit one of the candles. It shone a shy light down what seemed a never-ending passageway.

"Where are we going?" asked Sido.

The valet turned around with a finger to his lips. "No talking, mademoiselle."

Sido followed in silence. Every now and again cat's cradles of light shone from one wall to the other, through peepholes. Luc opened a door.

"This will be your bedchamber. The marquis will call you when he is ready."

"What are the corridors for?"

"The marquis does not like to see his servants," said the valet, his face expressionless, and with that he closed the door behind him. It disappeared perfectly into the painted panels so that if you didn't know it was there, it would be impossible to tell.

This was a plain room, paneled in powder blue. The four-poster bed had thick dark blue velvet drapes, a fabric screen stood near a dressing table, and above the fireplace hung a painting of an Italian masked ball. There were no flowers to welcome her, no bowls of fruits, no sweetmeats, though these were given to all the other guests.

For her part, Sido was just grateful to be away from the convent. She stared out of the window. The sky was snow-laden, her breath a shadow on the windowpane, and it saddened her that she could not recall her mother's face.

Hours passed, so that she was wondering if she had been forgotten, when the valet reappeared. "The marquis wants to see you now, mademoiselle."

Sido straightened her skirt, took a deep breath, and concentrated with all her might on not limping as she was taken downstairs. Through an open door she glimpsed the dining room with its seven tall windows and polished parquet floor, its walls painted with exotic birds and vistas of undiscovered lands. The long table, with its silver, china, and cut glass, looked abundant and welcoming, waiting for the fever of conversation, the rustle of silk to bring it to life. Sido felt a shiver of excitement. Tonight she would be sitting at this very table.

The marquis was waiting in his study. He had a large, needy, greedy face that gathered itself into a weak, undefined chin and had about it the promise of perpetual disappointment. He stared down his aristocratic nose at his daughter as if summing up a work of art and finding it wanting.

"I see, Sidonie, that you are not much changed since last we met. A little taller, maybe? Unfortunate. Tallness is unattractive in a girl."

The abruptness of the criticism and the use of her full name made all Sido's skills of navigation abandon her. She felt clumsy and out of place in the marquis's study, which was paneled with gold leaf and filled with valuable objects. She was so fearful of putting a foot wrong that she stepped back, narrowly avoiding a table displaying the marquis's latest acquisition, a collection of scientific instruments.

"Look where you're going!" His voice was sharp and cold, his lips pursed together as if they had just tasted something sour.

Sido felt herself blush. Blown backward by his words, she bumped into another table, sending it and its arrangement of leather-bound books crashing to the floor. The noise was shocking in the quiet room.

"In heaven's name, are you as stupid as you appear? And I see you still have that unpleasant limp. It seems not to have improved in the slightest," said the marquis irritably.

Sido stood there wishing with all her heart that the floor would open and swallow her up.

At that moment Count Kalliovski was shown into the chamber. At his heels was a large black wolfhound, his famous dog, Balthazar.

Sido had not seen him since she was small, and her first impression was that she would not like to be left alone with either the man or his dog. She dropped her gaze and curtsied as she felt his sharp inquisitive eyes upon her. Glancing up quickly now and then for a discreet look, she saw a tall thin man, elegantly dressed, his skin smooth and ageless, without lines, as if it had been preserved in aspic. He had the perfume of wealth about him.

"That," said the marquis abruptly, "is my daughter. Why I went to the expense and inconvenience of bringing her back here, I cannot imagine."

"To humor me, I do believe," said Count Kalliovski, setting the table to rights but leaving the books where they had fallen. He sat himself in a chair and stretched his long legs out before him, placing his hands together to form a steeple in front of his mouth. They were large, ugly hands that somehow didn't seem to go with the rest of him. The dog settled near his master. Sido saw that the pattern on the count's embroidered silk waistcoat was of little black skulls intertwined with ivy leaves.

"Charming," said the count, studying Sido with an expert eye. "But is there no food at your convent?"

"Not much, sir," Sido replied.

The count smiled. "Tell me then, are the nuns all as pale and thin as you?"

"No, sir."

"I thought not. Do they eat at their own table?"

Sido nodded.

"And which convent is this?"

When Sido told him, the count laughed out loud.

"I know the cardinal. I have lent him money in the past to settle his gambling debts."

The marquis looked most uncomfortable.

"My dear friend, I may not have your eye for art, or the finer details of architecture, but I do consider myself to be a connoisseur of women. Your daughter has the most bewitching blue eyes. Give her a few more years and you will find her to be ravishing."

The marquis stared at Sido. He looked like a spoiled overgrown child who is being asked to play nicely. "With respect, my dear count, plain she is and plain she will remain. I fear you have been taken in by the beauty of my study and the afternoon light."

"Not in the slightest. I am just concerned to hear that your daughter has been sent to such an indifferent school. Tell me, Marquis, what use is a dull and charmless wife? No, to make the most of your daughter I suggest that from now on she should be educated at home."

Sido stood there, surprised to find that she had an ally in the count.

The marquis rang for his valet.

"The girl is to be bathed and the dressmaker summoned," he said grudgingly. "She will be dining with us this evening."

It took Sido a moment to realize what her father had just said. Perhaps she might be allowed to stay here after all. She wondered if just for once fate was smiling kindly on her.

chapter three

$\mathscr{I}$t was eleven thirty, and the guests had just finished eating. It had been a feast to be savored, and glasses clinked as the wine flowed. Upstairs the gaming tables had been laid out and a group of musicians played in the long sitting room.

On their arrival, Topolain, Têtu, and Yann had been shown into the library, where a small stage had been erected, with a makeshift curtain. The only light in the room came from the fire and the candles on the mantelpiece. When the candles blazed up you could see that this was a large semicircular room. The walls were lined from floor to ceiling with bookshelves, divided halfway down by a wooden walkway. At each end was a spiral staircase. It was hard to fathom where the ceiling began or ended; the books looked as though they might go on to eternity.

Topolain was not in a good mood. When they reached the

house he had been in a deep sleep and he had stumbled badly as he got out of the coach, making a fool of himself in front of the footman.

"Shouldn't have let me nod off," he snapped at Têtu, who deliberately ignored him. He stood near the fire doing his best to get some warmth back into his frozen limbs, for in spite of all the fur rugs in the coach, he still felt chilled to the marrow.

Only Yann was alert and excited enough to explore. He moved away from the fire into the dark recesses of the library. He had never seen so many books. He took one out of the shelf. It was brand-new, some of its pages still uncut. He put it back and took out another, smiling to himself. Whoever owned the château used this room more to impress than for the knowledge it held.

It seemed extraordinary to Yann that a château should be owned by one man, and it made him feel insect-small. Still, for all its grandeur, there was something uncomfortable about the place, as if the foundations were having an argument with the earth. A bad omen, he thought, for tonight's show.

The large double doors at the end of the room opened and in the draft that followed, the candles flared up. Yann turned to see a tall man enter the library. He was dressed in black, his hair powdered white, and he walked with an assured step, the red heels of his shiny buckled shoes clicking loudly on the parquet floor. A black wolfhound followed him. He was holding something that Yann couldn't quite make out. Now in the firelight he saw clearly what it was—a human skull carved in wood.

The sight of it made Yann move farther back into the darkness of the bookshelves. There was something sinister about this man. He supposed him to be the Marquis de Villeduval.

Count Kalliovski ignored Topolain and Têtu, and he hadn't seen the boy. Turning his back on the fire, he put the wooden skull on the table, opening it up to reveal a magnificent timepiece. On its face was the image of the Grim Reaper.

Topolain rushed forward, accidentally tripping and making nonsense of his low bow. Balthazar growled, showing a perfect set of sharp, pointed fangs. Topolain hastily moved back. Kalliovski didn't look up.

"It is an honor, Count Kalliovski, to be called to your splendid residence," said Topolain. "May I congratulate you on your fine taste?"

"This is not my residence. It belongs to the Marquis de Villeduval. Let us hope your magic shows more skill than your words do."

Topolain was still not fully awake. How could he have forgotten what he had already been told? He attempted some more toe-curling flattery, making matters worse. Balthazar snarled again, a low menacing rumble of a sound like the coming of thunder, his ears pinned back, his eyes shining yellow, watching every move the magician made, longing for one word from his master to tear him to pieces. Topolain took another step backward. He was terrified of dogs.

Têtu, watching this, had a sense of rising panic. His mind

whirled as he tried to remember exactly where and when it was he had last seen this man.

It was the sight of the count's hands that finally loosened Têtu's memory. He knew now with a dreadful certainty that they were all cursed. For all Kalliovski's airs and graces, he still had the hands of a butcher, the hands of a murderer.

Yann had never been able to read Têtu's mind, though tonight that didn't stop him from realizing that something was wrong with the dwarf, and it wasn't just his usual tiredness after the show. It was something altogether more worrying. He listened as the count began to speak.

"I called you here tonight because I was impressed by your performance at the Theater du Temple. I too have a great interest in automata," said the count.

Topolain smiled feebly. He was only half listening. He was positive he had met this man before, though where, for the life of him he couldn't remember.

"Do you know who first came up with the idea of man as a living machine?" said the count. "It was the philosopher Descartes. It might interest you to know that he even had a replica of his dead daughter Francine constructed for him."

"I didn't know that," said Topolain. He realized with a start that Kalliovski was staring at him intently. He had never heard of Descartes, and knew nothing of philosophy. Nervously, he took out his handkerchief and blew his nose.

"And then there was Jacques de Vaucanson," continued the

count musingly. "You may remember that he came up with that wonder of the world, the defecating duck."

Now Topolain felt safer. Everyone in France knew about the defecating duck. He coughed and drew himself up.

"I never had the privilege of seeing the duck. It must have been most amusing to see it take the grain from your hand, appear to eat it, and then expel it just like a real duck."

"Quite," said Count Kalliovski dryly. His face was expressionless. "And do you know that it was nothing more than a clockwork toy? The Age of Enlightenment, and all it brings us is a defecating duck! I trust your Pierrot holds more magic than that."

"Oh yes, sir, much more," said Topolain. Then, without thinking, he inquired, "Forgive me for asking, but haven't we met before? I never forget a face and yours is one that—" He stopped, realizing too late that his tongue had run away with itself. He knew it was a fatal mistake.

Kalliovski's eyes narrowed to scrutinize the man in front of him. He turned to look at the dwarf, a spark of recognition showing on his face. Only then did the poor magician remember when and where he had last seen the count. Under his blotched white makeup all the color drained from his face. The count smiled inwardly.

He turned on his red heels and left the room. Têtu and Topolain listened to his footsteps retreat into the distance. They were well and truly trapped.

"What have I done?" said Topolain.

Yann could suddenly feel Topolain's fear, though his thoughts were jumbled together and made no sense at all.

"Quiet," Têtu grunted. "The boy is here. You'd better leave the pistol out of the show."

Topolain poured himself a generous glass of cognac from a decanter, his hands shaking. He drained the cognac in one gulp. "No pistol. I think that's wise. But we're dead, aren't we?"

The memory of the voice early that evening began to haunt Yann again. There must, he thought, be a way to escape.

Above him on the wooden walkway came the sound of footsteps. A footman appeared as if from nowhere, and started to walk down the spiral staircase with a dish of sweetmeats. Quickly Yann made for the staircase at the opposite end of the room. He watched the footman leave the dish beside the decanters on the table before returning the same way he had come, through an invisible door in the bookshelves. Yann, catlike, went up the stairs after him and caught hold of the door before it fully closed.

"See if you can find a way out of here. I'll keep the door open. Go!" hissed Têtu.

Yann found himself standing in a dark, musty-smelling passage-way. Up ahead he could see the flicker of candlelight as the footman disappeared down the rabbit warren of corridors. It reminded him of walking between the painted flats in the theater. But why did the château have this hidden labyrinth of corridors? What was it trying to hide? What illusion was it hoping to create?

Sido had been dressed and ready for hours, but no one had come for her. She could hear music and laughter wafting up the stairs as doors down below opened and closed. It was late. Supper must be over. She had been forgotten. Hungry and disappointed with waiting, she lay down on the four-poster bed and closed her eyes.

This was how Yann first saw her. He had discovered that there were peepholes in all the doors, and by looking through them he had a good idea by now of the layout of the château. It was like watching different scenes from a play, with guests getting ready and putting the final touches to their finery. He felt drawn to this girl, certain that she wouldn't cry out if he were to venture in. He pushed against the door and it opened silently. Not wishing to wake the girl up, he sat down and waited for her to stir.

There was something about her that fascinated him, and he was curious to know why she had been left up here all alone. She reminded him of a china doll, with long eyelashes that fluttered like a butterfly's wings, and an abundance of dark hair that cascaded across the pillows.

Sido woke up with a start, then, seeing the boy, sat bolt upright in bed.

"Who are you? What are you doing here?"

She pulled the curtains around her and peeked out, wondering if she should call for help.

"Even if you did, no one would come," said Yann.

This was very unsettling. Had she been talking aloud and not known it?

"What is your name?" she asked.

"Yann Margoza. What's yours?"

"Sido de Villeduval. Why are you here?"

"I am with the magician. We are doing the show tonight, downstairs in the room with all the books."

"The library?"

"Whoever it belongs to hasn't read any of them. They are all new."

"Everything in the house is new. My father has only just built it."

"Are you a princess?"

"No," Sido laughed, "I am not."

"I couldn't live like this," said Yann. "The walls would close in on me. It would become a pretty prison."

The boy shouldn't be here, Sido thought, yet the strange thing was that she had no desire for him to leave. He made her feel less forgotten and less hungry. She tried hard to think what she knew about boys, which was very little. Unlike the other girls at the convent, she had no brothers or cousins to help her out. Now there was a strange boy in her bedchamber. If she were caught with him, she would be sent back to the convent to be forgotten again.

"You won't be, not now that you are here."

"How do you do that, know what I am thinking?"

Yann picked up a book and said, "It's all the same, thinking and saying. Can you read?"

Sido nodded.

"Are you sure I won't be sent back to the convent?" she asked.

"You will stay here."

His words thrilled her.

"I would like to read words. Thoughts can be so confusing. Why does this house have secret corridors?"

"My father had the corridors built because he doesn't like to see the servants. Thank you for what you said. Still, I think you should leave."

Yann knew he should, but there was something intriguing about this girl that made him forget the reason he had gone off exploring.

He smiled at her. "There's no need to worry. No one will come for you until the show begins."

This was a strange boy indeed. It was like being in church and feeling that you were opened up and all of you could be seen.

"The doors have peepholes. I looked through one. That's how I saw you. Would you like to see?"

Sido nodded.

"Come on, leave your shoes."

In her dress of watered silk that rustled as she moved, she followed Yann through the hidden door and down the secret passages. Together they took turns looking through the peepholes. A lady in a boudoir adjusted her impossibly tall wig, complaining to her maid that it was too heavy and that she had a headache.

In another room, a man was kissing a lady on the neck. She was blushing and Sido saw her step quickly aside, fanning herself as her husband appeared at the door. Ladies and gentlemen were sitting in a sumptuous salon, and the scene looked almost golden in the glow of so much candlelight.

She felt Yann touch her arm lightly.

"We must go back," he said.

They retraced their steps. Sido quickly straightened out the bed and put her shoes back on. When there was a sharp knock on the door her heart nearly missed a beat.

Then she realized that the boy with the all-seeing eyes had vanished.

$\mathcal{S}$o it was that on the last stroke of midnight the scene was set. All that was keeping the performance from beginning was the late arrival of the marquis. The guests were waiting as an argument broke out between two of their party, a cardinal and an intensely earnest-looking young man called Louis de Jonquières.

"The clergy are the First Estate of France, the nobility are the Second, and the Third Estate are the rest of the country. We're seriously outnumbered. It is imperative that we question our role," said the young man.

"I suppose you think the Third Estate should have a voice. Are we expected to give a say to every peasant? Have you thought through the consequences?" asked the cardinal with distaste.

"You are a man of the church. The Bible commands us to consider the poor," replied Louis de Jonquières, warming to his theme. "In my view, if their lot is to be improved, they should have a say in the way things are run. Come, you must agree that at present our society leaves much to be desired."

The cardinal looked pained. He cleared his throat to make his point.

"My ancestors fought to make this country what it is. We are a great nation, the envy of the world. You surely do not imagine that this has been achieved by the people? It is our duty to retain our position and lead the way."

"But the nobility cannot be relied upon," said Louis de Jonquières. "We are not going to change our ways in order to put bread on the tables of the starving. Look what has happened in America! The people rid themselves of English sovereignty and now, with our help, it is a republic. Many of my friends would argue that absolute monarchy is dead."

The cardinal's cheeks were now as red as his silk gown.

"Society," he said haughtily, "will have to evolve, and that, monsieur, will take time. Nothing is going to be achieved in a day."

"But why should the poor pay for the privileges of the rich? They are so many, and we are so few," said Louis de Jonquières passionately.

Count Kalliovski, who was enjoying watching the cardinal's discomfiture, interrupted with a laugh.

"Enough, enough," he said. "For tonight, my friends, let's leave politics alone. The subject makes dreary companions of us all."

Now, with the timing of a great actor, the marquis entered the room, accompanied by Sido. He took his seat at the front of the makeshift stage. Sido sat down beside him.

Her attention was caught by the Duchesse de Lamantes, with her fashionably tall coiffure. On top, amongst an assortment of ribbons and flowers, sat a coach made out of gold thread, drawn by six dapple-gray horses of blown glass. This brittle design sat oddly with the sour face of its wearer, who looked as if one smile might crack the piecrust of her makeup.

"Who," inquired the duchess, lifting up her spyglass, "is that plain-looking creature? Can it be the marquis's daughter? What a disappointment for him."

The marquis silenced the company. "I hope I haven't missed any of this intriguing little performance of yours, Count Kalliovski."

"Not at all, my dear friend," said the count. "As you can see, the curtain has not yet been drawn." He clapped his hands for silence.

"Messieurs et mesdames, to thank the marquis for this splendid evening I have brought him a show from the theater at the rue du Temple—a show so popular that it has been sold out for the past four months. I give you the People's Pierrot."

There was a round of applause as the curtain was pulled back and Topolain brought the Pierrot to the front of the stage.

The magician started as always by demonstrating to the audience the working of its wooden limbs and its lack of strings.

"Monsieur le Marquis, Count Kalliovski, my lords and ladies," he announced with a flourish, "I have here the wonder of Paris. He can walk! He can talk! Moreover, he can look into the future, see into the depths of your hearts, and know your darkest secrets."

"Why would it want to do that?" interrupted the marquis. "It seems most impertinent."

A titter of laughter echoed around the room.

Topolain stopped, uncertain whether he should continue or wait.

"My dear count," said the marquis, who in truth was irritated that it hadn't been his own idea to bring this show here, "these are mere street entertainers. I am surprised that you have brought them here."

"Be patient. I can assure you that this little notion of mine is going to prove most entertaining."

Topolain was so put out by all the delay that he found himself tongue-tied, unable to remember the questions that he usually asked the Pierrot. To his relief, the Pierrot stood up and opened its steely glass eyes. It stretched out its wooden fingers and moved its wooden limbs. There was complete silence.

Topolain recovered himself and began to work his audience. With care, he lifted up the Pierrot's baggy blue top to show the carved wooden torso. He tapped it with his hand; it made a pleasingly solid sound.

"Bravo! An artful mystery indeed," said the marquis.

Count Kalliovski stared fixedly at the wooden Pierrot; he too was intrigued to know how the strange doll worked.

Topolain, his voice no longer faltering, said, "Ask the Pierrot a question. Any question will do. I promise you the answer will not disappoint."

Yann, from his vantage point hidden in the shadows, could see the stage and the audience clearly. Têtu, standing beside him, was working the Pierrot, though how he did it remained to Yann a profound mystery. It was their combined talents that made the show the success it was.

"Tell me then, what kind of dog have I got?" said a lady with beauty marks and a painted fan.

This was what Yann could do, read minds and throw his voice so that it sounded as if the Pierrot was talking.

"A spaniel. She had puppies three days ago."

The lady laughed. "How charming, and how clever."

Now it started just as it had done in the theater earlier that evening, a ribbon of silly questions neatly tied up and answered to everyone's satisfaction. Yann felt pleased that nothing more taxing had been asked of him. Two shows a night was hard work, especially for Têtu.

Just then Louis de Jonquières remarked, "If the Pierrot is right about small things, things of no importance, then maybe he can inform us on the bigger questions of the day."

"Really, monsieur!" said the Duchesse de Lamantes. "Why do you insist on being so disagreeable? Why not save your talk for the coffeehouses of Paris instead of asking a wooden doll to take part in your idiotic debate? Let it rest. It is most inappropriate."

"Forgive me," said Louis de Jonquières, "but I am curious. Tell me, Pierrot, will the present regime fall?"

With this question the room changed. Yann saw in the slipstream of his mind an audience of headless people, blood running down their fine clothes. He heard the Pierrot say, as if from many miles away, "A thousand years of French kings are coming to an end."

The audience began to shift on their chairs. Topolain rushed toward the front of the stage. "The doll jests," he cried. "Please now ask him a question he can answer."

Louis de Jonquières pushed back his chair and stood up.

"Without wishing to make a dull fellow of a wooden doll, perhaps he would care to give us his candid opinion as to whether France will evolve itself into a constitutional monarchy."

"Please, monsieur," said Topolain, "my doll is no political fortune-teller."

"But you said, sir, that he can see into the future, into the minds of men. I am merely asking what he sees."

"Watches, snuffboxes, trinkets, bonbons, and the like," said Topolain. He felt he was losing his grip. What on earth had come over Yann, that he would say something so dangerous?

"Humor me," the young man persisted.

Yann looked out at all the fine ladies and gentlemen, at the emeralds, rubies, and diamonds that glittered on wilted flesh. Louis de Jonquières appeared to be holding his blood-soaked head under his arm. Yann blinked, hoping the vision would go away, only to see Death walk into the room. He wanted to keep silent, but it was as if he were possessed.

He heard the Pierrot say, "I see you all drowning in blood."

This remark was so unexpected and so shocking that Topolain burst out laughing. "As you see, messieurs and mesdames, on the question of politics the Pierrot is but a wooden doll."

None of the guests were laughing. Instead their faces were grave and the atmosphere in the room became uneasy.

"A doll indeed," said the marquis solemnly. He turned to his guests. "I can assure you, my dear friends, that such a thing would never happen here. It must be an English doll!" There was a ripple of nervous laughter. "In England, that country of barbarians, yes, maybe. Look at what they did to their King Charles the First—chopped off his head! We would never fall so low."

There was a murmur of approval. Everyone applauded.

Count Kalliovski watched with interest. He had sat there, judge and jury on the fate of Topolain and Têtu, and had come to his verdict. This would be their last ever performance. After tonight the old fool and his friend would be dead.

"Thank you, that will be all," said the marquis, dismissing Topolain. "I believe the entertainment, if you can call it that, is over. We will adjourn."

"Not quite yet," said the count. "The show is not finished. I believe Monsieur Topolain is celebrated for a trick that he does with a pistol. Monsieur Topolain is the only man in Europe who claims that no bullet can harm him."

"Impossible!" said the marquis.

"Well then, let us see for ourselves," said the count.

Topolain was on his own. In his mind's eye he saw the Grim Reaper climb out of the wooden skull, grow in size, and stand there watching him, just like Kalliovski. For one moment he contemplated escaping, but he could see Milkeye standing guard at the library doors. If he ran, it would be the end for all of them. He took a long, deep gulp of air. He who thought himself a coward now showed the bravery of a lion. Always the showman, he brought out the pistol and a bullet and showed them to the audience.

"I will prove to you that I am invincible. This bullet will be fired at my very heart, and yet I will live to tell the tale. Now, I require an assistant."

He looked out into the audience, knowing full well who would stand up.

"You need someone with an accurate eye. I flatter myself that I am that man," said Count Kalliovski.

Topolain wished that he had at least drunk more of the marquis's very fine cognac. He loaded the pistol and handed it to the count, who took his time inspecting it. Only Topolain saw that with sleight of hand he had interfered with the weapon.

"When I raise my handkerchief, you will fire."

"Wait," said the count. "Have you forgotten? Should you not say some magic words to keep you safe?"

Oh, Topolain remembered all right, but he knew there were no words to keep him safe.

The count's voice broke through his memories. "No bullet . . ."

"No bullet," repeated Topolain, "can harm me. I have drunk from the cup of everlasting life."

With these words he walked away bravely as if he were about to fight a duel, though, unlike Kalliovski, he was unarmed. He looked his murderer straight in the eyes as he lifted his white handkerchief.

"Fire!"

The count pulled the trigger. There was a loud retort, followed by the acrid smell of gunpowder and scorched flesh. Topolain stumbled and the audience gasped as they watched the handkerchief he was holding turn bright red.

Topolain straightened himself up. In his sweating palm he held up the bullet and showed it to the audience. He staggered forward to take a final bow.

The curtains were drawn and the audience clapped politely. By now they had lost interest.

"Most peculiar," said the marquis. "Come, I think we are all in need of champagne. Let us go upstairs, where the card tables demand our attention."

The great library doors were opened and music filtered into the room. The marquis led the way out, quite forgetting his daughter, who stood staring transfixed at the curtains as the other guests filed past her. All seemed unaware of the drama unfolding behind the velvet drapes. None of them turned around as there was a thud from backstage. None of them saw Topolain slumped down on the chair.

Death had made his entrance upon the small stage. He was all too visible to the magician. As a trickle of blood ran down his chin, he had the strangest sensation of becoming detached from his body, connected only by spider threads of silver memory. Now he was floating up over the guests, past the crowded bookshelves toward the bright painted ceiling with its angels and cherubs.

The silver threads snapped and he was free. Caught in a gust of wind, he was blown out of the library and into the hall with its marble busts and winged statues, where the doors had been opened to let in a latecomer. The snow flurried in as Jacques Topolain, the magician, glided out into the dark night. He saw no more, he heard no more, he was no more.

Yann had rushed with Têtu to help. He had taken one look at Topolain and seen Death's black gown trail across the stage. Sido too had witnessed Topolain's end, but the count had turned her around and led her from the room, locking the doors behind him. The candles flickered in the draft.

Têtu put his head to Topolain's chest, listening for a heartbeat. He shook his head. There was nothing to be done.

"It has never gone wrong before. Why now?" cried Yann.

Têtu was examining the weapon. "It didn't go wrong this time either," he said. "The pistol has been tampered with. Topolain didn't stand a chance. He was murdered."

chapter five

$\mathcal{Y}$ann had never before stared death in the face as he did now. It looked to him so absolute, a final curtain fallen. The essence of Topolain had gone, snuffed out like a candle. Only the body that housed him was left lying on the stage in a pool of congealing blood, with Têtu kneeling beside him, tears rolling down his cheeks, rocking back and forth on his heels and sobbing.

"I should have listened to you. We shouldn't have come. Then this would never have happened," he said defeatedly.

Yann put a gentle hand on the dwarf's shoulder and bent down to whisper to him. "We have to leave."

Têtu was silent. In the dim light of the room Yann could see him shaking. He was in a bad way. He was already exhausted from doing two performances in one night, and now the shock of losing such a dear friend had taken all his strength away and robbed him of his senses.

All Yann could think was that they must somehow get out of here.

Out in the hall, the guests were making their way up the grand staircase to where the Marquis de Villeduval stood, champagne glass in hand. Sido felt perplexed by their indifference. Surely they realized that the magician wasn't acting, surely they realized he had been seriously hurt. Why did no one summon a surgeon to help?

She turned in desperation to the duchess. "I think the magician has been wounded."

"Nonsense, child! It was just playacting."

Could these people not see what had taken place? Sido wondered. Did they not care? She felt she had arrived in a foreign land, where the language seemed twisted and words possessed double meanings.

"There is really no need to alarm yourself, my dear child," said the duchess, hardly glancing down at Sido. Her eyes searched the room for more distinguished company. "I can assure you that your magician will live to work another day." She walked away, leaving Sido alone.

I don't want to grow up to be like that, thought Sido. She looked up at Count Kalliovski, who was surrounded by ladies. They reminded her of hens bobbing up and down, preening their feathers, all vying for his attention, all hoping to be first in the pecking order.

Sido would have liked to go back into the library to see for herself what had happened to the magician, but one of the count's men was standing guard outside and she knew that if she moved any closer she might attract unwanted attention. She moved behind a pillar and watched with a sense of relief as Kalliovski escorted two ladies up toward the card room and out of sight.

Beside her on the first step of the staircase stood a young lady in an elaborate pink silk dress, with a hawk-nosed gentleman.

"Do you remember the time the marquis brought in a fortune-teller?" the young lady was asking.

Her admirer shook his head. "Alas, I was not invited. I suppose it was Count Kalliovski's doing."

"The count was not even there. The marquis sent his gamekeeper out into the countryside and he brought back this old Gypsy. She refused to tell our fortunes, no matter how much gold she was given. She would only speak to the marquis and no one else."

"What did she say?"

"It was so ridiculous, it made us all laugh. She told the marquis he would lose everything to the king of the Gypsies."

Sido, who had been half listening to this and half looking about her, caught a glimpse of light coming from under the staircase. A door opened and a footman came through, carrying a tray of champagne glasses. Behind him Sido could just see the beginnings of a passageway. She knew then what she was going to do. Without giving it a second thought she slipped over to the door and found herself at the bottom of a flight of stone stairs. She knew there must be a way through the secret corridors to the library. It was just a matter of finding the right door.

Gently, Yann helped Têtu to stand and with difficulty guided him up the spiral staircase and along the wooden gantry to the concealed door in the bookshelves. By now all the color in Têtu's face had drained away. Yann knew that it was up to him to save the dwarf. His exhaustion had robbed him of his instinct to survive. What surprised Yann was that although he himself was well aware of the danger they were in, he felt no fear. His vision was clear, colors were electric, and everything seemed sharper. Every nerve of him felt completely alive.

But the concealed door was shut fast.

"Don't worry, I'll get you out of here," he said soothingly, knowing full well that the shutters of Têtu's mind had closed down. He heard the library door open and then close with a firm click, and pulled Têtu back into the shadows.

Count Kalliovski called out, "I know you're both there. My man tells me there is a boy as well. There's no point hiding. Listen to me carefully. If you don't want to go the same way as Topolain, you'd better tell me how the Pierrot works."

He waited for an answer. Yann kept quiet. He could hear the count walking to and fro, trying to determine where they were.

"I have examined the doll. It is a piece of solid wood: It could not have been worked from the inside. I am a man of science. Come now, tell me its secret."

"Why did you murder Topolain?" shouted Yann.

"Quiet, boy. Dwarf, answer my question. Tell me the secret of the automaton and I will protect you. If you refuse me, I tell you this: No matter what you do, no matter where you hide, I will find you. Think carefully before you answer, for I never make an offer twice."

Têtu's small legs had started to shudder as if caught in a trap. Yann heard the scrabble of Balthazar's claws up the spiral staircase and there was the dog staring at them with his yellow eyes, his mouth snarled back, his fangs shining bright with saliva. Balthazar growled.

"Bring them to me," commanded the count.

Têtu's legs twitched all the more as the dog's shadow was thrown large against the bookshelves. Yann stood up. Holding his hands out in front of his body, he pointed his fingers directly at the dog's eyes and spoke softly in a language that Balthazar seemed to understand. The beast dropped on all fours as if the firm hand of a giant had suddenly crushed him.

Yann did not blink or break his stare. Defeated, Balthazar, his tail between his legs, went back down the stairs whimpering to his master.

"What have you done to him, Têtu? What Gypsy sorcery is this?" demanded Count Kalliovski angrily.

Yann said nothing but moved silently toward the banister rail. To his despair he saw Milkeye enter the room. The count spoke to him. Yann couldn't hear the words, but knew what he was saying. Quickly, he moved back to the darkness of the bookshelves and tried again to push with all his strength upon the concealed door. He could hear the count below as he walked with Balthazar toward the library doors. The dog's clicking claws told him they were leaving.

"I want the dwarf and I want that boy," said the count. "Don't let them get away."

"Yes, master." Milkeye was already at the bottom of the staircase.

For the last time Yann tried the door, feeling it desperately with his hands for hidden locks or latches. He could hear Milkeye getting closer. He was near the top of the staircase and still the door wouldn't give. Yann could almost see the top of his head. It was no use. He would have to stand and fight—that was all that was left to him.

Suddenly the door opened. Standing in the darkness of the passageway he could see the girl.

"Help me," he whispered, and together they pulled Têtu through.

By the time Milkeye had taken the last few steps to the top of the gantry, there was nobody there.

chapter six

It wasn't easy to drag Têtu along the narrow passageways. He was heavy, as if his bones had turned to stone. Only when they were in Sido's chamber with the screen moved to block off the peephole did Yann finally feel safe, safe enough to say, "We must lie him down."

"Of course," said Sido, pulling back the bedcovers.

"He'll be better once he's slept," said Yann.

It took all his strength to get Têtu's heavy body up on the bed. He was an alarming sight, with all the color drained from his face. Hastily he covered the dwarf with a quilt, his anger subsiding a touch when he saw Sido standing there anxiously watching. By some twist of fate she had become unwittingly involved in what was happening. The only hope he had of escaping lay with her. If she lost her nerve, he and Têtu wouldn't stand a chance of getting out alive.

"Who is he?" she asked.

"His name is Têtu. He's looked after me since I was born. We work together, with Topolain."

"Will he be all right?"

"Yes, but he should stay hidden. If anyone comes in, it just looks as if the bed has been turned down."

"What about the magician?" asked Sido. "Is he dead?"

"His heart gave out," said Yann.

"I don't believe that." She said it so bluntly that he knew she couldn't be fooled.

"No, it isn't true, but there's no time to explain. We have to get out of here. I need your help."

"But what can I do?"

"Be brave."

"I don't think I am brave."

He smiled at her. "I know you are. Will you stay here with Têtu while I search for a way out?"

The thought of being alone in the room with the sleeping dwarf terrified Sido. With a sickening feeling in her stomach she nodded, hoping that Yann could not read her mind. She wanted to scream *No, I am not brave*, but when she looked into his dark eyes she knew she would do as he asked.

"I'm not good at lying," she said, hoping that this might make him change his mind.

"I know that too."

The silence after he had gone felt almost solid, as if it were pressing down on her chest, squeezing the air out of her. She sat on a chair by the bed and told herself again and again to be calm.

A few minutes later there was a knock on the door. Sido felt every nerve in her body tighten. Checking that Têtu was completely covered, she stood up, took a deep breath, and said, "Come in."

Count Kalliovski stood in the doorway, Balthazar at his side.

"I came to see if you were all right. You vanished so quickly after the little show." He entered the room, closing the door behind him. "Why, my dear child, how pale you are. You look as if you've seen a ghost."

Sido moved toward the bed.

"It was only an illusion, you know. No harm was done."

Despite herself she began to shiver, and as if in response, Balthazar started to growl softly. Count Kalliovski looked around him suspiciously.

"I was feeling very tired, sir," said Sido hastily. "I came up to my chamber to lie down. I have not eaten since early this morning and there has been more excitement than I am used to."

"Your life at the convent is, I imagine, a quiet one," said the count. He looked around the bedchamber again. His gaze fell upon the screen before returning to the bed. "I suppose by now you would be fast asleep?"

Sido nodded and wondered if her legs would continue to support her. They felt like hollow reeds shaking under her petticoats. The count stood facing her, his shadow casting a monstrous figure on the wall behind him, one that appeared to possess a multitude of hands, all poking and prodding into the dark recesses of the bedchamber.

The bed with the sleeping body of the dwarf was only three steps away. Balthazar had begun to edge closer, his growling becoming more insistent.

"You are alone, of course?" asked the count.

"Why, yes, sir."

"Do you mind if I see what has caught Balthazar's fancy?" The count moved forward. Now only two steps separated him from the dwarf.

"Please, sir," pleaded Sido. "I am frightened of dogs, and it is clear that yours does not like me."

"You have no need to fear Balthazar," said the count with a smile. "He will not harm you. He only growls at strangers."

If Count Kalliovski moved one more step, it would all be over. Everything would be discovered. She would be sent back to the convent in disgrace. As for the boy and the dwarf, she hardly dared think about it.

"Please, sir, it is not right or proper for a man to visit a girl's chamber. The Mother Superior would be shocked to hear of such a thing." She found to her surprise that she had tears in her eyes. "Please," she begged again, "don't let your dog come any nearer."

The room began to spin and a metallic taste filled Sido's mouth. She thought she was about to faint. She grabbed at the four-poster bed, holding on to consciousness with all her might.

The count's voice softened. "My dear child," he said, "I had no desire to alarm you. You must be faint for lack of food. I will see that some supper is brought up to you straightaway. It is outrageous that you should be so neglected."

He gave a deep bow and called for Balthazar. "Forgive the intrusion," he said, closing the door softly behind him.

Sido leaned her head on the bedpost, trying to stop the room from spinning. She remained statue-still, listening to the scratching of claws and the clicking of heels as they retreated into the distance. Only then did she loosen her grip. She sank to the floor, resting her head in her hands, and prayed that Yann would hurry.

Carefully and soundlessly, Yann made his way along the secret passages to the stone staircase and looked over the wrought-iron banister. He caught a glimpse of the kitchens below, saw the doors swing open and shut, heard the clatter of pans and the murmur of voices. A man stood in the stairwell and stamped snow from his boots before disappearing from sight. There must be a door to the outside world there.

He was returning the way he had come when a pinprick of light caught his attention. He looked through the peephole into a grand bedchamber, with huge displays of white tulips and black roses on the table. Maybe it was the flowers, maybe it was the lavishness of the decor, more likely it was the large dog bowl sitting on the floor that told Yann that this was where Count Kalliovski slept.

If nothing else, they were owed the blood money that had

been promised to them at the beginning of this nightmare. How would they get back to Paris without a sou to their name?

Yann pushed against the door and slipped inside. An eerie red light shone from the coals in the grate. The walls were painted with hunting scenes that in the spit and hiss of the firelight appeared to be moving. The wooden skull sat on the table beside the vase. It might have been valuable, but he knew also that it was cursed, and would bring whoever took it nothing but bad luck. Next to it was a necklace—a bloodred ribbon with seven crimson stones set into it. Without thinking, he put it in his pocket. It would be something to show Têtu.

He began to search the room for money.

This is what Yann knew, what he had always known: All objects, great and small, have a spirit. Sometimes, if you listen carefully, you can almost hear the sound they make.

Hidden deep in among the drapes of the bed was a purse. Yann picked it up and put it in his pocket, where it felt pleasingly heavy. Now he had to get out of here as fast as he could.

Sido hadn't dared move since the count had left. Yann found her still sitting on the floor, her head in her hands. She looked up at him.

"Where have you been? Count Kalliovski was here."

"It took longer than I thought. We'll be gone in a minute." He went straight to the bed and pulled back the covers. "Wake up," he said gently, shaking Têtu back into life as he helped him to his feet. He was pleased to see that the dwarf's eyes were purple-black once more and his skin no longer pale.

"Where am I?" said Têtu, who for a moment thought that he must have woken from a bad dream. Yann said something to him in a language Sido had never heard before. Têtu gulped as the memory of what had happened came back to him.

Yann turned back to look at Sido, sitting crumpled and abandoned on the floor, and for a moment he had an over-whelming desire to take her with them, to save her from being one of the headless ones.

There was a knock at the door. Sido scrambled to her feet. Quickly Yann and the dwarf disappeared behind the screen and through the panel, sliding it back into place just as the count entered, followed by a footman carrying a tray with Sido's supper. This time the dog at the count's heels was silent. The tray was laid before her. The sight of the food made her mouth water. Eat slowly, she said to herself. Don't rush.

The count's eyes darted around the room as he ordered the footman to straighten out the bed.

"There is no need," said Sido quickly.

"Continue," said the count smoothly, addressing the footman. Balthazar had begun sniffing the air.

"I hope you don't mind if I keep you company while you dine?"

Sido knew that the longer he stayed, the longer the dwarf and the boy had to make their escape.

"I would like that," she said.

Count Kalliovski sat down on a chair by the bed. The dog at his feet let out a heavy sigh and, putting his head on his outstretched paws, closed his eyes.

"I think your dog is more used to me now," said Sido.

"So it seems. When you have finished, I will take you down to see the fireworks. Your father assures me that they will be magnificent."

Sido watched the count as with hooded eyes he searched the room once more, looking for evidence to confirm his suspicions. In the quicksilver candlelight he made a menacing figure, and she knew then that he was no friend. Her instinct told her that there was no escape: This dark spider was waiting patiently to catch her in his gold-spun web.

chapter seven

$\mathcal{T}$he kitchens of the château were busy. Even after the main banquet had been served there was more than enough to do. The gambling tables demanded a constant supply of drinks and *petits fours*. Jean Rollet, the chef, and his staff would be working all night until the very last guest had left or retired. The arrival of two more in the kitchen went almost unnoticed except as extra pairs of hands to help.

"Hey, you there, lackey," a valet shouted at Yann, "the viscount needs this tray taken up to him at once."

Yann shook his head. "We are the entertainers, hired for the count's show. We need to get back to Paris tonight."

The valet threw up his hands in disgust. "What are you doing in here, then?"

Yann felt bewildered. He had never been in such a large kitchen before, with servants running backward and forward, the chef swearing and stamping his foot, bells ringing, the noise, the smells, the heat. It was like a furnace.

Têtu started to sway. He was going to fall over if he didn't sit down. Yann grabbed a stool.

"No you don't," said one of the cooks, snatching it back and lifting her wooden spoon as if it were a weapon. "Away with you, Gypsies."

"We have to get back to Paris."

"Well, what are you doing asking me? Do I look as if I have a magic carpet?" Then, seeing the state of Têtu, she softened. "You'd better go and ask the coachmen in there."

Yann helped Têtu through the kitchen to a small antechamber where a group of men were sitting at a table, their plates wiped clean, their glasses full.

"My friend needs to sit down," said Yann, and one of the men pulled out a chair for him.

"He don't look too perky. What's wrong with him?"

"We need help. Are any of you Paris-bound tonight?"

"Not if I have anything to do with it," said one of the men, pushing his chair back and lighting his pipe. "With luck, they'll be playing cards till dawn and then some."

Suddenly Yann felt as if he had hit a wall. He had gotten this far without being discovered, and now, just when there seemed hope that they might escape, all was lost. Time was slipping away from him; he knew it would not be long before the count found out about the secret passages.

"Here," said a man with a shining bald head, pouring some wine from a large clay pitcher into a glass. "Give this to Titch. He looks as if he could do with it."

"Thank you," said Yann, helping Têtu with the wine. Slowly he began to look more like his old self.

"Has he always been that small, or will he grow?" asked the bald-headed man, laughing.

If Yann had been given a gold coin every time he had heard Têtu insulted they would be rich by now. Still, it riled him as it always did to hear his friend slighted, though he knew better than to react.

A footman opened the door and poked his head around. "The Viscomtess de Lisle will be staying."

"Good to know it," said her coachman. "First sensible thing the old bat's done in ages."

"You think so?" laughed the footman. "Well, she wants her pet monkey brought back from Paris. She thinks it'll be lonely. It's not your night, Dufort, my old friend."

"Hasn't she seen the snow outside?" said Dufort, gesturing toward the window.

"That's why she wants her monkey."

"Oh well," sighed Dufort, "here we go again. Doubt I'll make it back before tomorrow. Tell you this much," he muttered into the last dregs of his wine, "one day I'll be my own master. No more of this come here, go there, lucky-to-have-a-job nonsense."

All the men laughed. "You know what you can do?" said the bald-headed one. "Write all your grievances out and send them to the king."

"That's a good one," said his friend, slapping him on the back. "Maybe the king will be able to get her to behave."

Everyone burst out laughing, everyone except Dufort, who looked furious as he pulled on his heavy coat, loath to be leaving the warmth and comfort of the kitchens.

"To make matters worse, the roads aren't safe these days, what with all the bandits and brigands, and she's too mean to pay for a lackey to help," he grumbled.

Yann seized his chance. "We will keep you company," he said.

"What, take a couple of Gypsies like you? Forget it."

Têtu, now able to walk unaided, followed Yann back through the kitchens past a rack of freshly baked bread that was cooling from the ovens. With the swiftness of hand that takes a lifetime to master, he took two of the loaves and hid them in his topcoat before making his way out into the snowy courtyard.

"It's no good you two following me," said Dufort. "I'm not taking you and that's final."

"Would money change your mind?" asked Yann.

"Would the man in the moon giving me a silver eye make me think different? Of course it would. It ain't going to happen, though."

Yann, as if from thin air, conjured up five coins and handed one of them to Dufort. He looked at it carefully, then put it in his mouth and gave it a good bite to check its worth. He didn't know what to make of this strange pair, the street urchin and the little fellow with the girly, squeaky voice.

"Where did you get this kind of money?" he said.

"We were brought here from a Paris theater to entertain the guests. We're magicians. We were paid handsomely for our trouble," said Têtu.

"Then where's your driver, Titch?"

"We can't find him. He must have left earlier to avoid the worst of the weather."

"We were held up," added Yann quickly, "because my friend was feeling unwell." He knew that Dufort was wavering between doubt and the certainty of the coin that he held in his hand. "I'll give you this now and as much again when we reach the city. Is that fair?"

"All right," said Dufort reluctantly, "as long as you don't tell anyone. The old bat's most particular about who is allowed in her carriage. Monkeys yes, dwarfs and dogs no."

The coachman led the way across the yard to the marquis's stables. They were the height of luxury. He might not have cared much for his servants or his daughter, but the marquis's horses were a different matter altogether. He liked them to be well looked after. He had a notion that after his death he might be born again as a fine stallion, in which case the marquis wanted to be housed here with crystal chandeliers to illuminate his hay, and underground heating to warm his hooves.

"Look at that," said Dufort. "His tenants live in hovels with barely enough to eat and the horses live like lords. It makes my blood boil, it does."

He opened the door of the carriage and let Têtu in. "If you don't mind, I'd like the boy to ride with me and keep an eye out for thieves. When we're near Paris, I'll lock you both into the carriage. Don't want the riffraff trying to hitch a ride, do we?"

He handed Yann a heavy coat to wear. It nearly drowned him. "Always keep two handy, in case of rain."

It was a small carriage with two young horses to pull it, both of whom seemed high-strung and reluctant to leave the warmth of the stable. Finally, with much urging, they made their way down the avenue of trees whose branches were full of little lights that twinkled like stars. Beyond the estate lay a vast black abyss, waiting to swallow them up.

"I hate driving at night," said Dufort miserably, his breath coming out of him in a foggy mist. "It gives me the creeps."

The darkness had never bothered Yann, especially not tonight. There was safety in a starless sky.

"We may be less than four leagues from the city, and this may well be the best road France has to offer, but with no moon . . . Ah, what's that?" The coachman flinched as the sky above the château erupted with the sound of fireworks. They exploded into the darkness, painting patterns of light in the shape of stars, serpents, comets, and chrysanthemums. It was an astounding sight in this landscape of ice and snow.

Terrified by the noise, the horses reared up. Dufort, distracted by the fireworks, lost control of the reins, grabbing at the sides of the carriage to stop himself from being thrown to the ground. The horses, now wild with fear, were galloping. Up ahead the road turned, and Yann could see that at this speed the coach would skid on the ice. He could hear Têtu shouting as he was thrown from side to side. With difficulty he scrambled down from the coachman's seat.

"You're mad!" yelled Dufort, as with one measured leap Yann managed to mount the first horse. Holding on to its neck for all he was worth, he leaned forward and whispered into its pinned-back ears. At the sound of his soft voice both horses became calmer and slowed down until they finally came to a halt, steam rising from their glossy coats. Yann climbed down and stroked their muzzles, talking to them in a language that the startled coachman was sure he had heard before.

"You're a brave one and no mistake," said Dufort, wiping the sweat from his forehead. "I thought I was a goner back there." He handed Yann his flask as they set off again. "There's a thing! What did you say to them?"

Yann shrugged, looking back to see the last of the fireworks as they illuminated the château before it too disappeared altogether.

"The only other person I've seen talk to horses like that was a Gypsy man. I had a feeling you two had Gypsy blood."

Yann wasn't listening. He was wondering if Sido had been allowed to see the fireworks, or if she was still locked in her chamber. He smiled as he stared at the road in front of him. The thought of how angry the count would be to discover that the purse and the red necklace were missing warmed him.

Dufort shivered. "I always think them forests are full of eyes, all watching and waiting." He laughed. "Tell you this, boy, I'll be glad when I see the lights of Paris."

Yann looked into the woods of beech trees, their silvery barks catching the reflection of the carriage's lights. An owl hooted, and its haunting cry followed them as they made their way down the icy road. An hour and a half later he was allowed into the carriage, where, half frozen, he quickly fell asleep.

Têtu woke him just before dawn. The coach had reached the gates of Paris. Through a gap in the curtains Yann could see crowds of people all waiting to be let into the city in the hope of earning the price of a loaf of bread. The carts that had food to sell were being heavily guarded by police and soldiers. They were the first to be let in, while the begging and pleading from the crowd rose in volume.

"Get away with you," bellowed the gatekeeper. "There's no work in the city. It's frozen solid like the rest of this blasted country."

Groups of starving people were being forcibly turned back, while others yelled that they had papers.

At last the carriage came to a standstill.

"How are you, Dufort?" they heard the gatekeeper inquire.

"Why, Monsieur Gaspard!" said Dufort with genuine surprise. "What are you doing here? A new job, I see, and a good one."

"A good one, this, dealing with the rabble every day? You must be joking! I only got it because the old chap had a heart attack. They say one man's misfortune is another man's misfortune." They both started to laugh.

"Is the viscountess with you?" asked the gatekeeper.

"No, thank the Lord."

"So why did she send you back empty?"

"She wants me to fetch her monkey. I'll be back this way as soon as I've got the little beast."

"A monkey," chuckled the gatekeeper. "I've heard it all now. Away with you."

The carriage set off again, lurching from side to side as it made its way over the cobbles and over the Pont Neuf, and then they were on the right bank of the Seine. There, in a narrow side street, Dufort stopped, climbed down, and unlocked the door.

"You did well, my friend," said Têtu.

Yann was too tired to do anything other than take some coins from the purse and hand them to Dufort.

"This is too much," said Dufort, looking longingly at the money in his hand.

"Keep it," said Têtu.

"Very decent of you. You're good people," said Dufort, climbing up again and taking hold of the reins. "I reckon it's me who should be thanking you for saving the coach. I owe you one."

The snow had started to fall again. Yann put his hands deep in his pockets. He could feel the purse, and the weight of it reassured him that they had money left over; but the red necklace had vanished.

"Come on," said Têtu.

With heads bowed, coats pulled tight around tired, cold bodies, they walked toward the theater manager's apartment in the Marais, knowing they had the unpleasant task of breaking the news of Topolain's death to him.

Count Kalliovski, returning to his chamber in the early hours of the morning, looked into the heart of the fire. It had been a good night. He had watched as more money was lost than won at the gaming tables. The little black leather-bound notebook that he privately called the Book of Tears was full of IOUs with the trembling signatures of desperate souls longing to borrow more, sure that their luck would change.

Men's morals were as insubstantial as tissue, and about as transparent, he thought. Oh yes. He had bought himself more foolish-minded men and women, who would soon be asked to pay him back with interest.

He put the Book of Tears on the desk. It was only then that he noticed the absence of the red necklace. A cold fury overtook him. Balthazar made a low growl, and he spun around.

"Who's there?" he said to an empty room.

The count went over to the bed, felt in the drapes for the

purse, and cursed out loud when he found it gone. With rising anger he summoned Milkeye.

"Where are they?"

"We're still looking, master."

"Why haven't you found them?"

"They could be anywhere in the labyrinth of secret passages behind the walls," said Milkeye. For such a big man he seemed to have shrunk in size.

"Show me," said the count coldly.

Milkeye opened the hidden door.

The count took a candle and disappeared into the passage. Coming back into the room, he turned his icy gaze upon his servant, and pinned him up against the wall.

"I made you and I can destroy you, and I will. I want both of them. Do you understand?"

"Alive, master?"

"No, dead."

chapter eight

*M*onsieur Aulard was not a morning person. The previous night he had been out drinking with some actors. Now, red-faced and snoring, he was fast asleep.

It took him a few minutes to realize that the terrible banging sound was not coming from the inside of his head, that it was something quite detached from him.

His parrot, Iago, who was sitting on his usual perch shipwrecked amongst the shambles of the bedchamber, joined in the commotion by screeching, "Wake up, naughty boy, wake up!" In a desperate attempt to silence the noise Monsieur Aulard threw his wig at the parrot. The knocking just kept on, getting louder and more urgent.

Finally, barefoot and shivering, Monsieur Aulard dragged himself out of his warm bed. His head felt like a rotten apple. His apartment looked as bad as he felt. The source of the noise was coming from the front door. He fumbled with the lock until he finally managed to open it. Two Yanns and two Têtus floated before him. They were swaying back and forth, overlapping each other.

Something was missing from this unsettling picture. There should be a third person.

"Where's Topolain?"

Têtu walked into the apartment, followed by Yann. Even half awake and with a thumping headache, Monsieur Aulard could see that the dwarf was in a bad way.

"My dear friend, are you unwell?" He looked back at the door, expecting to see Topolain come panting up the stairs behind.

"Topolain's dead," said Têtu with a sob.

"Dead!" repeated Monsieur Aulard. "Dead? Not Topolain! He was larger than life. How can he be dead?"

"A bullet," said Têtu, his face collapsing as tears appeared in his watery red eyes. "He was shot like a dog."

"No, no, no! *Mort bleu!* Yann, speak to me, tell me this is a nightmare!" He grabbed hold of the boy's flimsy coat so that the sleeve came away from the armhole with an unforgiving ripping sound.

"Count Kalliovski shot him," said Yann.

"But why would Count Kalliovski kill Topolain?" His teeth were beginning to chatter. He pulled his housecoat tight around him and abstractedly went over to the fireplace, throwing a few wet coals onto the burning cinders. It had the immediate effect of puffing clouds of smoke back into the chamber and he started to cough as Yann opened the window.

The bitter coldness of the air cleared the smoke and Monsieur Aulard's head too, long enough at least for him to realize that he was in deep trouble. He sat down heavily on an armchair whose horsehair insides were spilling out. It creaked alarmingly under the weight of his hangover.

"The trick must have gone wrong. It must have been an accident."

"It was no accident," said Têtu. "The count knew exactly what he was doing. He tampered with the pistol."

"But why would Count Kalliovski, who is famous and respected, murder a mere magician?"

It was the question Yann had been asking himself all the way back to Paris, a question Têtu up to now had refused to answer.

"Because," said Têtu wearily, "Topolain recognized Kalliovski, and instead of keeping quiet he let his tongue get the better of him. Topolain knew him from a long time ago, when he was called by another name." He spoke so quietly that Monsieur Aulard was not sure that he had heard him correctly.

Yann could see that if Kalliovski was a fraud he would want no one knowing it. Still, Têtu's explanation raised more questions than it answered. He put a half-frozen pan of wine on the fire to boil, searched through the mess to find some glasses, and cleared the table as Têtu took one of the loaves from out of his jacket, where it sat before them like a golden brown sun.

At the sight of the loaf, Monsieur Aulard's attention wavered from his immediate grief. "Where did you get that?" he asked.

"From the Marquis de Villeduval's kitchen." Têtu broke off a piece and handed it to him.

The hot wine and bread worked their magic on Monsieur Aulard. With a huge sigh he went to get dressed, reappearing with his wig placed lopsidedly on his head, his waistcoat buttons done up wrong, and his shirt hanging out.

"I have a full house, all tickets sold and no performer!"

"You'll have to find someone else," said Têtu.

"*Mort bleu,*" said Monsieur Aulard. "I tell you, if I weren't so kindhearted, I would have you two thrown onto the streets for your failure to protect Topolain. Why, he was one of the greatest magicians France has ever seen!" He wiped his eyes and, putting on his heavy outer coat and scarf, opened the front door, letting in a blast of icy wind from the stone stairwell. "You can't stay here, you know."

"Don't worry, we'll soon be gone," said Têtu. "Count Kalliovski is after us too. We had trouble getting out of the château alive."

"*Mort bleu!* You know who he is too, don't you?"

"Yes, for my sins, I do."

"Who is he, then?"

"That," said Têtu, closing his eyes, "would not be worth my life to tell you."

Monsieur Aulard arrived at the theater and started to make inquiries to see who could fill Topolain's place for the evening performance. He sat at his desk and opened the bottom drawer, where he found what he was looking for, a none-too-clean glass and a bottle of wine. He pulled out the cork and poured himself a drink. It tasted good. He closed his eyes, taking another sip.

He opened his eyes with a start. There, sitting in the chair before him, was someone he had never seen before, but who he knew at once was Count Kalliovski. It was as if the devil himself had appeared from nowhere.

The shock made him choke on his wine, spraying it over his desk. Desperately he tried to recover himself.

"*Mort bleu,* you gave me the fright of my life," he gasped. Pulling out an overused handkerchief, he wiped his mouth and then the desk. "I didn't hear you, monsieur!"

"Where are they?" demanded the count.

"Where are who?" said Monsieur Aulard, hurriedly refilling his glass.

The count's hand in its black leather glove moved effortlessly toward the stem. With his fingers spread, he pinned the glass firmly to the table. "You know very well who I am after. The boy and the dwarf."

"I know no such thing," said Monsieur Aulard, trying to summon up much-needed indignation. "Perhaps you would be kind enough to tell me where Topolain is."

"Topolain is dead. I'll wager you've been told as much by the dwarf. It was I who pulled the trigger. A most unfortunate *accident*," said the count with emphasis.

Sweat was beginning to form on Monsieur Aulard's forehead. The room felt uncomfortably hot.

Kalliovski leaned forward and stared menacingly at him. "I need information."

Monsieur Aulard felt an icy trickle of sweat creep down his back.

"You will tell me where they are hiding. I know you know where they are," said the count, standing up.

"I assure you I do not. I haven't seen them," said Monsieur Aulard. Each word he spoke sounded shakier than the last.

"You have until the curtain goes up at seven to tell me," said the count. "If you fail"—here he gave a mean, thin-lipped smile—"if you fail, I hope for your sake that you have made peace with your Maker."

The door closed behind him as poor Monsieur Aulard waited to make sure that he had gone. Then, grabbing hold of the bottle, he drank what was left.

It was three o'clock and still snowing when Monsieur Aulard trudged up the stone stairs to the front door of his apartment. It swung alarmingly back and forth on its hinges.

"Hello," called Monsieur Aulard, his heart beating so fast that he thought it might give out altogether. There was no answer.

"You been popular," said his neighbor, a lady with a face like a ferret, sticking her head out of her front door. "A big man with a cloudy eye came looking for you and your friends."

"What friends?" said Monsieur Aulard.

"The boy and that there dwarf. He said he knew them."

Monsieur Aulard took out his wine-stained handkerchief and wiped the snow away from his face.

"He said he knew where to find you."

Monsieur Aulard, dry-mouthed and terrified, pushed open the door. The apartment looked worse than it had this morning. His possessions had been thrown across the room, papers scattered, the table knocked over, and glasses smashed. Even his mattress had been pulled from the bed. Iago, his feathers all ruffled, was hiding in a cupboard. He looked wretched. Monsieur Aulard stroked the parrot's head and put him back on his perch. Then he sat down in his armchair, and, feeling a piece of paper beneath him, pulled it out to see that it was a poster for the greatest show on earth, with Topolain and the People's Pierrot, the first walking, talking, all-knowing automaton.

"I am ruined," wept Monsieur Aulard. "The only time I have a success in my theater, it vanishes in a puff of smoke."

Finally, exhaustion overcame him and he fell fast asleep. He woke with a start, changed, and made his way miserably back to the theater, terrified of telling the count that this time he truly did not know the whereabouts of the boy and the dwarf.

Monsieur Aulard arrived at the theater just before seven to

be told that he had had no visitors and that no one had asked after him. He went up the stairs to his office and opened the door. The room was dark. Why had no one bothered to light the lamp? he thought irritably, fumbling for the tinderbox. He stumbled, steadying himself on his desk. In the dark he could see an unfamiliar shape.

"Who's there?" he called.

He lit the wick.

Slowly and terribly, the dead body of Topolain was revealed, sitting in his chair. Around his neck was a thin line of dried beads of blood. In his lap was the sawn-off head of the Pierrot, its glass eyes glinting in the lamplight.

Monsieur Aulard's scream could be heard all the way through the theater and out on the rue du Temple.

chapter nine

$\mathcal{T}$êtu and Yann had left the apartment earlier that morning, not long after Monsieur Aulard, for they knew that was the first place Milkeye would look for them.

The apartment block was never quiet. The lives of its inhabitants seemed to spill out onto the landing rather like the stuffing of Monsieur Aulard's chair. A terrible fight was taking place between a husband and wife on the floor below, witnessed and commented on by the other tenants. There was a cacophony of sounds: shouting, screaming, babies crying, dogs barking, the background noise of lives lived on the edge of existence. In such chaos Yann and Têtu went down the stairs almost unnoticed.

At the bottom sat a child of about seven, who looked older than his years, thin and half frozen.

"Best you go inside, *mon petit.*"

The boy stared at the dwarf, terrified. He didn't know what to make of the strange fellow who conjured up a loaf of bread from out of his coat. He looked at it in disbelief before grabbing it and running up the stairs. Only when safely out of reach did he lean down over the wrought-iron banister and shout, "Thank you, monsieur."

It had been one of those twilight days when the gloom of night still lingers on. The sky was so heavy with snow that it appeared to have collapsed under its own weight onto the buildings below. It was not a day for having your sleeve come adrift from your coat. Even the church bells had a muffled half-heard sound. No one was out by choice in these icy streets, with the snow piled high against the sides of the buildings, so that the walkways were narrow and treacherous.

The months of December and January had produced a bitter harvest, a crop of starved and frozen corpses, the money it brought in lining the pockets of the coffin-makers.

The lights and smoky warmth of Moet's Tavern seemed like a slice of heaven in this frozen city. As usual, it was full of hot-headed youths and men arguing over the state of the kingdom. Têtu found a table tucked away in the corner out of sight. Here he ordered the dish of the day for himself and Yann. Only when his fingers finally felt that they belonged to him again did he begin to sew the sleeve back onto the boy's coat.

Yann felt not only that his coat had come apart but that his world had been torn to pieces. Everything had changed the minute the pistol had gone off, killing Topolain.

What he knew about the past amounted to no more than a few facts, bright beads from an unthreaded necklace, reluctantly given to him by Têtu, who refused to join them together. He had no father that he knew of; his mother had been a dancer in a circus, and had died soon after he was born; Margoza, his surname, was the name of a village of which Têtu had fond memories. His survival had been due to Têtu, and Têtu alone.

What he knew about the dwarf was not much more. He had once been a jester to a king; which king, he wouldn't say. He had traveled the world with a dancing bear. All that had happened a long time before he had found himself with a baby to care for. Never once had he mentioned Count Kalliovski, or who he might be. So why now had the count tampered with the pistol? What exactly was it that Topolain and Têtu knew?

The more Yann thought about it, the more certain he was that there was one question that, if answered truthfully, might string together all the beads on the necklace.

"Who is Count Kalliovski?"

Têtu shrugged his shoulders.

"One day I will tell you," he said finally, cutting the thread with his teeth. He shook out the coat and handed it back to Yann.

"I'm old enough to know right away."

Some secrets are best kept, Têtu thought to himself. "Yannick, you know I love you as if you were my son. Don't you trust me?"

"I do."

"Then believe me, I will answer all your questions, but not now. Now is not the time. Now is not the place."

The food arrived and they set to eating.

Three tables away sat a group of young men, one of whom had a nose that looked as if it had been in an argument with a fist. His skin was pockmarked and he was talking loudly about the rights of citizens. He had no doubt drunk more than a skinful of wine, for he kept standing up and shouting out: "Citizens, the wind is changing! The old regime will be blown away. All is dust, all is dust!"

His friends quickly pulled him back down onto his seat.

"I have the right to say what I damn well please," he shouted, glaring at another man sitting alone at a table. "Don't you agree, citizen?"

Yann had been watching all this intently and did not at first notice Têtu wrapping his scarf about him and putting on his hat.

"Where are you going?"

"I have someone to see. I'll be back in a couple of hours. You are to wait here for me. If Milkeye comes looking for us, make yourself scarce."

Têtu set off purposefully, walking away from the Marais across the Pont Marie toward the left bank, where he stopped as he had done several times before to make sure that no one was following him.

He knew that he had to get the boy out of Paris. It was too dangerous for him to stay. The only hope of doing so lay with a friend of his, the English banker Charles Cordell. He walked on, remembering the night all those years ago at the theater in Le Havre, a memorable evening all around, for it was the first time that Topolain had successfully performed the bullet trick and the first time Têtu had met Cordell. The two of them had struck up an unlikely friendship. Their mutual interest, to begin with at least, was magic, for Cordell fancied himself something of an amateur conjurer.

Cordell soon realized that prejudice made people underestimate the dwarf. Têtu was not taken seriously, so he was told things other men would never have heard. Ladies confided in him, young men spouted their views. The dwarf listened to the gossip of the coffeehouses, the prittle-prattle of the salons, and the oratory of the clubs. Cordell, like Têtu, knew that these places were where the real intrigue lay.

The two would meet regularly at the Café Royal, where Têtu would tell Cordell all he had heard and seen. This information gave the banker a clearer idea of what was going on and how best to advise his clients.

The snow was still falling as Têtu made his way toward the rue du Dragon, with its grand, imposing houses. They had a smug quality, as if they had folded their arms across their frilled façades, and looked down judgmentally from tall disapproving windows onto the tree-lined boulevard below.

Têtu stood waiting for what felt like a lifetime before a housekeeper came hurrying out, carrying a lantern.

"Is Monsieur Cordell in?"

"Is he expecting you?"

"No, I came on the off-chance. I need to see him urgently. Will you say that Têtu is here?"

The housekeeper went inside, closing the door behind her. Têtu stood waiting, stamping his feet and blowing on his frozen hands. The door opened again and he was shown into the hall. His teeth were chattering as the housekeeper took his coat, hat, and scarf. The snow that had formed itself into frozen clumps on his stockings was melting onto the wooden floor. He stamped the rest off his shoes as he heard the door above him open, and looked up the stairwell at Charles Cordell.

Têtu had never been more pleased to see his friend's grave, bespectacled face staring down at him, and for the first time since the murder the night before he felt a glimmer of hope.

"Why, my dear friend, you look half frozen," said Cordell, coming forward with his hand outstretched.

"I need your help. I am in a great deal of trouble," said Têtu. And before he had even been taken into the elegant drawing room he had told Cordell the story of Topolain's death.

"This is a great loss," said Cordell, taking Têtu over to the fire and bringing out a bottle of cognac. "So . . . Kalliovski . . ."

Têtu nodded. "I have been a complete idiot," he said angrily. "I let my guard down, believed we were safe after all these years.

Fool, fool that I am not to have known who he was. I, of all people, should have suspected. I walked straight into a trap."

Têtu got to his feet as if sitting still was impossible, and started to walk up and down the room. "I knew he was a master of disguise, yet I too was nearly taken in by him. Do you know what gave him away? His hands, his large, ugly hands."

He made a sound that could have been mistaken for a laugh, though Cordell heard it as pent-up fury.

"Yes, his face may be smooth and ageless, but you can never change your hands, they never lie," Têtu continued.

"May I ask why you are so afraid of Kalliovski?"

"Sometimes you meet someone you know is touched by evil. Kalliovski is such a man. I believe he came originally from Transylvania. We met when Topolain and I were working in St. Petersburg, where he made his money by cheating at the card tables. He was a cheap trickster, a gambler. He was interested in us because of the magic; we didn't much like him, stayed out of his way. But he became obsessed with a friend of ours, a young dancer. In the end, in fear of her life, she ran away from him and we went with her. The idea was that we would protect her, for we had seen what he was like when he didn't get what he wanted."

"What happened?"

"He followed us to France. He found us, and he killed her with his bare hands. I could do nothing to save her. After that he was wanted for murder, and he disappeared. Later I heard that he had made his way back east toward Transylvania, and had married. I believed—or rather I wanted to believe—that no good would have come to him. I first heard the name Kalliovski shortly after I met you, but I had no inkling that it was the same man. The Count Kalliovski I learned about was a mysterious figure, who claimed to be on the verge of creating an automaton that could pass as a human. From all accounts, he was a man who would sell his soul to the devil to learn the secret of creating life."

"My dear friend," said Cordell, "it seems to me that you have unwittingly turned over a stone and found there a deadly creature."

"There is one other thing you should know," said Têtu, and he pulled from his pocket the red necklace. "This is what Yann found in Kalliovski's room." He handed it to Cordell, a thin red ribbon with seven crimson garnets set into it like drops of blood.

"If this were to be worn round the neck," said Cordell, examining it, "it would look as if your throat had been cut."

"Precisely," said Têtu. "The only people who have ever been found wearing such a thing, so I have been told, are dead. I am sure that Kalliovski is in some way involved. This being found in his chamber proves it."

"Têtu, I can't bear to see you in such a state. What can I do to help?"

"I need to disappear. I can't take the boy with me, it would be impossible. I want him out of the way, for a while at least. I want him to go to London, be given a chance to learn to read and write. Just a few months, that's all, then he can come back."

"I am sure Henry Laxton, my colleague in London, wouldn't mind looking after the boy until things are back to normal. Coincidentally, Laxton has some knowledge of Kalliovski," said Cordell, refilling Têtu's glass. "Laxton has a French wife, whose sister was married to the Marquis de Villeduval. Some years ago, when Mrs. Laxton's sister was killed in an accident, he went to Normandy, to the château of the Villeduvals. It was very odd. The marquis appeared to have no interest in his wife's death, or in what would happen to their only daughter, Sido."

"We met the marquis's daughter," said Têtu. "She helped us escape."

"What small circles we all travel in. It was Kalliovski who stopped Henry Laxton from bringing Sido back to London to be brought up by his wife. The marquis didn't care one way or another about his daughter, yet for some peculiar reason Kalliovski did." Cordell went over to his desk. "Tell me one thing," he said. "What part did the boy play with the Pierrot?"

"He was the voice, and he read people's minds."

"Interesting," said Cordell, handing Têtu an envelope. "Now, here is enough money to pay for your expenses."

"No, I don't need it."

"My dear friend, take it. I know the proprietor at the Hôtel d'Angleterre, a Madame Saltaire. You'll be safe there. I take it that the boy has no passport?"

"No."

"Then I will have to get that organized. It will take a day. You must stay in your room until you hear from me. By the way, how old is the boy?"

"Fourteen. He is like a son to me. I love him as if he were my own flesh and blood."

Charles Cordell smiled. "I will let Henry Laxton know to expect him."

The two men shook hands.

Têtu sat in Charles Cordell's carriage, grateful for the lift back to Moet's Tavern, and thinking to himself about what he hadn't told his friend. A secret that Têtu hoped to take to his grave, for some words can do as much damage to the living as a shot fired from a pistol.

It was at about the same time as the carriage pulled up outside the tavern that Monsieur Aulard lit his lantern.

chapter ten

*Y*ann had waited in Moet's Tavern until it had grown dark. He was beginning to think that Têtu was never coming back when, to his great relief, he saw the dwarf's small shape push and jostle his way to where he was sitting.

"Everything is arranged," said Têtu. "Come, we must get out of here."

They walked swiftly away from the Palais Royal and down a tangle of narrow streets.

"Where are we going?" asked Yann.

"To a hotel. We'll stay there for the night, and then you'll get the coach to Calais and go to London," said Têtu.

"London!" said Yann, stunned.

"Come on, keep up." Têtu was now walking as fast as his

legs would allow him. He looked anxiously around him. "Don't dawdle. The sooner we're off these streets the better."

The entrance to the Hôtel d'Angleterre was a wooden door that opened into a courtyard overlooked by two other apartment blocks. At the far end, under a stone arch, stood a narrow door that led out onto the rue du Richelieu, a two-minute walk from the Palais Royal.

Here Têtu, as Cordell had suggested, took a room for the night.

"Why are we going to London?" asked Yann, the minute they were alone.

"Not we; you. You are going to London."

"No!" said Yann. "I'm not going anywhere without you."

"Paris is not safe. Kalliovski wants us both dead. I can disappear—I've done it all my life."

Yann started to interrupt.

"Wait, wait. Before you say anything, listen. I have a great friend, an Englishman called Charles Cordell, who is a banker based in Paris. He has agreed to send you to London and put you in the care of his partner Henry Laxton, who will teach you to read and write and speak English."

"I'm not leaving you."

Têtu's face looked as hard as ever Yann had seen it.

"Listen to me. You are not a baby. It will only be for a few months. You will do this and that is the end of it."

Yann was too exhausted to argue any more, too angry to sleep.

He lay facedown on the bed, furious, only to find that when he woke up it was morning.

Whether or not Têtu had slept, Yann couldn't tell. The dwarf was pacing to and fro, mumbling to himself. On a table sat a bottle of wine and a loaf of bread.

Yann sat up and said, "I still don't understand why I have to go away."

"I'm going to explain. I'm going to tell you things you want to know. Will you listen, or are you going to block up your ears with anger, so that you won't hear anything but your own thunder?"

Yann shrugged.

"You've often asked me about your mother, and now I will tell you," said Têtu. "Your mother loved you dearly. She wanted no harm to come to you, and I promised her I would keep your Gypsy origins quiet."

"Gypsy!" said Yann. It was a word like an old tin mug that had followed them wherever they went . . . a swearword, a figure of speech, an insult. It confirmed what he already knew, that he and Têtu were misfits, outcasts living on the edges of society. He had never imagined it to be the truth. He and Têtu spoke Romany for their own protection, Têtu had told him, because few people understood it or knew where it came from. Now he could see that these roots went far deeper than he had ever thought, and he wished with all his heart that it were not so.

"Yannick, we are an ancient and noble people," said Têtu.

"Take from this what is good, and learn from it. I regret that you couldn't grow up in a Gypsy world where you would have known our ways and secrets."

"I've asked you so often if we were Gypsies, and you've always shrugged your shoulders and said no," said Yann.

"It was for your own safety. You know there is a price on every Gypsy's head. The gallows and the huntsman's gun wait for us."

The seriousness of what Têtu was saying took away all Yann's anger. Maybe this explained why they were not like other people. Maybe it at last explained why he could read minds and see into the future.

"I have done my best by you, Yannick," said Têtu. "I have given you a piece of your Gypsy origins by teaching you our language. Your mother didn't even want me to do that, for fear that you would be taken away from me, that you would be branded like cattle and sent away to sea. It was for the best that I kept silent."

Yann sat down on the edge of the bed. "Go on."

Here Têtu stopped, as if reconsidering all he had said so far.

"Your mother was called Anis, and she was beautiful. She had your eyes, dark as ebony and deep as a well. When I met her at the circus in St. Petersburg I knew straightaway that she was Romany, like me. She told me that each year her people followed the ancient routes, wintering in caves, and when the snows passed they traveled deep into the forests, far away from the house-dwellers.

"Anis's mother was the keeper of the arts of sorcery among her tribe. She had extraordinary powers. She could move objects without touching them. Her daughter could do it too."

"And so can you."

Têtu continued. "All objects have threads of light coming from them. Living objects have the brightest threads of light, energy that flashes like lightning. Lifeless objects, such as cups, jugs, or beds, have dull threads of light. If you can see this light, then you can become a master, able to move things at your will. Think, Yann, what power that would give you."

"Is that how you work the Pierrot? Is it? Tell me."

Têtu said nothing.

"All right," said Yann. "If you won't answer that, tell me how my mother ended up in a circus."

"Something terrible happened. It was Anis's wedding day. She was fourteen and the boy was sixteen. She believed that they were one soul divided into two bodies, and that only when they were together were they whole.

"The ceremony started at daybreak round the campfire, when the marriage was sealed with a cut made on the bride's right wrist and the groom's left wrist; then their hands were bound together and they took an oath to free each other when love had left their hearts.

"There was singing and dancing to celebrate—and then the huntsmen came to kill the Gypsies. Anis's mother saw them sitting on their fine horses watching, waiting. She ordered her people to carry on dancing, shouting out "Life is life!" in Romany. The

Gypsies went on playing their fiddles and singing their songs. They didn't run. Until the shooting started."

"But my mother must have managed to get away," said Yann.

"Anis said she never knew how. It was as if her mother had made her invisible. But she remembered the last thing her bridegroom said to her: 'In death they will never catch us, my beloved one. We are birds, we are free.'

"She remembered nothing more. When she woke up she found herself in the hollow of a tree. It was getting dark. She stood in the middle of that clearing and saw them all hanging in the trees like songbirds, colorful but lifeless: her bridegroom, her mother, every one of her tribe. Even the babies had been slaughtered. Blood dripped from the oak leaves. That day, her wedding day, she lost everything.

"She ran far away and joined a circus, never speaking of her Gypsy roots, though her dark hair and eyes told the truth of it. She never spoke of it, that is, until I met her."

Yann was very quiet. Of all the things he had imagined about his mother, he had never once imagined this.

It was Têtu who broke the silence.

"It is nothing to be ashamed of. Far from it—it is a source of pride."

"Are you a French Gypsy?"

"No, I come from Romania. It is another story for another time. I have told you how I met your mother. That is enough."

"So am I only half Gypsy?"

"No."

"You know that for certain?"

"Yes."

"My father was the Gypsy boy my mother married?"

"No, Yannick, he was killed some seven years before you were born. Who your real father was, I do not know, but Anis believed you were a gift from the spirit of her one true love. We Gypsies know and understand things that those attached to houses and land will never comprehend. We have outlived and outwitted great civilizations."

"Do you think I have inherited those gifts?"

"You are a natural. You have an exceptional talent already."

"Will you teach me to work the Pierrot like you do?"

Têtu laughed. "In time, Yann, in time."

There was a knock at the door. On Cordell's instructions, Madame Saltaire had brought a package up to Têtu. It contained Yann's travel documents and a passport.

"You leave tonight," said Têtu after she had gone. "I'll take you to the coach at seven. A man called Tull, an Englishman, will escort you to Calais, where there will be a boat waiting to take you to Dover. We must hurry, so as not to miss the tide."

Yann wanted to say again that he didn't want to go. This time, though, he knew it was useless. Instead he made up his mind that in this new country he would let no one know of his Gypsy origins. There he would have a fresh start. For once in his life he would be like everyone else.

As they left, Têtu had pulled Yann's coat about him and buttoned it up as if he were a child. Yann had then an image of his mother, and a terrible sense of loss rushed in upon him.

"I can do that," he had said.

Still Têtu insisted, standing on tiptoe to put the scarf around Yann's neck and tucking it carefully into his coat.

The hall of the hotel was empty. The lantern outside was shining on the snow, making it look blue. A cat came meowing across the courtyard, lifting its paws in disgust at the depth of the snow and curling itself around their legs before going into the warmth.

Têtu seized Yann's hand. "Now. We'll make a run for it."

Far too late did Yann sense the menace in the general silence. The windows of the building overlooking the courtyard were shuttered as if they had closed their eyes against what was about to happen.

"Here goes," said Têtu.

A shot rang out, and suddenly Yann realized he was dragging a dead weight behind him. He stopped and stared down at Têtu, who was lying crumpled in the snow.

"Get up! Get up!"

The dwarf's eyes were closed. His skin had already started looking translucent.

"No!" shouted Yann. "No!" He tried with all his strength to lift Têtu.

At that moment he saw the red necklace lying there in the blood.

"It's no good," whispered the dwarf. "Go, run like the wind. Life is life, Yannick."

Yann felt a cold leather-gloved hand come down hard on his shoulder.

"Got you!" said a voice as the shadow of Milkeye fell over him. "There's no escaping."

Yann could feel the burning heat of the pistol butt as it was pushed into the side of his head. Suddenly everything both slowed down and speeded up. Yann shut his eyes. In that second, when life and death hung in the balance, the trigger clicked, the barrel jammed. Yann opened his eyes to see Milkeye staring ferociously at his weapon.

Madame Saltaire ran out of the hotel screaming, hands flying. Yann twisted himself free, conscious of nothing but escape. He was already at the street door when the second bullet ricocheted off the stone wall. He ran as fast as he could, soon to be lost from view in the maze of streets.

The sharp air rasped his throat painfully but still he ran, and soon the sound of the city enveloped him, calming him. Near exhausted, he stopped, and checking that no one was following him, backtracked toward the Palais Royal. He could hear the clocks chiming the hour. Seven o'clock.

A coach was waiting, its driver huddled against the icy wind in a great cape, his groom beside him.

The coach door opened and a man with an English accent asked, "Are you Yann Margoza? Where's the gentleman who was supposed to bring you here?"

"Dead."

"Too bad. Get in," said the man. "There's no time to lose if we're to catch the tide."

Stunned and grief-stricken, Yann climbed in. The man, the coach, all became a blur. He looked out of the window as the terrifying reality overwhelmed him. Topolain had performed the ultimate trick. He had taken with him Yann's world, the theater, the actors, the scenery—all vanished, all gone, in a wisp of smoke from a pistol.

The coach rattled and shook. He could hear the horses snorting, their bridles jangling; and he could hear too the unmistakable voice of Têtu as he whispered to him, "Life is life."

chapter eleven

$\mathcal{H}$ere, in London's fashionable Bloomsbury, is a newly built town house that faces a tree-lined square, with streets leading to Piccadilly and Whitehall. To the back its windows look out to the rolling hills of Hampstead and beyond. The house, which is decorated in the French style, is charming, comfortable, welcoming. It is the home of Henry and Juliette Laxton.

Henry Laxton could not be described as handsome. He had, though, an engaging face with undistinguished features made attractive by the fact that he was a rich banker who had the good fortune to be married to a beautiful woman.

This morning he was to be found in his study. A letter from Charles Cordell had just been delivered. It should have reached him two days ago, but the messenger had been held up by bad weather and a lame horse. He now read with increasing alarm that a boy called Yann Margoza was due at the Boar Inn, Fleet Street at three o'clock that very afternoon, giving him no time to prepare for his arrival.

Henry Laxton stood by the fire lost in thought. Taking on such a boy would, he knew, be a challenge, especially as he and his wife had no children of their own.

He rang the bell and his valet entered the room. "Is my wife still in her boudoir?"

"I believe so, sir."

"And does she have any visitors with her?"

"One, sir, Lady Faulkner."

Henry Laxton smiled inwardly. He knew how bored his wife would be. Lady Faulkner's sole aim in visiting her friends was to pick up the latest tittle-tattle and add it to her cauldron of malicious small talk. He went up the stairs to his wife's boudoir.

Juliette Laxton was the younger sister of Isabelle Gautier, who had married the Marquis de Villeduval. Their father, a widower, was a wealthy bourgeois businessman, and the marriage was seen as beneficial to both sides. The Villeduvals would have an injection of much-needed money and land, and Monsieur Gautier would see at least one of his daughters settled with a title, and could claim an aristocrat as a son-in-law.

Only Juliette had had any idea of the depths of Isabelle's misery, married to a much older man who cared only for himself.

Then, shortly after the death of Monsieur Gautier, Isabelle

was killed in an accident when a coach was overturned. The only survivor was three-year-old Sido, whose leg had been badly broken.

After his wife's death the marquis did something so strange, so out of character, that the only rational explanation was surely insanity brought on by grief. For it had turned out a double tragedy: His half brother, Armand, his father's favorite, had gone missing at the same time. All attempts to find him had failed.

Isabelle was not buried in the family vault in Normandy. Instead, her coffin was taken to a small church by the sea. There were no mourners and little ceremony. She was placed in a simple grave and the headstone merely recorded her name, Isabelle Gautier, without title, inscription, or date.

The marquis was never to speak of his wife again, and his half brother's disappearance proved to be the death of his father.

Juliette had never gotten over the loss of her beloved sister. Her only consolation had been the hope that she might be allowed to bring up Isabelle's daughter, Sido, but it was not to be. For reasons Juliette had never understood, Sido's father, the marquis, had written to say that he wanted nothing more to do with the Gautier family.

For Juliette it had been a double bereavement. Not only had she lost her sister and her closest friend, but shortly after this she had had a miscarriage and been told that there was little hope of her conceiving again. It had been her greatest sadness, for she had always imagined herself surrounded by a large and noisy family.

She sat now in front of her dressing table mirror, wishing her visitor would leave. Not for the first time, Lady Faulkner was giving Juliette the benefit of her advice.

"My formula for looking perpetually young is to avoid laughter and excessive use of the facial muscles. That, I can assure you, leads to wrinkles and the falling of the flesh. Best by far to keep one's face emotionless. Only by such a means can one hold back time's cruel hand—"

She was interrupted by a knock at the door. Juliette's face lit up with a charming smile when she saw her husband enter the room, while Lady Faulkner's remained masklike and rigid.

"I trust your family is well?" said Henry Laxton with a bow.

"Quite well," replied Lady Faulkner stiffly.

"And does your son still spend all his time at the theater, sporting with pretty actresses?" The question was designed to speed the guest's departure.

Lady Faulkner's features knew not quite how to react to this. Her lips longed to purse themselves together in disgust at such a suggestion, but lines, as she had just informed Mrs. Laxton, must be avoided at all costs.

"I have no idea what you mean, Mr. Laxton," she said, standing up and waving her fan vigorously. "Jack is at Oxford, where he is studying diligently. Now I must leave you. I have other calls to make where I will, I know, be very welcome." And with great indignation she swept out of the room.

The Laxtons waited until they heard the front door being closed, then both burst out laughing.

"She seems more absurd every time I see her," said Henry Laxton, pouring himself a cup of tea. "Jack hasn't been near Oxford all term, from what I can gather. The woman is a fool."

Juliette sighed. "*Mon chéri*, please remind me to laugh and smile and to use every muscle my face might possess, lest I end up looking as sour and miserable as that woman."

"That would be an impossibility. Now, on a more serious note, I have had a letter this morning from Charles Cordell, and I have news that will hearten you. It relates to Sido de Villeduval."

"To Sido? What is it?" asked Juliette urgently.

"Apparently Sido was brought home from her convent for a party that her father was giving in honor of Count Kalliovski."

"That odious man!"

"Quite. That odious man had a whim to see her, and has persuaded the marquis not to send her back to the convent."

"How do you know all this? It's incredible!"

Henry Laxton grinned. "I have my spies."

"No, don't joke. Tell me. I know! You heard it from a client of the bank."

"Not quite, but tonight you will be able to ask after Sido yourself. You will meet someone who spoke to her only a few days ago."

"You're talking in riddles! Who is it?"

Henry Laxton walked toward the window and then turned back.

"Cordell has asked if we would be willing to take in a boy for a few months. He is fourteen years old, an orphan, brought up by a contact of Cordell's in Paris, a man called Têtu."

"But what has this boy to do with Sido?"

"Aha!" said Laxton. "I am coming to that. Têtu and the boy are traveling entertainers—"

"Traveling entertainers! What strange company Mr. Cordell keeps," Juliette exclaimed.

"—and a couple of days ago they were invited, with a magician called Topolain, to perform at a party the marquis was giving."

"The same party that Sido was at?"

"Precisely. And at this private performance the magician Topolain performed the bullet trick for which he was famous in Paris. It was Kalliovski who fired the pistol, and he shot the magician dead."

"But why?"

"Why indeed? He claims it was an accident, a trick gone wrong, though neither Cordell nor Têtu believes that. Têtu is certain that it was because both he and Topolain knew something about his past. Whatever the reason, Têtu is now terrified that Kalliovski will come after him and the boy. He went to Cordell for help. Cordell has asked that we look after the boy for a few months."

"And this boy met Sido?"

"Yes. Evidently she helped them escape."

"And what is the boy called?"

"Yann Margoza. He hasn't had many advantages in life. Maybe we can help him, give him some education. If we are true to the principles of enlightenment, then a pauper is fit to be a king, and there is no reason why this boy cannot live on equal terms with us and learn to be a gentleman."

Juliette's face lit up with excitement. "There's no question of it. This boy met Sido! He will live with us as a part of the family, not in the servants' quarters."

Henry Laxton came over and kissed the nape of his wife's very white neck.

The carriage bringing Yann to this rough dark diamond of a city made its way over Blackfriars Bridge. Mr. Tull, whose job it had been to transport the boy here, had one last stop to make, at the inn on Fleet Street where he had been instructed to wait for Mr. Laxton's carriage.

The courtyard of the Boar Inn was full of stagecoaches and horses, ladies and gentlemen, assorted parcels and trunks, all taken up with the hectic business of arriving or leaving. Mr. Tull decided upon a well-earned breakfast. He stopped at the door of the inn and looked woefully at the boy. It struck Mr. Tull as nothing short of an insult to have to take a foreign ragamuffin into this decent God-fearing place. He sighed. Orders were orders. He was to hand the boy over to Mr. Laxton. Until that was done, he would have to keep him close by, for the boy had the look of one who might scarper. He took Yann by the scruff of the neck and steered him, as one would a dog, into a seat by the window.

Yann shook himself free of Mr. Tull's clutches and sat huddled up in the corner. The journey had been a blur of misery and grief. He didn't like his jailer, for that was how he had come to think of Mr. Tull, a bulldog of a man who had made it quite clear that the feeling was mutual. He had said as much in very bad French. "*Stupide garçon.* All this trouble! For what? For you?"

After that they had traveled in silence. It suited them both, for Yann needed time to think about what had happened. Never had he felt more alone and wretched than he did now. He regretted that he had ever agreed to come to this country, brought here by a man he didn't like and didn't trust, to stay with a man he had never met.

The inn with its low wooden beams was paneled and stained near black by tobacco. Smoke filled the air as well as the sharp smell of burned fat and stale ale. It was full of hungry people, travelers' appetites demanding constant satisfaction.

"Bring me a tankard of the finest ale, a steak, and a dozen oysters," said Mr. Tull to the innkeeper.

The innkeeper looked at Yann as he might look at a dirty plate. "The same for him?"

Mr. Tull reluctantly nodded his head. "Only a small beer for him, mind you."

When the innkeeper had gone Mr. Tull said angrily, "I don't

know why a gentleman like Mr. Laxton would be wanting to give a street urchin like you a roof over your head. If you were to turn up on my doorstep, I'd have you taken down to the workhouse without a second thought. I wouldn't want one of your kind near me or my kin."

Yann might not have understood the language, but he got the gist of what Mr. Tull was saying all too clearly.

Mr. Tull fidgeted impatiently as he waited for his ale, tapping his short stubby fingers on the table.

They ate in silence. Mr. Tull mopped his plate clean with the last of his bread, finished his ale, and burped loudly.

"I would say 'Excuse me, Your Honor,' if I were in *good* company," he said, emphasizing the word *good*, "which I ain't, so I won't be saying nothing."

He stood up and shook himself.

"Now you stay put while I see if the carriage has arrived." He leaned across the table, grasping the lapels of Yann's coat. "If you so much as move one of them there miserable muscles of yours, you'll be in for it and no mistake. Do you get my drift?"

Yann watched as Mr. Tull wove his way across the courtyard and in that instant he decided to take his chance. His one aim was to get back to Paris to find where Têtu had been buried, and kill Kalliovski. The idea of doing away with the count was all that had kept him together on the long journey here.

In his haste to leave, he ran into the innkeeper.

"Hey, where do you think you're going, you blasted scallywag?"

the man shouted as the tray he was carrying went flying. There was a loud crash as pewter tumblers and plates of food fell to the floor. For a moment the whole room fell silent, and heads turned to see a boy running for the door as if his life depended on it.

Yann didn't stop to look back at the mess he had caused. Quickly, he swerved past a coach driver who made a desperate attempt to catch him. He ducked and dived around horses and carriages. Turning back he ran straight into a well-dressed man who firmly but kindly put his hand on his shoulder.

"Yann Margoza, I take it?" said Henry Laxton in flawless French.

Mr. Tull came panting and puffing after him, shaking his fist.

"Where's that ruddy boy? That little heathen, I'll wring his scrawny neck, I will. He's been nothing but trouble since I first clapped eyes on him."

"You will do no such thing," said Mr. Laxton, still holding firmly on to Yann. Pushing him into his carriage and climbing in after him, he nodded to his coachman, who handed Mr. Tull an envelope with his money in it.

Mr. Tull started counting.

"It is the agreed sum," said Mr. Laxton.

By now the carriage was making its way out through the arch, disappearing into the main thoroughfare.

"Wait a minute! Not so ruddy fast!" shouted Mr. Tull to the disappearing wheels. "I need money for the breakages."

Mr. Tull was not in a good mood as he walked toward the Fleet

River and the Red Lion Inn, a tavern renowned for the company of rogues.

If you couldn't make an honest penny by hard work, then perhaps it would be more worthwhile to make a dishonest pound instead. "Where is the justice?" said Mr. Tull to himself. "The rich get everything and do nothing for it, and all the while they expect the likes of me to risk life and limb for them. And they don't even pay for breakages."

He had heard the talk of clever people in Paris and in the London coffeehouses, people who knew what the tomorrows of life had in store. Civil war, that was what they were predicting. As far as he was concerned it couldn't come soon enough. There was money to be made in upheavals.

chapter twelve

The savagery of grief tore at Yann, filled him with rage, stripped him of his gift for reading people's minds. All that was left was the silence of heartache. His past and his future had vanished, had been gobbled up and spat out again as if the very marrow had been sucked from his soul with the murder of Têtu.

Lost in the fury of his thoughts, he hadn't heard one word Mr. Laxton had been saying, until finally, standing in the hall of the house in Queen Square, he realized that by some twist of fate he had entered another world, and he didn't want to be here.

Henry Laxton's valet, Vane, had been with his master for many years and spoke tolerable French. He took Yann upstairs and showed him a large bedchamber, dominated by a four-poster bed and smelling of oranges. They reminded Yann of hot summers and journeys with Têtu. Behind a screen at the far end was another door that led to a small antechamber, and there by the fire sat a bath filled with steaming hot water. What it was doing in the room Yann wasn't sure until Vane started solemnly rolling up his sleeves and said that sir was to take a bath.

Yann stared at him in disbelief and then, seeing that this was no idle threat, made for the door, but to no avail. Vane was doglike in his determination, with a wiry strength that took Yann by surprise. Finally, defeated by exhaustion and the lack of sleep, he resigned himself to drowning.

He was washed and scrubbed until the water was as filthy as the Seine and his skin tingled all over. Wrapped in a large housecoat, he sat in front of the fire while a barber set about cutting off his long black locks and vigorously rubbing a lotion into his scalp, for the express reason, so he said, of ridding Yann of fleas.

From an assortment of shirts and breeches, Vane then set about dressing Yann as if he were a tailor's dummy. Finally, he tied a cravat around his neck and set a looking glass before him. What Yann saw there was a stranger. If it hadn't been for the anger in his face he would have said he was staring at someone else.

Vane inspected his handiwork and took Yann down to the sitting room on the first floor to present him to Mr. and Mrs. Laxton.

"Well, look at you, sir," said Mr. Laxton in his perfect French. "To the manor born, I would say."

Yann, not knowing what was expected of him, bowed stiffly. All this felt as if it were happening to someone else, that he was simply an actor upon the stage.

"You have met my niece, Sido de Villeduval, I gather," said Mrs. Laxton.

Yann looked at her. Was he dreaming, or did she look like Sido?

"Yes."

"And was she well?"

Was she well? He had to think what he was being asked. Was this the reason he had been brought here, to answer this one question—was Sido well?

Finally he said, "She is unhappy."

After an awkward supper that seemed to go on and on, with many courses and unanswered questions, Mr. Laxton took him into his study. On hearing of Têtu's death, he told Yann that this was to be his new home. What he meant by this, Yann had no idea. The only family he had ever known was Têtu. Home couldn't be counted in candlesticks and cutlery, of that much he was sure. Home for him had been simple: Home was Têtu.

That night he lay awake, finding the soft mattress worrying, the smell of oranges unsettling. Finally he got out of bed and fell asleep in front of the fire, like a cat.

The days that followed were encompassed by ticking clocks and dull, meaningless routine. Time dragged its weary feet for Yann in this grand house. The long, empty momentum of the minutes and the passing hours was something he had never been aware of before.

A tutor had been employed for Yann, a Mr. Rose. He was as thin as a sheet of paper left flattened and forgotten in a book, and had about him the smell of dried-up ink. Knowledge had been beaten into him and he saw no reason why it shouldn't be beaten into every other child. His philosophy of education was not one he had shared with Mr. Laxton.

On the first day of his employment, what appeared before Mr. Rose was a well-dressed, intelligent-looking young gentleman.

"Appearances can be deceptive," Mr. Rose was to grumble three weeks later. "The boy is nothing more than a savage. No tailored garment is going to alter that fact."

This cutting remark had been his first complaint, followed by, "The boy has no aptitude for learning."

Mr. Laxton had spoken firmly to Yann, who stood in his study and said nothing.

Another two weeks passed, by which time Yann felt as if his very life was beginning to be drummed out of him by this wizened leaf of a tutor. He would gaze out of the window, longing to be down in the street where life went on, until he could take it no longer.

One day Mr. Rose, in a fit of temper, threw a book at Yann, hitting him on the head. Yann got up and calmly took the cane from his terrified tutor, breaking it across his leg before delivering a knockout blow. Mr. Rose almost flew across the room. He lay stretched out cold on the wooden floor, his nose bleeding profusely.

Yann went down the stairs to Mr. Laxton's study and told him exactly what he had done and why.

There was a general commotion, a doctor was called for, and Mr. Rose, regaining consciousness, demanded that the boy be brought before a magistrate and sent to the clink for the savage he was. Then, seeing that Mr. Laxton was going to do nothing of the sort, he left, appalled, holding his handkerchief to his very sore nose.

Immediately he went hurrying around to Lady Faulkner, whose son Jack had benefited greatly from his tutoring. For her part she had swiftly and delightedly passed on the news that the Laxtons, for want of a child, had taken in an alleycat. The scandal kept many a lady happy over her morning coffee and many a gentleman at his club wondering what the respectable banker was thinking of.

The Laxtons took no notice whatsoever of the gossip, and employed another tutor who had no more control over Yann than the dreadful Mr. Rose. He lasted only a month before storming out of the house, announcing that the boy was unteachable.

Finally free of his tutors, Yann took to leaving the house without permission and going off by himself to explore London. The vulgar tongue of the streets began to intrigue him: It was a stewpot of words and sounds that he was hungry to taste. It took him no time to speak these earthy words with a near-perfect Cockney accent.

All attempts at keeping him at home failed. Locked doors and high windows were no barrier to him. He would frequently climb down the side of the house at night without being noticed by the night-watchman. He had always found the darkness friendly: It was like a huge overcoat, one he was well used to wearing. He could see almost as clearly in the dark as in the day, and had never understood people's fear of it.

For all the trouble Yann caused the Laxtons, they could not help liking the boy. There was nothing timid in his nature. He was fearless, stood up and fought, despised injustice, and cared little about the injuries he received. Mr. Rose was an ass of a man for not seeing how clever the boy was. Anyone who had a tongue that could master English this quickly was no fool. Têtu had been right when he told Cordell the boy had talent. The problem lay in how to make him see the opportunities he was merrily throwing away.

Mrs. Laxton understood better than her husband what Yann felt. She too had been sent near mad by grief, and it was the memory of what she had gone through that made her brave.

Late one foggy March night she waited in Yann's room for him to come back from one of his escapades. He looked sheepish as he climbed through the window to see her sitting there in the dark. He was certain he was going to be punished. Instead she lit a candle and invited him to sit down.

"What is it you want?" she asked.

"To go back to Paris."

"Why?"

"I want to find out what happened to Têtu."

"You know what happened, he was shot. It was a terrible tragedy for you. Why do you think he sent you here?"

Yann shrugged his shoulders.

"No, that won't do," she said sharply. "You are a clever boy. Now, tell me again."

"To learn to speak English, and I can now."

"You have the accent of the street and the manners of a ruffian. Your friend Têtu went to Mr. Cordell and told him you were talented, that you deserved to be given an opportunity, that there was a lot more to you than meets the eye. What I have seen is a stubborn, unhappy Gypsy who is too wrapped up in himself to see what his friend sacrificed for him."

"I *am* a Gypsy," said Yann through gritted teeth, realizing that he was about to break down. "I don't belong here, not in your world. Not in all this softness. Not imprisoned by walls—"

"When I was nine my mother died," Mrs. Laxton interrupted. "She was very pious, and I believed that the only reason she had left me was because I had been naughty. I was lucky; I had a loving older sister who helped me to understand that she hadn't left me behind for anything I had done." She leaned forward and touched Yann's hand. "It's not your fault Têtu died. You couldn't have caught the bullet; you are not a magician."

Yann felt burning hot tears sting the corners of his eyes.

"I should have stayed with him—I shouldn't have run."

He was suddenly aware that Mr. Laxton was standing in the doorway, listening.

"Stayed to be killed," Mr. Laxton said. "That would have been a waste."

"We are here to help you," said his wife softly, "but you refuse to let even a chink of light into that dark space in your head."

"I don't want anything from you. I don't want your help. I never wanted to come here!" Yann was shouting now, so angry at the tears that wouldn't stop rolling down his face, joining together under his chin. "Save your money and save your pity. I want none of it!"

Blast the tears, why didn't they stop?

"The door is open. If you want to go back to Paris, go," said Henry Laxton. "I am not your jailer. You are not a slave, you are a free man."

Yann bolted down the stairs two at a time. He pushed past the startled doorman and out into the foggy night air.

Henry Laxton leaned over the banisters and watched him go. "Well, that's that. What a fine mess we've made."

His wife put her arms around him. *"Mon chéri,"* she said, "don't despair. I promise you, this is not the end. It is just the beginning."

chapter thirteen

*Y*ann only stopped running when he reached Seven Dials. The sound of his feet on the pavement was the drumbeat that finally calmed him down. Gasping for breath he leaned against the corner of a building, grateful for the thick fog, and laughed out loud at his own stupidity. Well, he thought bitterly, I can't go back there again.

He felt certain that the Laxtons would be mighty pleased to be rid of him. Mrs. Laxton had called him a Gypsy! He *was* a Gypsy. What did any of it matter now? He pulled the collar of his coat up, the biting cold tickling its way through the seams. He could hear around him the distorted voices of people sounding as if they were underwater, their words swimming before them, their owners following, appearing out of the fog like phantoms before disappearing again.

As the cold found its way into his bones it dawned on him exactly how alone he was. Like a small pebble on a stony beach.

He shook his head. He had been a complete fool. What did he have? Nothing, just the clothes he stood up in, not a penny to his name. He looked down at his coat. In the morning he would pawn it. That should give him some money, at least enough for a day or so. For the time being he would just have to keep on walking.

He made his way toward Covent Garden, where the audiences were spilling out of the theaters. All those people, eager to be home! Sedan chairs vying for business, boasting how fast they went. Carriages lined up, horses snorting.

Maybe he should try to find work in the theater, though he wondered quite what he had to offer. The ability to throw his voice was surely not enough, not now that he couldn't read minds. That gift had abandoned him. It belonged to another time.

The bells of St. Martin's were chiming eleven o'clock as he walked away from the piazza. It was going to be a long, cold night.

On the last stroke he heard someone call out for help. It was a sharp, urgent cry that was strangled the minute it had found a voice.

Yann stopped and listened. It was the cry of a desperate man. The fog made it hard to work out where he was. He heard nothing more.

Then he caught the growl of voices coming from down an

alleyway that smelled worse than the river Seine on a hot day. Through the fog a little way ahead of him he could make out two men who seemed to have a third man held hostage against the wall.

Yann moved quickly out of sight. The men didn't notice him.

From what he could see, the one nearest him looked like a fish-eyed monster, his hand as wide as a shovel covering the third man's mouth, while the second, a ratlike creature, egged him on.

"What have we got here, Sam?" said the fish-eyed monster.

"A gentleman in a fine coat!" leered Sam. "With shiny buckles on his shoes! Hey, Joe, I reckon we've caught ourselves a plum pudding of a gent!"

"Go on, take it off," said Joe, taking his hand away from the gentleman's mouth and pulling at the coat.

"Please, my dear commodious sirs," cried the gentleman, "I am but a poor thespian and this is my humble costume. I wear it to trip the light fantastic and earn my meager bread and cheese. The buckles are nothing more than paste, for I am but a poor Malvolio whose yellow stockings are thus gartered."

"You what?" said Sam.

"Let's take him to Dr. Death," said Joe. "He'll shut him up. He pays handsome for a good healthy body, he does."

All this was too much for the actor, who let out a muffled moan. "My stars above, no I beg thee, let not my night's candle be so rudely snuffed out. I implore you, gallant gentlemen, to spare me!"

Sam was now rifling through his pockets. "Nothing," he said despairingly. "He ain't got nothing, not even a penny."

"*Must* be a bleeding actor, then."

"My dear sir, my name is Mr. Trippen of Drury Lane. You aren't going to kill the famous Touchstone the Clown, are you? Think what the papers will say."

Joe burst out laughing. "Nothing," he said. He put his hand to his face and pulled out his glass eye. "Like to hold it, would you?"

He was about to put the glass eye back when he heard a young girl's voice calling him by his name. He spun around to see where she could be.

"Did you hear that?" said Joe. "She was calling me."

Then the sweet voice called again. They had no idea what she was saying, except that this time it was Sam who recognized his name.

"How about that? She's calling me too. She sounds French, she does."

Yann called out, "*Mon ami.* If you understand what I am saying just answer *oui.*"

"Yes," mumbled the actor.

"*N'ayez pas peur.* Don't be afraid. Just tell them I am keen to meet them. When the moment's right, try and get free. I will say *Allez!* When you hear that, move."

"What's she saying?" said Sam in a state of great excitement.

"I can tell you, good sirs, if you would do me the honor of removing the knife from my neck."

Joe put down his weapon. "Tell us then, in as few words as possible."

"My French is a little rusty, but surprising as it seems she sounds mighty keen to meet you gentlemen," said the actor.

"Hey, hey!" said Sam. "What else is she saying?"

"She says she's lonely and would like some kind gentleman to keep her company and buy her a drink."

"We're in luck," said Joe.

"I tell you she's mine. I heard her first," said Sam.

His friend spat on his glass eye and polished it on his sleeve. "Give me a chance to get my looks back in, and then, when she sees us, she can take her pick."

The girl spoke again. "Are you ready?"

At that moment, apparently out of nowhere, Yann appeared. The two rogues were so startled that Yann was able to snatch Joe's looks from him before disappearing into the fog again.

"Hey, give that back unless you want me to wring your wretched little neck," cried Joe.

The sweet-voiced girl suddenly spoke again. "When I throw the glass eye, you are to make a run for it."

"What's she saying now?" asked Sam.

"She's asking what keeps you so long," said the actor, hardly believing that the gods could have been so kind as to send this angel.

Yann shouted, "*Allez!*" and threw the glass eye up into the air. Both men together made to catch it, as Mr. Trippen, free of their clutches, ran for his life, swiftly followed by Yann. Once back in the main square they both stopped, the actor holding a pillar and gasping for breath.

"My dear young sir, I cannot thank you enough for your bravery in the face of such terrifying and, may I add, murderous villains. May I ask the name of my savior?"

"Yann Margoza."

"I have to report," Mr. Trippen carried on, standing up, "I have to report that I felt my dying moment upon life's tentative stage had come. Its drama in its myriad forms rushed before my misty eyes, my courage slipping from me like a shadow when I thought of my darling Mrs. Trippen and the young Trippens all left fatherless."

"Do you always use so many words?" asked Yann, smiling.

"They are like bonbons for the tongue, my young friend." He took out his handkerchief and mopped his brow. "Lucky, weren't we, about the young girl being there. I can't imagine what she saw in those two rogues. But I can assure you that the fairer sex is one of life's mysteries, a folly of Mother Nature's creation, for never has there been anything more delightfully irrational and tantalizing upon the face of the earth than woman. If it were not for Delilah, Samson and the temples would still have stood; if it were not for Cleopatra, Caesar—"

"'Allo!" came a voice. "Why did you run away so quickly?"

Mr. Trippen spun around, his face pale. "Alas, my young man, she has followed us. Those two ruffians will be here in a moment. I tell thee, young sir, we are undone!"

"Didn't you realize?" said Yann. He began to laugh. "That was me pretending to be a woman."

"No! That is incredible," said Mr. Trippen. "Why, my dear sir, I had no idea I was talking to a fellow thespian." He looked earnestly at Yann. "I see now a touch of the Hamlet about you. A noble yet tragic face. Where did you learn to speak such excellent French?"

"In France," said Yann.

"You are French?" said Mr. Trippen, surprised.

Yann nodded.

"And English is not, I take it, your native language?"

"No. I have just started to exercise my tongue with it," said Yann with a chuckle.

"A natural, a born natural."

"Thank you, sir," said Yann. "I wish you a safe journey home. Good night."

"Wait, wait my dear young friend, not so fast. Mrs. Trippen would never pardon me if I didn't bring my savior home for supper."

"At this hour?" asked Yann.

"Why, this is the hour, sir, when the Trippens gather after the curtain has fallen on the day, to mull over an actor's life, to reminisce of days gone by, helped in no small part by a good port wine. My wife, having danced the Fairy Queen tonight at Sadlers Wells, will, I believe, have a chicken simmering in its juices on the fire, the bottle, ruby red, breathing in the air."

Up to that moment Yann had forgotten quite how hungry he was. The thought of the chicken simmering away was enough to make him say yes.

They walked toward the Strand together.

Mr. Trippen looked as pleased as punch with himself and did not stop singing:

> *"Hey ho the wind and the rain,*
> *For the rain it raineth every day"*

all the way home.

The Trippens lived in a ramshackle house in Maiden Lane, a cul-de-sac that ran parallel to the Strand. Mrs. Trippen was a little sparrow of a woman, and the four Trippen children ranged in age from nine downwards. The youngest was screaming at the top of his lungs in a crib made out of a box on which the words *Seville Oranges* were written. Clothes hung halfway across the room, but apart from the orange box and a few baskets, it appeared empty of all furniture. Mrs. Trippen, standing over the range stirring a pot, looked as if she had been crying, while the three older Trippens were standing in the doorway in descending height with tragic looks printed across their small faces.

"Why, love of my life, the apple of my eye, the rosebud of my bosom! Where are the table and chairs? Where is the cupboard?"

Yann didn't wait to be introduced. He went over to where the baby lay red and near hoarse with screaming and picked the little thing up, rocking him back and forth until peace was restored.

"The bailiffs," said Mrs. Trippen, when at last she could be heard above the din, "have taken the beds and all the furnishings of our humble lives."

"Not the chicken! Pray tell me they did not take the chicken, or for that matter the ruby wine."

"No," wept Mrs. Trippen, "but the shadow of the debtors' prison once more looms over our heads."

"We are not to despair," said Mr. Trippen firmly. "Tonight could have ended in tragedy. Mrs. Trippen, you could have been widowed and our children left fatherless if it hadn't been for that young Hamlet there holding the baby."

At this momentous news Mrs. Trippen threw herself into her husband's arms and swooned, reviving when smelling salts were administered. The children, obviously well-used to walking furniture and late-night meals, fetched more boxes while their father went outside and brought in a spare door, laying it across the crates to make a table. A sheet was thrown over that, and with the children and adults perching at various heights on a mixture of crates and baskets, the family sat down to eat. At one o'clock the meal was finished and the three Trippen children had fallen fast asleep in the next room while the baby slept contented in his orange box.

Yann lay on the floor by the burning embers of the fire,

stretched out on his back, his head on his hands, and thought how strange that one event can change a life. One stupid mistake and another path is closed.

The bells rang out on the hour, every hour, in the quietness of the night. In that topsy-turvy house he came to regret bitterly the opportunities that had been given him and not taken.

The next morning Henry Laxton was to be found in his study in Queen Square, looking tired and anxious. He had been out half the night searching for Yann and now, washed and shaved, he was staring out of the window and drinking his black coffee.

Vane, the valet, who had also been out looking, brought in a bundle tied up with string.

"Any news?"

"I have just retrieved this, sir," he said, unrolling Yann's coat.

"Dear God, don't tell me you found that lying in the gutter?"

"No, sir, in a pawnshop. It appears that young Master Margoza managed to get a fair sum for it this morning."

Henry Laxton laughed out loud with relief. "Then at least the boy hasn't been robbed or knifed, or worse. Do you know where he is?"

"This, sir, is the address he gave the pawnbroker. Maiden Lane."

Henry Laxton arrived at the house to find Mr. Trippen sitting on an upturned crate. A fire was blazing away and the room had a pleasing aroma of hot buttered toast; Yann, having gotten up early to pawn his coat, had bought provisions. Mr. Trippen was flabbergasted to see such a fine gentleman standing in the door-way and regretted much that he hadn't, as planned, gotten dressed, but was still to be found in his battered housecoat and cap.

"You find me at a disadvantage, sir," he said, bowing.

Mr. Laxton handed him his card and Mr. Trippen read it with interest. The word *banker* danced before him.

"I believe that you have a young man staying with you who goes by the name of Yann Margoza."

"I have that privilege, sir, and a finer and more talented young person I have yet to meet."

"I take it, then, he is not here?"

"No sir, he has taken the young Trippens out for the benefits of fresh air and——"

Mr. Laxton interrupted him. "The young man is in my charge."

"Of course, sir. I am in no way kidnapping him, I can assure you of that. By Jupiter, sir, he saved my life! A brave one is that boy, sir, a young Hamlet, indeed a Henry the Fifth on the battlefield of Agincourt."

With many theatrical gestures that near exhausted him, Mr. Trippen related what had happened in Covent Garden. Henry Laxton found himself warming to the actor, and an idea came to him.

"I am unfortunate, Mr. Trippen, in that unlike you I am not a father."

"Three girls, and one son and heir."

"You are a lucky man indeed. I wish my wife and I had been so blessed. I wonder, sir, if I might confide in you?"

"By all means! Discretion is my middle name."

Mr. Laxton told the actor as much as he thought he needed to know about Yann's background and the death of Têtu.

"He was placed in my care. I found him a tutor, a Mr. Rose, who, unknown to me, saw fit to try and beat the spirit out of him."

"I should think his petals were sent flying."

"Knocked out cold," said Mr. Laxton, smiling at the memory of all the chaos Yann had caused.

Mr. Trippen clapped his hands with delight. "In my humble experience, the cane only teaches the child to loathe the tutor, despise the lesson, and scorn all the benefits that education might bring."

"I entirely agree," said Mr. Laxton. "Tell me, how would you go about teaching such a boy as Yann?"

"I would never keep him tied to a desk. That way nothing would be learned. No, I would show him London, take him to galleries, the theater; fire his imagination. Then when it caught I would tell him about the magic of books. Never let him become bored, sir."

Mr. Laxton listened while taking in the lack of any furniture.

"Forgive me," said Mr. Trippen, suddenly changing the subject and looking dejected. "You catch the great Touchstone at a considerable embarrassment." He waved his hand around the room by way of explanation.

"Have you just moved here, and are waiting for your possessions to arrive, or are you in the process of leaving?" asked Mr. Laxton.

"Neither, sir," said Mr. Trippen. "I am between tides, so to speak. You know the expression 'There is a tide in the affairs of men.' In my case the tide was not taken. I was recently given the opportunity to be a full-time tutor. I turned it down, believing the stage to be my one and only true calling. A foolish moment. Now, alas, debt's dagger hangs over me."

"I have a proposition to put to you," said Mr. Laxton, "and if the idea suits, it may be one way out of your little difficulty with the debt and may help me with the boy."

"Sir," said Mr. Trippen, sitting bolt upright, "I am all ears."

Yann returned with the little Trippens to find the house remarkably quiet. The girls ran upstairs giggling, followed by Yann carrying the sleeping baby, and entered the room to see their parents seated on boxes, both looking solemnly ahead of them as if they were in church on Sunday, their attention held by a gentleman who was leaning on the mantelpiece. It was Mr. Laxton.

Yann stood there feeling stupid and embarrassed, as Mr. Trippen ushered his little family out of the room and left them together. He was thinking so hard about what to say that it took him a moment to realize that Mr. Laxton was already talking.

"I owe you an apology, Yann. I underestimated you. I didn't understand what Mr. Cordell meant when he said Têtu had told him you were talented. It was my stupidity not to see that straightaway."

Whatever Yann had been expecting to hear, this was most definitely not it. Mr. Laxton's kindness floored him. He looked up and was amazed to see genuine concern in the man's tired face.

Finally Yann said what he had thought he would never admit to anyone, least of all to Mr. Laxton.

"I bitterly regret leaving as I did. My only excuse is that I thought you would be better off without me."

Mr. Laxton sat down on an upturned box with his feet spread out before him. He leaned on his gold-topped cane.

"You could not be more mistaken if you tried. I have been out all night looking for you."

"Mrs. Laxton called me a Gypsy."

"She meant no harm by it. She is as desperate as I am for you to come home."

"What did Mr. Cordell tell you about me?"

"Just that you were brought up by a dwarf called Têtu, traveling round France and working in theaters."

Yann nodded. "So you know nothing more?"

"I know nothing about your parentage. I wrote to Cordell asking for more information, and had a letter from him describing how he saw the show you performed with Topolain and the People's

Pierrot. He was fascinated by the way the Pierrot could walk and talk, and particularly by the way it could read people's minds. He said that Têtu had told him the success of the performance was all due to your talent."

"That was nothing," said Yann. "Têtu did most of the work. But I used to be able to read minds. The gift left me the day Têtu died. Now all I can do is throw my voice and perform a few simple magic tricks."

"Grief can strip one of all sorts of powers. I am sure it will come back in time."

"I feel it's gone forever," said Yann.

"Let's hope not. I think you should know that Têtu's body was never found."

"But I left him lying in the snow, in the courtyard where he was shot!"

"Yes, the proprietor of the hotel said as much. She went to get help and when she returned, she found only a bloodstain where the body had been."

"It doesn't make sense. Maybe . . . maybe he's not dead after all."

"I doubt it. The man who shot him must have removed the body."

"But he just might still be alive. I must go back and find out what happened," said Yann.

"If that's what you want, then I will, of course, make the arrangements. But before you decide, I must tell you this. Têtu risked a great deal to get you here. If he is alive, his survival will only be assured by no one finding him, especially not you."

Yann felt as if he stood at a crossroads. One path he knew well, and one appeared too dimly lit for him to see where it led. Looking at the two of them he knew which one he was going to take. "I will try my best not to let you down, sir."

"Good, that's all anyone can do," said Mr. Laxton, looking mightily relieved. "Then we have an understanding."

Before Yann could say another word, the door burst open and Mr. Trippen entered, his arms spread out wide.

"At last the tide has turned! A wise decision, sir," he said, violently shaking Yann's hand, "a wise decision."

Yann looked baffled.

And Mr. Laxton said, "I took the opportunity of asking Mr. Trippen to be one of your tutors."

"Will that suit, sir?" said Mr. Trippen, looking anxiously at Yann. "If it won't, I will not force the point. It would gladden the heart of Touchstone to be of help to a fellow thespian. Clowns are often wiser than the cleverest of men. Not for nothing do jesters keep kings company."

Yann burst out laughing. "And you can get the furniture back."

"It's already settled," said Mr. Laxton.

"Yes," said Yann, "then it will suit very well indeed."

chapter fourteen

$\mathcal{T}$he Marquis de Villeduval's response to the growing political turmoil in France was to build a garden surrounded by a high wall. The garden was designed to enhance the beauty of his new château. He had employed numerous draftsmen, architects, and gardeners, and insisted that all his tenant farmers abandon their work in the fields to bring the elaborate project to life.

As part of the grand plan the marquis ordered the removal of a small, inconvenient hill that blocked the view from the château. The farmers, whose wheat fields he had confiscated, came cap in hand to beg him to leave it be. It was a sacred mound. To disturb it would mean spoiled crops, diseased animals, ruin and starvation.

This was not the first time a peasant delegation had annoyed him with saints and superstitions. The same thing had happened when he cleared the forest around his château in Normandy to make way for a park. That time they had warned him not to touch the ancient trees that belonged to the spirits of the earth and were guarded by the Gypsies. They said that misfortune would overtake him if he cut down a single one.

The marquis was determined to clear his land of the Gypsies, whom he held solely responsible for these nonsensical and irrational ideas, so one winter's day he set off in pursuit of them, with a group that included Count Kalliovski.

The party soon came across a Gypsy family fleeing through the woods. The marquis had thought to have them rounded up and transported. The count, however, had an altogether more immediate solution. The marquis, who had not quite the count's taste for blood, watched from a respectable distance, and the servants looked on in horror, as Kalliovski personally killed each and every one with less mercy than he would have shown a fox.

The dead bodies were left hanging in the trees like grotesque baubles, an example to all those who put store in old wives' tales instead of having a proper respect for reason and authority.

The small hill was duly removed. A long line of horses and carts went plodding back and forth, antlike in their industry. Then a lake was dug out and filled with water diverted from the surrounding irrigation ditches. When one of the farmers asked how they were now supposed to water the crops, the marquis replied irritably that he expected them to solve agricultural problems themselves, not bother him.

At one end of the lake a Grecian pavilion was constructed,

and from it grassy paths led to fountains and fishponds. The marquis imagined himself wandering through groves of linden trees, where birdsong followed his every step and flowers complemented the colors of his clothes. Oh, here he would be in perfect harmony with nature, in a paradise entirely of his own making. That the cost of this paradise would bring him to financial ruin was something he chose to ignore.

The task of telling him the true state of his financial affairs fell to the long-suffering Maître Tardieu, trusted adviser to the Villeduval family for over thirty years. In that time he had served both father and son, and after the old marquis's death he had watched with growing dismay as the family's fortune was mercilessly squandered.

Every time Maître Tardieu brought up the question of monies owed, the marquis's solution was to raise rents, regardless of the ability of his tenants to pay them. And if that did not bring in the required sums, he simply borrowed more from the count. In vain did Maître Tardieu try to explain that there would come a time when the count would want something in return.

And now it seemed that the day of reckoning had arrived. On the morning of the fourteenth of July, Maître Tardieu received a letter from the count for the attention of the marquis. It was written in white ink on black paper with three words inscribed in red at the bottom and embossed with a deep red seal. Maître Tardieu knew that he must inform the marquis of its contents immediately.

The elderly lawyer looked not unlike a mole with his thick round spectacles stuck firmly on the end of his nose. They were besmeared with the grime of ages, and gave everything he viewed a tinge of gray. His waistcoat and breeches were of molelike black velvet and to complete the picture he lived in a small house down a covered passageway where candles were needed both night and day.

He called for his carriage while Madame Tardieu, terrified by the idea of her husband traveling when Paris was in such turmoil, pleaded with him not to go.

"*Chéri*, please," she begged. "Look at what happened yesterday. The people are arming themselves. What if the king's soldiers come into the city while you are away? There will be fighting in the streets. We shall all be killed." She crossed herself.

"Stay calm, my dear," said Maître Tardieu. "I shall be back before nightfall. You are to stay indoors and not set foot outside, my pet."

She watched from the safety of the front door, her small, anxious face peering out to see her husband make his way out of the passage into the bright, alarming sunlight as an angry crowd grudgingly let him climb into his carriage.

With the curtains drawn, Maître Tardieu sat back in his seat as the carriage rumbled through Paris. Twice, men with cockades in their hats and brandishing pitchforks stopped the carriage and demanded that Maître Tardieu get out while they searched it for firearms. It was with a great sigh of relief that he finally arrived outside the wall that encircled Paris, and set out on the road to Versailles.

The journey gave Maître Tardieu time to reflect on the past, and he felt a profound sadness when he thought of the late marquis. He had lost his adored younger son, Armand. His elder son, mean-spirited and extravagant, had always been a trial to him. He would turn in his grave to know of the present marquis's current debts. Maître Tardieu remembered how appalled the old marquis had been to see the indifference with which his son greeted the news of his wife's death.

When Maître Tardieu finally arrived, he was greeted by a valet and shown into an antechamber. Here he was made to wait for a further hour and a half, without refreshment, before the marquis deigned to receive him. Even then he refused to talk business until he had first shown the lawyer around his grounds. The marquis, parasol in hand, sauntered lazily along the grassy avenues, stepping with care to avoid getting the silk bows on his shoes dirty.

If there was beauty here it was lost on Maître Tardieu, who was limping by the time they reached the Grecian pavilion that overlooked the lake. He saw it as a mournful place, the afternoon sun casting a leaden light over the water.

Maître Tardieu tried to raise the question of the letter, but the marquis strolled on, put out that the lawyer seemed so unappreciative of his enterprise and the beauties on offer.

"Have you noticed that the flowers match the colors of the bows on my shoes?"

To the tired eyes of Maître Tardieu, all looked gray and dead.

The marquis now said that he never discussed business in the afternoon, but was prepared to listen to the lawyer's concerns over supper. With a sigh Maître Tardieu resigned himself to having to spend the night at the château, and sent the coachman back to Paris with a message for his wife.

While the marquis was resting, Maître Tardieu took the opportunity to talk to the steward and to examine the household accounts. He was appalled to discover just how much money the marquis had spent on the garden. Not only had there been the designers, the hothouses, and the rare flowers and shrubs to pay for, but the marquis had had a network of secret tunnels built under the flower beds so that the gardeners could crawl down them each morning and discreetly change the flowers to match his outfit. The birdsong that followed his every step came from aviaries strategically hidden behind the greenery. Such folly came at a high price.

What shocked Maître Tardieu even more was what he learned about Sido. Apparently she had been confined to her chamber for the past seven months—why, he could not fathom. The marquis's valet, by way of explanation, said his master viewed her as an inconvenience. Maybe it was this, and the remembrance of what she had meant to her grandfather, that finally made Maître Tardieu decide to throw caution to the winds and to speak his mind, whatever the outcome.

At last the lawyer and the marquis sat down to dine, the

marquis at the head of the long table. Maître Tardieu was used to plain food and was quite overcome by the pomp and ceremony of this meal and the many dishes on offer. Five footmen stood in attendance. The room was ablaze with candles, even though it was still light outside.

"Sir," Maître Tardieu said, "as you know, I have come at some considerable inconvenience—"

"If you have come here to tell me any more ridiculous tales about the disturbances in Paris," the marquis interrupted, "I am not interested. The whole situation has been grossly exaggerated."

At the word *exaggerated,* a candle blew out and a footman came forward to relight it.

"No, no, no!" shouted the marquis, bringing down his bejeweled hand on the table. "How many times must I tell you? Always use a new candle, never relight an old one."

Again Maître Tardieu tried to speak. Again his host interrupted him. "Did I tell you that very amusing story about the duchess and the writing desk?"

Maître Tardieu sighed. "Please, sir, I beg you, we must talk."

"I see," said the marquis, "that you are determined to be dull. In that case, let us have some champagne." He snapped his fingers at a footman. "Politics is such a flat affair."

In desperation Maître Tardieu decided to force his employer to pay attention. He took the letter from his waistcoat pocket and handed it to one of the footmen to give to the marquis.

"What is this?" said the marquis, waving the letter away. "Do you intend to ruin my digestion?"

"It is from Count Kalliovski."

"Oh, I see. Well, read it to me if you must."

"Perhaps, sir, it would be better if the letter were read in private."

"We are in private."

"Forgive me, but we have in this room a butler and five footmen who can hear every word I am about to say."

"Don't be absurd, man. They are merely here to serve me and have no opinions of their own. They are less important than the furniture and definitely less valuable."

"Very well," said Maître Tardieu. He took the letter and began to read slowly and carefully so that master and servants could hear every word.

"What does he mean?" said the marquis.

"Exactly what he says. He wants his money back with interest and he wants it before the end of the month."

"That is ridiculous. What has gotten into him? I think the best course of action is to take none. Kindly acknowledge the letter and point out that there seems to have been a misunderstanding."

Maître Tardieu had reached the end of his tether. Throwing diplomacy and caution aside, he said, "Sir. You are near bankrupt. There is no money left. I have warned you on many occasions, but you have refused to take my advice. Now I fear it is too late."

"What! You sit at my table and have the impudence to talk to me so? How dare you!"

Maître Tardieu brought out a bundle of household accounts. "Mindless extravagance," he said. "Thousands of candles squandered, over a hundred suits a year, half of which are never worn, not to speak of the expenditure on your garden."

The marquis, red in the face, tried to interrupt again, but Maître Tardieu silenced him.

"There is more, and it is of even more consequence."

He returned to the letter and read the last paragraph, in which the count inquired after Sido's health and asked for reassurance that she was being well cared for.

At this the marquis looked most uncomfortable. The champagne, combined with his gold lace and silk embroidered suit, was making him hot, and the powder from his hair and the makeup on his face were beginning to run.

"The count ends his letter by saying that he is looking for a wife. He believes your daughter could well be suitable. If that is the case and you agree to the marriage, all your debts will be canceled. He says that an engagement at fourteen and a marriage at fifteen is what he has in mind."

It had never occurred to the marquis that the count of all people would desire his daughter, and the idea of the man being even more closely linked to the ancient and noble family of the Villeduvals worried him. On the other hand, when he thought of his financial situation, the proposal had some merit.

"She will, of course, be married into an aristocratic family. That goes without saying," he said.

One redeeming sentence, thought Maître Tardieu. Still, he was sure it had more to do with the marquis's pride than his daughter's well-being.

"And for how long do you intend to keep her imprisoned in her chamber?" asked the lawyer as his glass was filled, this time with fine claret.

"What? Do you expect me to dine with the child and have her run around under my feet? She is well cared for and out of sight." The marquis dusted his thin, mean lips with a napkin. "I regret to say that she is most decidedly plain. Then there is her limp. She is, in my view, a broken vase, never to be made whole."

Tardieu's dislike of this man was growing with every remark he made. "I agree," he said, not without a touch of irony, "that for Sido to marry the count is not ideal. His title is unfamiliar and his lineage does not, I am sure, stretch back as far as the grand and honorable name of Villeduval. But that aside, are you aware of the significance of such a marriage?"

"If you mean she will be off my hands, all well and good. Let some other soul suffer her. I have had more than enough."

"Your father's will—"

"What of it?" said the marquis with a dismissive wave of his hand. "The subject bores me."

"I take it, then, that you have no objection to the fact that once your daughter is married she comes into the inheritance from her grandfather's will, which of course her new husband will have at his disposal."

Maître Tardieu could see that for the first time this evening he had rattled the man. Relishing the moment, he said, "Shall I read again what he says at the bottom of the letter?" He leaned forward into the light of the candles. "'Your daughter is your greatest asset.' Think about it, sir. She is twelve years old, so that gives you two years to find your way out of your debts and therefore be free to marry her to an aristocratic family worthy of the connection."

The marquis looked thunderous. In all his previous dealings with Maître Tardieu, the lawyer had never spoken to him in such a manner.

"I still have my estates in Normandy," he said loudly.

"No," said the lawyer, "you have the right to take all the income from the land and the tenants until your daughter is married. On her wedding day they will become her property and that of her husband, Count Kalliovski."

"Impossible! I will not allow it!" said the marquis. "How much do the estates bring in?"

"Not as much as they should. I have been reliably informed," the lawyer continued, "that your tenants have taken flight without paying their rents. The crops have failed. Your barns have been ransacked by starving peasants. Instead of attending to these matters you have remained here and built a garden and a wall. In short, there is no money to pay off your debts, if that is what you were hoping."

Finally the marquis understood. Of course Kalliovski would be paid back in full with this marriage. The thought was intolerable.

"I don't want to hear any more," he said, putting his hands over his ears. "Your sermons are putting me out of humor."

Maître Tardieu had no intention of stopping. "There is something written at the very bottom of the letter, not in white ink but in red. Three words only. 'Remember your wife.'"

Through the grime of his spectacles the lawyer hardly noticed the deathly pallor that had come over the marquis. He did, though, observe with interest his shaking hand.

"Write and tell him I will give his proposition some thought."

"And what, pray, will you do if the situation in Paris worsens and there is a revolution?"

For a moment the marquis said nothing, just stared fixedly at the candle. "That is inconceivable," he said at last. "The king will put down any such revolt."

But for the first time he was experiencing the odd sensation of doubt. The letter that wretched little man had brought him had upset him more than he cared to admit. It wounded him to think the count should turn on him like this.

"The king has already lost his power," the lawyer went on. "His army will not fight against its own people. The sovereignty of France now rests with the National Assembly."

"Rubbish!" shouted the marquis.

There was a sudden din outside in the corridor. The marquis ordered Jacques, the butler, to go and investigate. He returned with the marquis's valet, who could hardly contain his excitement.

"What is going on?" said the marquis, standing up. "Can the servants not be controlled?"

"Sir," said Luc, "we have just received extraordinary news from Paris. The Bastille has fallen."

"Fallen?" repeated the marquis. "What do you mean, fallen?"

"The citizens have stormed it. They fired cannons at the wall and brought it tumbling down."

"The Bastille is no more!" said Jacques. "The governor and the provost have both been killed. Their heads are being carried through the city on pikes!" He was carried away by his enthusiasm. *"Vive la Nation!"* he cried.

The marquis collapsed on his chair.

The day the Bastille fell was the day Sido was released.

chapter fifteen

It was the Comte du Verrier who had brought the extraordinary news of the fall of the Bastille, on his way to Versailles. The poor man had taken fright and fled Paris, certain that they would all be killed in their beds if they stayed. Little did he know that three years later, as he cried like an infant, his head would be guillotined from his body.

The Comte du Verrier's valet, Baptiste, found himself that warm July night in the kitchen of the marquis's château in an unusual position of authority, for he alone there had borne witness to the making of history.

The marquis's staff gathered around, dumbstruck, as he related what he had seen.

"Did you take part, then?" asked a young groom called Philippe.

"Not exactly," said Baptiste. "I wish I could have done. For my sins, I was stuck with my master. I can tell you this, though—he was trembling when he looked out of the window and saw the crowds."

"What was he doing in Paris when he should have been at court?" asked Luc.

"What are all men doing when they are where they shouldn't be? Seeing their mistresses, that's what. No doubt he had his breeches down about his stockinged ankles while the Bastille fell." He laughed. "When he's old and he is asked where he was on this great day, how will he account for himself, I wonder?"

"If he's lucky enough to live that long," muttered Jean Rollet, the chef.

"I heard cannon fire," said Baptiste, not wanting to lose this moment in fame's fickle flame. "I saw men and women, fearless citizens of Paris, take to the streets. I was told that they tore at the Bastille with their bare hands. They stopped the clocks and started them again to show that the world had begun afresh. You could see smoke for miles around and the sky went white with papers. I ran out and caught one, I did." He brought a singed piece of paper out of his pocket and held it up for them all to see. "I'm going to keep this and show it to my children as proof that I was there." He began to put it back in his pocket.

"Wait, wait!" said Luc, grabbing it from him. "Not so hasty. What does it say?" He looked uncertainly at the paper, disappointed that he was unable to read it.

His fiancée, Lucille, came forward.

"My mistress can read. Why don't I show it to her?" she said, taking the paper and folding it up before putting it in her apron.

"Did they release hundreds of prisoners?" asked Jean.

"Seven."

Everyone started talking at once. "Only seven!" "That's all?" "That can't be right."

"The rumor on the streets was that the prison was emptied ahead of time," said Baptiste. "They'd been tipped off about what might happen."

"It doesn't matter how many," said Luc, getting to his feet. "What matters is what the Bastille stands for and the fact that the king's army didn't shoot at the crowd. This is the end of the old regime. Today, ladies and gentlemen, is the dawning of a new age."

Jacques also got up from the table. "This demands champagne, for today we are all equal, we are all kings."

The wine soon loosened everyone's tongues and their pent-up grievances against their master.

"The truth is," said Jacques, "that if the marquis had been half as much liked as his father—"

"Or his half brother," interrupted Madame Gournay, the seamstress. "Now there was a nobleman who knew how to look after his servants and land."

"Hear, hear!" They raised their glasses to the memory of Armand de Villeduval.

"I tell you this," said Alain Grimod, the gamekeeper, "I always thought there was something not quite right about that business."

"Now, now," said Bernard. "No good will come of raking up the past."

"As I was saying," said Jacques, "if the marquis hadn't been a tyrant and a bully, he might have won our loyalty."

"What did he call us?" said one of the footmen. "'Less important than the furniture and definitely less valuable.'"

"I'll tell you this for nothing. I hate my master. He's just a painted peacock," said Jacques. "I say if the people can bring down such men as he, then long live the Revolution!"

"I'll drink to that," said Jean Rollet. "Here's to the fall of the Bastille."

"Well said!"

There was another loud cheer and Baptiste stood up. "Do you know what they called out on the streets? They were shouting for liberty, for all men to be equal!"

"Equality! Do you think in the future we might all be equal, men and women, servants and masters?" asked Luc.

"For all our sakes, let us hope so," said Jean.

Upstairs, the moon shone brightly into another chamber, that of the marquis. Behind his walls with their gilded panels he could not hear the celebration below. He was not concerned one jot with the political turmoil in Paris. His thoughts were taken up by the count's letter, which taxed him greatly.

He could not for the life of him work out what had overcome

his friend, whose generosity up to that point had been faultless. Why should he so unreasonably demand his money back now? He wondered for a brief moment quite how much Sido stood to inherit. He remembered once being told the figure and had noted it only in that it could be called on at a later date. It must be a fair sum if it would cover all his debts.

On further reflection, he decided that such a proposal had a lot to recommend itself. After all, had not the queen herself been married at fourteen? And the Duchesse de Lamantes had been fifteen at the time of her wedding to that old libertine the duke. Tomorrow he would tell Maître Tardieu that he would agree to the marriage. It might not have been his first choice, but nevertheless it got rid of two unpleasant things that niggled at him—his debt and his daughter.

Lucille had come rushing into Sido's chamber at midnight, through the secret paneled door, to rouse her mistress.

"Look, mademoiselle!" She held before her the key to the main door.

Sido, half awake, propped herself up on her elbow as Lucille lit a candle. "What are you doing?"

"Watch," said Lucille, opening the door as if she herself were freeing a prisoner from the Bastille. "I'm sure you needn't be confined to your chamber any longer. You're at liberty! Isn't that a wonderful word—liberty?"

"I don't understand."

"Oh, mademoiselle, the most exciting thing has happened! The Bastille has fallen!"

Sido was now sitting up, fully awake. For a moment she had no idea what Lucille was saying. It seemed unthinkable. The Bastille, that huge blackened fortress that sat like a rotten tooth in the mouth of Paris, gone! Impossible.

"Are you sure?"

Lucille came over to the bed and took her mistress's hands.

"Oh yes, mademoiselle, certain. It's the start of the Revolution." She was now talking so fast that the words fair skipped over themselves as she related all that she had been told.

"Here," she said, gasping for breath, "see what Baptiste brought." She handed Sido the piece of paper. "He said the sky went white with letters like these, thousands of them, there were. What does it say, mademoiselle?"

Sido read aloud, " 'Give me a sign you are still alive and I may breathe again.' It's part of a love letter," she said, looking at its burned edges.

After Lucille had gone, Sido sat by the light of the candle for a long time, thinking about all that she had been told and wondering how it would change the future. And suddenly the image came to her of all the love letters from the Bastille, raining down over Paris like tears from the sky.

The next morning the marquis took his time dressing for an audience with the king at Versailles, making sure that he was properly wigged and powdered. He had decided to wear his finest dusty pink silk brocade coat, embroidered with small diamonds. The silver buckles on his soft leather shoes were decorated with diamonds and pearls. Finally, dressed and perfumed and meeting with his own personal approval, he called for the lawyer.

He was an imposing sight as he looked down his curved aristocratic nose at Maître Tardieu.

"I have decided to agree to the count's request," he announced. "I see much that is agreeable in this marriage, and leave it to you to discuss terms."

"Sir," said Maître Tardieu, "forgive me, but last night I thought—"

"Count Kalliovski is a very presentable choice, and there's an end to it," interrupted the marquis.

Maître Tardieu followed him out through the main entrance. His hip was hurting. He hadn't slept from worry.

The marquis said to his valet, "My daughter is to be brought down from her chamber." Then, waving a dismissive hand at Maître Tardieu, he said, "I leave it to you to inform her of my decision."

He walked out to his waiting carriage, passing the footmen who stood lined up like toy soldiers, and was helped up inside, his coat rearranged with much fuss so that he would not arrive creased. "I think I should wear the king's cockade," he said, leaning out of the open carriage door.

Luc clicked his fingers and a footman went rushing back indoors to fetch it.

Maître Tardieu stood on the gravel, silent and watching. He wondered if foolish men ever became wise. If the marquis was anything to go by, the sad answer had to be no.

The marquis, only half looking at him, said peevishly, "You have not noticed the buckles on my shoes. What say you to their elegance?"

The lawyer stared down at them, baffled. The Bastille might have fallen, France might be standing on the brink of civil war, but all the marquis could think of was buckles. Maybe, in the end, all that would be left of his great fortune would be buckles.

"I thought of wearing the ruby ones, but I felt they might clash with the brocade."

"Quite," said Maître Tardieu. "Quite."

The footman came back and handed the white cockade to Luc, who pinned it onto the marquis's coat. As he did so, his master stuck his chinless head forward like a turtle coming out of its shell.

"The queen's black cockade," said the marquis, "would of course have complemented my coat better than the king's white one. But I am not about to support the insupportable."

With this, the carriage door was finally closed. Maître Tardieu and the servants stood and watched the coach disappear into the distance.

Lucille had brought Sido a message to say that Maître Tardieu wanted to see her. Madame Gournay, the seamstress, came in carrying a white muslin gown run through with blue stripes, and a red sash.

"What do you think?" she asked.

Sido clapped her hands with delight. "It's lovely! It must have taken hours to make."

Madame Gournay, who was employed solely to look after the marquis's wardrobe, had found his daughter to be an altogether more delightful model. The marquis was forever changing his mind, ordering bolts of silks and satins that were immediately discarded, demanding alterations that, when made, were never satisfactory. She found in Sido an appreciation that her master never gave.

"Making clothes for you feels as if I am playing my part in the Revolution. There," said Madame Gournay, standing back. "You look beautiful."

Sido stared at herself in the mirror. Beauty she did not see, only that her leg appeared stiffer from lack of exercise.

"Perhaps," said Sido, turning and smiling at the seamstress, "if I were to be pulled along on a cart I might be passable. The moment I walk I am afraid all is lost."

"No," said Madame Gournay firmly, "you make too much of it. A little hesitation in a lady adds to her charm."

Maître Tardieu saw before him an anxious-looking young girl with large blue eyes, dark hair, and pale porcelain skin. It made the count's letter and what he had to impart all the more distasteful.

"I wish I had happier news for you, mademoiselle," he said,

"but I have not. I think it is best that you read this yourself." And he handed her the black letter.

Sido, unlike her father, needed no explanation. Her response was immediate.

"I can't marry him."

Maître Tardieu sighed. This young girl was not to be duped as her mother had been. He had known at the time that Isabelle Gautier did not love the marquis: She had been blinded by his wealth and the promise of luxury, the seduction of jewelry.

Maître Tardieu cleared his throat. "I greatly regret it, but your father has instructed me to agree to the marriage. You have no choice in the matter when his debts can be so easily solved by this union."

Sido looked at the letter again, taking in the three words written in red ink at the bottom.

"Do you know what he means by 'remember your wife'?"

"No, alas, I do not."

Sido bit her lip and said, "Why have I no family to advise my father against this ill-judged marriage?" She looked up at the old lawyer, fighting back tears.

He suddenly took pity on her and said something that had been locked away for many years, something he had been forbidden to pass on.

"You have family in London," he said quickly.

Sido stared at him, uncertain if she had heard the lawyer right.

"Family in London?" she repeated.

Poor Maître Tardieu looked appalled by what, without due legal consideration, had just tripped off his tongue.

"Oh dear. I have always been under strict instructions to say nothing on the matter. What is to be done now?"

"Where in London are they?" asked Sido, hardly able to contain her excitement. "How can I find them?"

"I have no idea. I know your mother had a sister there at the time of the accident. She married an Englishman, a Mr. Laxton. Whether she is still alive, I cannot say."

"What is her name?"

"Please, mademoiselle, do not press me. Truly, I shouldn't have said a word. And do not put too much store by this news. She is surely dead by now."

"Why?" asked Sido.

"Because," said the lawyer, floundering, "because the English have a very poor diet. They live a shorter time than the French."

Sido looked at Maître Tardieu and felt sorry for him. He looked quite exhausted and his face was gray. She could see that he was not a well man.

"I must leave. I am too old to be doing this, too old and powerless to know how to help you. I wish it were not so."

She knew it was no good questioning him further. He looked half terrified by what he had already said.

"Are you going back to Paris now?" she asked.

"I am. Immediately. I am worried about my wife. She is not in the best of health and with the state of things in the city . . ."

She followed him out to his waiting carriage.

"Before you go, may I ask you one last thing? Do you think the Revolution might save me? Or is it already too late?"

"I think the world we knew has gone," said Maître Tardieu. "What that means only time will tell."

An early-morning mist hung like a veil over the garden. Sido, still reeling from all she had been told and the joyful knowledge, for what it was worth, that she wasn't alone in the world, lifted her skirts and for the first time in seven months ran down the grassy paths. Nearly falling, she steadied herself on the statue of Pan. At last, finding her balance, she took the walk at a slower pace, pleased to feel her leg becoming less stiff. She wandered down paths where statues of goddesses watched over her. She saw a vista of fountains, and the lake beyond. The groves were full of birdsong.

It did not take her long to discover the metal cages. Pushing back the leaves, she saw aviaries full of wild birds, thrushes, blackbirds, nightingales, wrens, chaffinches, hidden amongst the foliage. She walked back up the path and discovered that the aviaries ran along every one of the groves. What cruelty, she thought, to do this to birds that own the sky.

She was trying to find out how the aviaries might be opened when a group of people appeared ghostlike out of the mist. They were armed with pitchforks, swords, and guns. She stood still with her back to the aviaries, recognizing some of the servants.

"Where are you going?"

"To Paris," said Jacques. "We have come to free the birds." He pulled out a key and said almost shyly, "Would you like to do it, mademoiselle?"

One by one, Sido unlocked the cages. They stood there, all of them silently watching the birds thrill to find the wind once more beneath their wings. Only when every cage stood empty did they part, the servants taking one path and Sido another.

chapter sixteen

Under the shade of the oak tree Sido could see in the flickering patterns of the leaves her life already mapped out, her future decided, her husband chosen. It was to be Count Kalliovski.

To Sido he seemed soulless, with his impossibly smooth skin, his face stripped of lines and wrinkles, his features wiped clean of life's tempests. She wondered what pact he had made with the devil, that time itself should not wish to embrace him.

She thought back to that evening of the party some seven months earlier when he and his great black hound had sat in her chamber watching her. It had felt as if the very air was being sucked out of the room, his presence as heavy as mercury.

It was after the fireworks, when she was alone again, that Sido had her dream. She was walking along snowy treetops. The road up ahead was a silvery ribbon in the starlight; it appeared to be far off, yet it wound its way toward her. There on the highway she could make out a coach standing diagonally across the road, as if it had just avoided some terrible catastrophe. The coachman was mopping his brow, looking shaken. By the side of the horses stood Yann. He was holding the bridles and she could clearly hear him talking to them in his curious language. She reached out to touch him, and in that moment he turned toward her and smiled.

Then with a jolt she was back in her room. That was when she knew, as if she had always known, that Yann Margoza would be in her life forever.

At the convent there was a nun called Sister Ignatius, whom Sido liked very much. She was kind and wholesome, her feet firmly planted in the soil. She surprised Sido by telling her that when she was nine years old she had seen a vision of the Virgin Mary standing on ripe ears of barley, holding a baby made of light. In the gentle breeze she seemed to be walking on a golden sea. Sister Ignatius had known from that day forth that she would be a nun. Maybe, Sido thought now, you could have the same certainty about a living person. Maybe her dream too was a vision, a premonition.

In the days that followed, Sido told herself her premonition was just wishful thinking. As the days and weeks slowly tied themselves into months she gave in to her fantasy, for loneliness threatened to overwhelm her, to destroy her spirit.

Sometimes she wondered if dreaming about someone you

hardly knew was sinful. Then she decided she didn't much care if it was, for thinking about Yann made the isolation bearable. She told herself the same story over and over again, and every time it comforted her like thick hot chocolate on a cold winter's day.

This dream of Yann had idled away many desperate months, until at last he seemed so real to her that she could almost believe he was sitting on the chair by her bed watching her.

Today, though, the dream stopped abruptly, for in her mind's eye the smooth, soulless face of Count Kalliovski smothered her vision like a black velvet curtain, snuffing out her hope of freedom.

The Marquis de Villeduval returned home that same afternoon and called for Sido. She entered the room to find him with his back turned toward her, looking out over the garden. He did not turn around, but started to describe the building of the wall and the landscaping of the terraces as if his daughter hadn't been there while all this activity was taking place. She stood staring at him, wondering what she should say; but every word felt like dust on her tongue, so she said nothing.

Her silence had an immediate effect. For the first time in Sido's life, it seemed that her father was prepared to show a grudging interest in her. He took her to the locked antechamber where he kept his collection of shoe buckles, as if to see them was her reward for months of solitude.

It was like the inside of an ornate jewelry box, and glimmered with diamonds, rubies, emeralds, sapphires, and pearls.

The marquis said with pride, "What do you think of this? My collection is priceless. Not even the king can boast of such fine buckles as these."

Sido didn't answer. She had discovered a treasure all of her own: the golden power of silence.

It was the beginning of a strange time in her father's house. The marquis spent most of his time at Versailles and Sido was left alone to explore the château and read the unread books. On his return her father would talk of the parties he had attended and how well he had been received, of Madame this and the Duchess of that. He never discussed Sido's forthcoming marriage, just as he never discussed politics or the Revolution. The closest he came to acknowledging that anything untoward was happening was when he bemoaned how many of his friends had seen fit to leave for long vacations abroad. Of Paris all he had to say was that it had become "dull, very dull indeed." Of Versailles he talked more favorably, of balls, parties, and the card tables, though here too he had his complaints.

"I observe," he said, "that standards of dress are slipping. It is a tragedy, the loss of whalebone in corsets. Whalebone gives women such excellent stature. Now the fashion is all for ladies to look like milkmaids in their white muslin gowns, without proper support or lacing. As a result," he announced, as if it were the most shocking piece of news ever, "women are slouching! So inelegant."

Sido listened quietly, relieved that there was no need for her to comment, for what could she say to such a kaleidoscope of folly? She had become a silent witness to her father's idiocy. She realized that, like the king himself, the marquis was out of touch with what was happening all around him. The decadence, the waste continued, and still the poor stayed poor while her father and his acquaintances determinedly danced, dined, gambled, gossiped, and spent their way to disaster.

It was only after the murder of his friend Madame Perrien that the fact that something terrible was happening dawned upon him. By then, it was all too late.

chapter seventeen

It had started with one of the marquis's extravagances, a grand fête, given for all his friends that late summer after the fall of the Bastille, and designed to take their minds off the tedium of the Revolution.

It was held on an overcast day full of clouds that whirled menacingly, windmill-like, across the sky. The skeleton staff of gardeners who had not yet left for Paris had been obliged to work around the clock, for the marquis refused to acknowledge any change. His only concession to economy had been to hold no parties for the past eight months.

Now that the National Assembly had collectively lost its mind and agreed to pass this ridiculous declaration of the rights of man, he felt it his duty to throw one of his spectacular parties, a reminder, if one was needed, of how preposterous this Revolution was. For the idea that all men were equal was laughable; no one in his right mind could believe it. In his opinion, the sooner the populace was crushed the better.

For the time being the marquis was more concerned about deciding on a theme for his fête, and he called for the painter Etienne Bouchot to design the setting and the winged chariot in which he was to make his entrance.

After days of deliberation he settled on the idea that everyone would come dressed as a character from the Commedia dell'arte: Zannis, or clowns, with interesting costumes and witty masks, were much in fashion. An informal picnic would be held in his Arcadian garden. The guests would be transported across the lake to an Italian piazza, where they would dine and be entertained by jugglers, fire-eaters, and tightrope artists.

The marquis fussed and threw tantrums over every detail of this fête. His fury at finding that the cages had been emptied of birds knew no bounds until one of the gardeners suggested a novel idea that the marquis immediately claimed as his own, and set all his poor tenant farmers to work with butterfly nets.

On the opposite side of the lake a stage was built, while in front of the temple itself a wooden floor was laid and painted to look like a marble piazza. Scores of scene painters, carpenters, and metalworkers were needed to make such an ambitious vision a reality.

The invitations had been sent out, with one notable and fatal exception. The marquis had not asked Count Kalliovski.

His reason for leaving the count off the guest list was childish, with, alas, no thought to the consequences. The marquis was bitterly jealous of Count Kalliovski's new acquaintance with Robespierre, a bourgeois lawyer from Arras, one of the leaders of the Revolution. It was beyond his comprehension as to why the count would want to keep the company of such a humorless, dull man, of little or no consequence. Misguidedly, he believed that once the count discovered he had not been invited to this party, he would come back full of remorse: for how could he ever have risen so high in count circles without the marquis's help and guidance? You could say the marquis had a talent for rearranging unpalatable truths to suit his narrow point of view.

What concerned him the most at the present time, and had almost turned the pink clouds of his mind gray with worry, was what to wear so as to outshine all his guests. Finally he concluded that none of the characters from the Commedia dell'arte reflected his noble nature or did justice to the ancient name of Villeduval, so he decided upon a costume that would truly enhance the glories of his personality. He would be the sun itself. To create the desired effect, tailors, shoemakers, glovers, and perfumers, fan- and mask-makers, and suppliers of gold and silver stuffs were called for.

All this fevered activity shook the château awake as if it were emerging from a long afternoon's sleep. The marquis felt alive again, with a total disregard for any form of self-restraint. It was as if the Revolution had only been a glint in a starving man's eye.

Sido, on hearing that the count was not coming, had felt a huge sense of relief. Now she could enjoy the fête without any worries about her forthcoming betrothal. Yet in all the preparations, her father never once asked to see her, and as the day drew nearer she realized that she had once again been forgotten.

On the eve of the party the marquis, as if at last remembering her, called for Sido to be brought to his chamber.

He was sitting in his dressing robe, his feet in a bowl of rosewater while his fingernails were attended to, a tall glass of champagne in the other hand, and beside him on the table a small pyramid of confectionery.

As the last rays of sunshine broke forth through the shutters, he looked at Sido and said irritably, "Don't stand there. The light is most unbecoming." He dusted the corners of his mouth with a napkin and addressed Luc, his valet. "She may observe the party from the side room in the temple, but that is all. I don't want her wandering about tomorrow. Everything must be charming." With that he lifted his pampered hand and waved her away.

Not for the first time did Sido wonder why it was that her father disliked his only child so very much.

On the day of the fête, the servants were up at dawn, bringing down long tables and laying them with fine damask, porcelain, and silver. An ice sculpture in the shape of a harlequin was placed in the center, and cut-glass chandeliers were hung from a series of ropes. They looked like strange, elaborate beehives floating in the sky above the tables. All around were urns filled with huge displays of flowers.

Boats shaped like swans and peacocks, their painted wooden feathers splayed out, were brought down to the lake on carts, and sackfuls of pink rose petals were floated gently on the metallic surface of the water.

Before the party started, Sido was taken down to the temple, where a concealed door in the wall was opened to reveal a cubbyhole with a good-sized window to look out of, and a spyhole to see into the temple itself. Gazing out of the window, she was reminded of the toy theater she had had as a small child. The scene before her had the same magical quality.

The orchestra struck up, and the guests began to arrive.

They came as Punchinellos, Scarpinos, Scaramouches, Pantaloons, Pierrots, Columbines. Tumblers and jugglers from the Paris circus performed amongst them, while a tightrope walker in a harlequin costume crossed back and forth above their heads.

At last the marquis made his entrance to the sound of trumpets, his winged chariot pulled by four men dressed in tunics with headdresses in the shape of the sun, their bodies oiled and shining. The marquis was helped out, an apparition in gold silk brocade. He wore a breastplate with the face of the sun on it. His wig was gold, studded with gems. His mask was made of thin gold leaf, and looked as if it had been blown across his face. The effect was dazzling—so much so that the sun might well have decided not to shine, out of envy

From Sido's vantage point, not only did she have a perfect view of the proceedings, but she could hear equally well all that was being said, for many of the guests came to gossip under the round dome of the temple, where their voices echoed.

By late afternoon the sky had turned the color of iron. Sido watched as the guests floated off in their swan and peacock boats and the footmen surrounding the lake opened baskets, letting out hundreds and hundreds of butterflies that in the eerie light of the oncoming storm looked like jewels taking flight.

The highlight of the afternoon's entertainment was the arrival of an Italian singer who was enjoying a great success at the Paris Opera House. Her voice soared through the gathering clouds, calling to Zeus himself, who answered in his deep bass voice with a mighty rumble of thunder as lightning forked its way toward the lake, followed by a sudden downpour of torrential rain.

The guests hastily abandoned their tables, spilling wine and knocking over chairs as they ran for cover, tall wigs flopping in the rain. Servants rushed here and there with umbrellas while the guests, like hissing geese, took flight back toward the château. They were followed by the musicians and the opera singer, who waddled behind like a flat-footed duck, her dress trailing in the mud.

Sido watched as the rain washed away the cakes, their pink icing running down damask tablecloths, the weight of the water half sinking the wooden boats that were illuminated, electric white, against the inky darkness of the waters. The scene, so wonderful, so magical at the beginning of the day, lay in ruins.

She was just opening the door of the temple to leave when, to her surprise, she heard her father's voice above the sound of the rain. He was deep in conversation with a lady. They were taking shelter in the temple—she could see them all too clearly through the crack in the door. Sure that at any moment she would be discovered, she decided that it was best to stay where she was.

"I have no money to repay the count," said the lady.

"Surely Monsieur Perrien can help you out of your little difficulty," replied the marquis.

"My husband's château was destroyed last week by a fire. He has lost everything, and after all he has been through I dare not tell him about my gambling debts. I am terrified of what the count will do. He wrote me a letter on black paper with white ink. You know what that means."

"There has been a little misunderstanding," said the marquis. "It signifies nothing."

"It is no misunderstanding," said Madame Perrien. "I implore you to lend me the money. You are my last hope. If you do not, I am as good as dead. I promise to repay you." She reached out to take his hand, but the marquis quickly pulled it away, disgusted.

"Madame, this is no way for a lady of your rank to behave," he said curtly.

She laughed a hard laugh. "I tell you this, Monsieur le Marquis, not inviting the count was a grave mistake. Do you really think it will be that easy to have nothing more to do with him? I think you will come to regret this oversight bitterly."

"I have no idea what you are talking about, madame. I advise you to pull yourself together."

"This is no child's game we are playing."

"It is, alas, one of the faults of the weaker sex to take matters of little consequence far too seriously. Madame, my advice to you is that this will resolve itself. Let us go back to the château for a glass of champagne. I find that champagne always lifts the spirits when one is feeling a little flat."

Madame Perrien was not listening. "The count could destroy all of us if he wanted to!"

"Madame," said the marquis stiffly, "this has gone far enough." He tried to step away but was stopped by Madame Perrien, who grabbed hold of his gold costume and collapsed to her knees.

The look of revulsion on the marquis's face would have been comical if it were not for the seriousness of what Madame Perrien was saying.

"At the beginning I thought, like you, that it was just a silly game. I had to give him something precious in return for the loan. When I explained that I could not give him jewelry as security, he said he wanted no such trinkets, he was after just a few little secrets. I gave him letters; letters which I now fear incriminate me. When I asked for them back he laughed and said he had them under lock and key and would use them to his own advantage if I did not repay him."

Madame Perrien now had the marquis's full attention. He took off his gold mask as a flash of lightning skimmed the lake. She let go of his coat and pulled herself up, leaning on the pillar.

"What secrets did *you* give the count, I wonder, in return for his generosity? They must have been worth a king's ransom that he should have lent you so much. I dread to think what he will want in return."

The marquis pursed his lips. "This does not apply to me. He did it purely out of friendship."

Madame Perrien made a mirthless sound. "What folly! Tell me this, then. If he did so much for you as a friend, what do you think he would do if you were to become his enemy? He once told me what his private motto was. Shall I tell you it? 'Show no mercy, have no mercy.'"

The marquis, who had swum all his life in the shallow waters of polite society, avoiding at all costs any meaningful conversation, suddenly realized that the largest pike in the river was after him. He straightened his back and looked at Madame Perrien coldly.

"I cannot speak for you, madame, though I would say that your dealings with the count have been unwise. Now, if you would excuse me, I must join my other guests."

Sido watched her father turn his back on Madame Perrien to walk down the steps, where two footmen were waiting with umbrellas to escort him to the château.

"We made a pact with the devil," she called after him, "and the devil is coming to get us!" The marquis did not turn around.

Madame Perrien called louder this time, not caring who heard her. "Count Kalliovski has bought our souls!"

Sido stood frozen to the spot, not daring to move. She could see Madame Perrien holding on to the pillar with her white hand, watching as the marquis walked away. A low rumble of thunder seemed to shake the earth, followed by a flash of lightning that snapped a rope that was holding up one of the glass chandeliers. It crashed down onto the table below, knocking the ice sculpture into the lake. Unforgiving raindrops of glass showered onto the painted marble floor.

Oblivious to everything, Madame Perrien started to walk slowly down the steps, her Pierrot costume soaked through, her white makeup running, her skirt of watered silk trailing in the mud through the broken glass, the wasted food, the spilled wine.

Sido had heard every word Madame Perrien had said. She had sounded lifeless, stripped of all hope, as if she had seen into the eternity of darkness and knew it to be waiting for her.

She had said, "I am done for, I am dead."

chapter eighteen

*A*t the beginning of October the marquis received a letter from Madame Claumont, who wrote to inform him that after the dreadful business with poor Madame Perrien she had decided to cross the Channel and go to visit her friends in London. She advised the marquis to do the same.

What dreadful business? The marquis had no idea and immediately sent a servant to Paris to inquire after Madame Perrien's health. The man returned with a letter from Monsieur Perrien. It made shocking reading. Madame Perrien had been murdered. It was, wrote her husband, unimaginable to think who could have done such a terrible deed. She had been found wearing a necklace of red garnets. Her maid said that she had never seen it before. The matter was now in the hands of the police, although, since the country was on the brink of ruin, he doubted that much would come of their inquiries.

The marquis was shaken to the very center of his being by this news. He remembered with terrifying clarity what she had said that day of the fête: "We have made a pact with the devil!" No, he wouldn't think about it, he would put this unpleasant subject out of his mind. It had nothing to do with him. What could he possibly have done? He was in no way responsible for her death.

Still, he felt ill, plagued by some malady that had upset his nerves, making him jump every time wheels were heard crunching on the gravel outside. He even started to see the ghost of his dead wife wandering silently around the house.

Finally, he took to his bed, complaining of a headache. A doctor was called for and he was bled. Despite all the treatments he was given, he still found little rest from the uncomfortable thoughts that kept tormenting him.

The marquis's health recovered somewhat when he received an invitation to a banquet in the Opera House at the Palace of Versailles. The guest list included the officers of the Flanders Regiment, the Montmorency Dragoons, the Swiss Guards, and other officers and noblemen. It convinced the marquis that at last the counterrevolution had begun. He dressed in his finest suit, his tallest wig, and shoes with red heels and diamond buckles, and set off for Versailles in his gold-painted carriage. To Sido he looked like a canary in a gilded cage.

In the early hours of the next morning the marquis arrived home shouting *"Vive le Roi!"* at the top of his voice, waking up the whole household. Sido got sleepily out of bed to see what the commotion was about and looked over the banisters to see her father in the hall, swaying from side to side and bellowing.

"The counterrevolution has started! The monarchy is to be restored to its former glory!" He lurched toward Jacques, the butler. "Then you peasants will know your place once and for all."

He stood in the hall, swaying like a full-rigged galleon on a sozzled sea of red wine.

"You should have heard how we drank to the king, and how we cried out with one voice, 'Long may you reign! *Vive le Roi! Vive la Reine!*' You should have seen the queen holding up the little Dauphin, a symbol of the continuation of kings, as the tears rolled down her cheeks! I tell you, we will deal with the rabble! We will bring down their Revolution! *Vive le Roi!*"

He spat the words in Jacques's face. "No one toasted the nation—the royal bodyguard would have none of it . . ." His voice was carried away in a wave of passion.

For a moment Sido thought the marquis was about to capsize. Two footmen rushed to steady him, and he pushed them aside angrily, holding on to the banister as he slowly righted himself, though his wig, like the rigging of a ship, was starboard bent.

Sido watched as Jacques and the footmen did their best to help her father up the stairs. As he passed Sido on the landing he stopped and said, "Who are you?"

Sido didn't answer.

"As I thought," said the marquis. "A ghost. Away with you."

The news of what had happened that night at Versailles spread to Paris and beyond like a forest fire on a hot summer's day, but it was not until three days later that the full impact of that disastrous banquet was felt.

It started in the afternoon when Michel Floret, one of the few gardeners who had not left the marquis's employment, had come into the kitchen to take shelter from the rain. He was warming himself by the stove, for these days the kitchen had become a meeting place for all the remaining staff.

Bernard, the coachman, was sitting there too. "I've been thinking," he said gloomily.

"Well, don't," said Jean Rollet, the chef, who with one look could reduce a cabbage to compost. "Thinking isn't going to get you anywhere."

"Go on, Bernard, take no notice," said Michel. "You have the right to think. Cooks aren't kings yet."

"That's it. That's what I think. If the king had agreed to the declaration of human rights, we'd all love him, wouldn't we?"

Jean sniffed. "*You* might. I have a more discerning palate myself. You can't change an old cockerel into a spring chicken. Anyway, he doesn't believe in human rights. He's made that clear enough."

"Shh," said Agathe, the scullery maid, "not so loud. What if the marquis were to hear you?"

"I wouldn't worry about it," said Michel. "What did he call the footmen? Furniture? He thinks we don't even exist when he's not around, let alone have a thought in our heads."

"I tell you, the king had better watch out," said Jean, "otherwise he'll find himself abolished."

"And the marquis too," added Bernard.

Just then the door to the kitchen opened and four of Count Kalliovski's grooms came in, their coats trailing water on the floor. No one in the kitchen said anything, for the count's men looked as mean and as brutal as their master. Jean snapped his fingers, and Agathe went to get wine, bread, and cheese for them.

"It took us an age to get here. The road to Versailles is blocked," said one of the grooms.

"What do you mean, blocked?" asked Jean. "Blocked by what?"

"Women. Women, heaven help us! Maybe ten, twenty, thirty thousand of them."

"Why? What are they doing?"

"Gone to get bread, and to kill the queen while they're about it."

Agathe was so startled by this that she dropped the lid of an iron pan on the flagstones with a deafening crash.

"Where do all these women come from?" asked Bernard.

"Women from the market in Paris started it, outside the Hôtel de Ville. Then other women joined them, thousands of them, all armed with pitchforks, swords, guns; they're even dragging a cannon."

Jean looked around at the kitchen staff. "We'd best be on the lookout. I've heard stories of lootings, burnings, and suchlike. We don't want them taking a fancy to this château as they march past."

Michel started to chuckle.

"What's so funny about that?" asked Jean.

"Nothing," said Michel. "It's just that he went and made that there wall with too much sand, didn't he?"

"What do you mean?" asked Agathe.

"I mean," said Michel importantly, seeing that he had everyone's attention, "that the thing will fall down when it's pushed, like children's building bricks, and serve him right."

"Well, whatever you do, don't tell the master," said Jean.

One of the count's men helped himself to another glass of wine and sat back in his chair. "Don't worry. I overheard him say he didn't think they'd bother with you today."

"Is that a threat or a promise?" asked Jean.

Upstairs in the library, the marquis, like a startled stag caught in a forest of books, was taken completely off guard by Kalliovski's unannounced arrival. It took him a moment or two to take in the count's appearance. His hair, instead of being powdered white, was black: The marquis would never have supposed the man to have such dark hair, and so much of it. Instead of his usual finery he was wearing a plain black woolen jacket and woolen breeches with black riding boots that did not even have a red heel. As he placed his hat on a table the marquis saw that pinned to it was the revolutionary cockade. He stared at it in disbelief. Could all that he had heard about the count be true?

"What foolish things you all did at your party this week, citizen," said the count, helping himself to a glass of cognac. "Drinking to the health of the royal family, in short forgetting your loyalties to the nation. Really, citizen, was this wise?"

"Citizen, citizen," repeated the marquis. "What nonsense is this?"

Kalliovski clicked his heels. "I am Citizen Kalliovski, a friend of the Revolution, at your service."

"Impossible!" said the marquis. Then he laughed out loud. "Very good! It is so long since I've seen you that I'd forgotten what a wit you are; you've come in disguise! Oh, very clever indeed."

"I am in deadly earnest," replied Citizen Kalliovski. "I am here on business. As soon as the papers are signed, I will be gone."

"What papers?"

"Have you already forgotten my very generous offer to you?"

The marquis said nothing. He was still trying to take in Kalliovski's new appearance.

Kalliovski rang a bell and a footman entered. "Fetch Mademoiselle Sido," he ordered. He turned his attention back to the marquis. "You have heard of the death of Madame Perrien, I imagine?"

The marquis had not encountered this bluntness in Kalliovski before, and it worried him.

"Why, yes. Dreadful."

Kalliovski smiled.

"She asked you for your help, I believe."

"I don't know what you're talking about," said the marquis hurriedly, his color changing. Even under the makeup his cheeks glowed red.

"Then let me enlighten you. Madame Perrien asked for your help with her gambling debt. The foolish woman asked the wrong person, of course, for you possess nothing but unpaid bills." He smiled again, the corners of his lips curling mockingly. "There are angry craftsmen in Paris still waiting for their money for your ridiculous fête."

"They will be paid in due course."

"Not by me," said Kalliovski, and he took from his pocket a necklace of red stones that he played with in his hand like a rosary.

The sight of it made beads of sweat appear on the marquis's forehead.

"Madame Perrien paid the price for disloyalty," said Kalliovski. "Madame Claumont believes that by emigrating she will escape me. If she thinks she can get rid of me that easily, she is very much mistaken."

The marquis bit his lip. The full impact of what had happened to Madame Perrien hit him like a blow to the stomach. He put out a hand to steady himself. With as much dignity as he could muster, he sat down heavily on a chair.

"Do you remember what we agreed when you last borrowed from me?"

The marquis said nothing.

"Then let me remind you. You have a choice, albeit a limited one, but a choice nevertheless. I could let certain papers find their way into the right hands. I am sure there are people who would be most interested to know how your wife died."

"No," said the marquis. His lips were white. "You wouldn't do that, would you?"

"Without a moment's regret," said Kalliovski.

"You were as much involved as I, if not more so," said the marquis, grasping at straws.

"That is where you are so very wrong. Nothing leads back to me. Your mark, your signature, is on everything. I made sure of it."

The marquis's mouth felt very dry.

"How can it be stopped?"

"By agreeing to this marriage. You see, citizen, the Revolution needs funds. The time has come for me to call in my debts." Relishing the worried look on the marquis's face, Kalliovski laughed. "Unlike you I have familiarized myself with the terms of your late father's will. He did not much care for you, did he? But oh, how dearly he loved his pretty little granddaughter. On her wedding day she inherits a fortune, and it will all be mine."

"I cannot let that happen! That cannot be the price I have to pay!" cried the marquis. "After all I have done for you, all the introductions I have given you! Your rise in society would never have taken place if I had not facilitated it."

"Believe me, I can do this. I will do this. Oh, how I have waited for you to fall so low! I have no mercy. I will show no mercy."

The marquis wiped his dripping forehead and regretted ever having had the fire lit.

"The body of Isabelle Gautier, now do correct me if I am wrong, was found in a field. Oh dear, I have forgotten. Was she found with a necklace similar to this? Do you remember?"

He held up the necklace with its bright red garnets that looked like drops of congealed blood.

The marquis swallowed hard, his mouth ash-dry. He trembled as a tidal wave of sound came crashing into the room from outside, engulfing the house with drumming, screaming, screeching, a wailing of women.

"We will have bread!"

The marquis got up to stare, bewildered, out of the window, at what appeared to be a never-ending stream of women passing close by his gates.

"What are they doing?"

"Going to fetch the king and queen, that's if they don't kill them first. They plan to take them back to Paris, where the National Guard can keep an eye on them, make sure that they don't get carried away by any more such extravagant banquets. I tell you, citizen, soon the streets will run with blood and no one will care. Now, back to business."

Above the noise the marquis let out a thin cry. It was the sound of his fragile mind breaking, like fine porcelain.

Sido knew the minute she entered the library exactly the reason for Kalliovski's visit. Her father, his face funereally grim, walked toward her just as a stone was thrown into the room, breaking the window and spraying glass onto the Persian rug. The marquis stopped and stared transfixed as if the stone were a fragment from a comet.

"You've brought this on yourself," said Kalliovski. "Fortunately for you, today they're out for bigger fish. But never fear, your time will come, you can rest assured of that." He walked slowly around Sido. "Do you now agree to the marriage?"

"I can't think. My head hurts," was all the marquis could say. "Later, leave it till later," and he turned to look once more out of the window.

Citizen Kalliovski touched Sido's face. She recoiled from him, stifling the words that were about to erupt from her. Yet again, she knew that silence was her only means of survival.

"Such soft skin, velvety like rose petals. Still too thin," he said.

Sido stood stock-still, hardly daring to breathe, Kalliovski's hand now resting on her neck.

"There is no later," he said, "just an urgent now. So I take it that you agree to this marriage?"

"Have I any choice?" asked the marquis.

"No," said Kalliovski. "It was, and it always will be, check-mate."

Outside the women shouted:

> *"We want liberty!*
> *We want bread!*
> *Give us what we want*
> *If you value your head!"*

chapter nineteen

*A*t fifteen, Yann looked older than his years. The gossip of where he had come from had long since ceased. It was generally agreed that he was a distant cousin of Juliette's whom the Laxtons had adopted.

Mr. Trippen had turned out to be an excellent tutor. By now Yann could read and write, was accomplished with sword and pistol, was a graceful dancer, and proved to have an uncanny way with even the wildest of horses. His great love, though, remained the theater. It was here that he felt the closest to Têtu and home. He would spend many an evening with Mr. Trippen watching famous actors performing Shakespeare and Sheridan; but the shows he loved best always touched on magic.

He had seen the great illusionist Katterfelto lecture on natural philosophy, and had paid close attention while Katterfelto performed tricks with dice, cards, money boxes, medals, and glasses, claiming that he knew the secrets of the occult.

Mr. Laxton had been most impressed by the show, and Mr. Trippen saw it as one of the wonders of the world. Only Yann stayed silent. He had not found in anything he had seen or heard what he was looking for.

The magic that he wanted to understand, Têtu alone had performed. He had read with interest about gold threads that the magicians used to achieve their illusions. Gold was lost to the human eye in the subdued light of the oil lamps, yet Yann knew for certain that Têtu had used no such devices. It made his magic all the more mysterious and tantalizing.

He felt sure that such magic came from deep within. It must be a force as powerful as anger, grief, or love—you had somehow to connect with it to make it work. It did not rely on sleight of hand, or baggy trousers from which a never-ending stream of handkerchiefs appeared.

Today, as he walked through Covent Garden, the sun was shining watery bright. The city looked as if it had put on its best clothes for the occasion. London in all her finery thrilled Yann. The piazza was, as always, full of people. There were street-criers selling bread and buns, shouting out their wares. Porters rushed here and there with parcels. Apprentices stood outside their masters' shops, begging passersby to go in and peruse the goods, each one shouting a little louder than his neighbor.

He had finished his fencing lesson, and had a tingling of

tiredness and a good hunger. He was on his way to his favorite coffeehouse to pick up the latest news when he saw a young couple, brightly dressed, with shiny rings in their ears and silver buttons on their clothes. The girl had dark eyes and jet-black hair, and she caught Yann's attention, not only because she was pretty but because she was speaking a language he understood. He stopped to listen, and the girl smiled at him.

"Would you like me to read your fortune, sir?" she said. "Cross my palm with silver . . ."

Yann laughed and answered in Romany, "Not now."

The girl and the young man looked surprised. Taking in Yann's fine clothes, the man asked uncertainly, "*San tu Rom?* Are you a Gypsy?"

For a moment Yann hesitated. Then he said, "*Da, pralo.* Yes, brother," accepting at long last the truth of what he was saying.

"Glad to meet you, brother. I am Talo Cooper and this is my wife, Orlenda."

They shook hands and the girl, smiling sweetly, asked, "Are you from the royal city?"

"No, I am not from London. I am from Paris, the city across the water."

After a while Yann walked away, looking back over his shoulder as Talo started to play his violin, the sound of his music filling the piazza with its sweet, aching melody.

Yann sat in the coffeehouse and ate his meal in silence, thinking back to the night of the marquis's party when Topolain had died. Deep down he had never quite gotten over the idea that he was responsible for what had happened, that if he had kept silent that evening when he was asked what the Pierrot saw, everything might have been all right. The memory of it made him bring his fist down hard on the table.

"Steady on, sir!" said the gentleman opposite.

Yann looked up, almost surprised to find himself in the middle of this busy eating house. In his head he was floating in a soundless sea of unanswered questions, driftwood for the mind. He stood up, his plate unfinished, paid for his meal, and left.

As Yann walked away he thought about Têtu, as he often did, and he wondered if the magic and the answers he was hungry for lay not in the theater but with the Gypsies themselves. There was also another reason for seeking them out. This one was less simple, a tangle of feelings that try as he might he couldn't untie.

For all the Laxtons' kindness and generosity toward him and their genuine concern to make him feel at home, Yann had known ever since he had first arrived in Queen Square that it was Sido who should have been there, not he. He understood all too well the longing Mrs. Laxton had to see her niece again, and when she told him about her sister and the accident, the girl with the sapphire-blue eyes whom he hardly knew had become a presence in his life. When he heard the news of her forthcoming marriage, his rage against Kalliovski surfaced once again.

The one comfort Yann took was the idea of how he would

revenge himself on the man he held responsible for the murders of Topolain and Têtu. Magic would be his weapon of choice, though how he was to achieve the powers he needed he did not know.

It was getting dark as he neared Seven Dials, where he knew the Gypsies camped in winter, and fog had begun to descend. The camp, a small city of tents, rolled out before him as far as the eye could see. It was not a place to go walking in unless you had business there. Groups of young men eyed his fine clothes and wondered which Gypsy girl had bewitched him enough for such a gentleman to come calling.

At last Talo Cooper appeared out of the fog.

"Orlenda knew you would come," said Talo. "She's never wrong in these matters. I will take you to my grandfather, Tobias Cooper. He is waiting for you."

A very old man sat at the entrance of his tent, smoking his clay pipe. Yann sat down beside him and stared out at the thickening fog that hung down over the camp like the muslin petticoat of some monstrous giantess.

"What is it you want to know?" said the old man, looking at Yann as if he could see right into his heart.

"I want to know how to move objects without touching them."

Tobias laughed. "What makes you think I would know such things?"

Yann shrugged his shoulders. "A feeling. I was brought up by a dwarf called Têtu, who was of the Romany blood. He worked a wooden Pierrot in a theater in Paris. He did it all from the wings; he never once touched it, still, he could make it dance."

"Then he knew the ways of the ancient magic. What makes you think you have any right to such knowledge?"

"My mother could do the same, and my grandmother. I never knew them. My mother died when I was a few weeks old. I worked in the theater with Têtu and the wooden doll. I made it talk, I read minds, and sometimes I even foresaw the future. Then one day I saw and said too much, and my gifts left me. Shortly after that Têtu was shot and I was brought to the royal city. All that is left to me now is that I can still throw my voice; but it is a cheap circus trick, nothing more."

"Show me."

Out of the fog came the noise of a man wheezing, gasping for breath, asking Tobias for a pipe of tobacco.

Tobias smiled and said, "Very good indeed. Choose an object."

Yann picked the first thing that caught his eye, the old man's hat lying inside the tent.

Without touching it Tobias appeared to lift it off the ground, where it hovered, as if listening to what was being said, before vanishing. In its place, suspended in midair, was a red rose.

"Yes!" said Yann excitedly. "That is what I want to be able to do, that kind of magic."

"You need, then, to be able to see into the spaces in between things," said the old man. "Can you do that?"

Yann squinted. "I see nothing. There is nothing to see."

"Then you are blind."

"I'm not!"

"The eye plays tricks, fills in the gaps, so that we see what we want to see. Objects are only solid because of our desire that they be so."

This did not make sense to Yann. He said, "A hat is a hat, a cup is a cup. I would prefer to trust in solid objects."

"Well, then, don't come knocking on my door," said Tobias with a shrug. "Go on believing in the flat lands of your mind. I tell you no magic lies there. If you see the world that way, that is all you will ever see of the world."

"I don't understand what you're talking about," said Yann furiously. Had he come all this way just to be told he was blind?

"If you will let her, Orlenda will read your palm. That might help me to know what it is you are fighting," said the old man.

He called for her and she came out of the tent with Talo. The firelight caught her pretty face, and she smiled at Yann, taking his almond-shaped hand in hers, looking carefully at his palm, moving it toward the light.

After a while she straightened up and said, "I am sorry, Grandfather. The gift has left me for tonight."

"Are you afraid of what your hand might reveal, boy?" Tobias asked.

Yann felt annoyed, as if somehow he had been cheated of what he needed to know. He wasn't going to be so easily put off having his palm read.

"You don't frighten me, old man," he said. "I am not afraid."

Orlenda stared deep into his eyes.

"You are a true Gypsy, and you could be a great shaman. You have a rare gift." She stopped, letting go of his hand.

"Go on," said the old man. "Tell him. Isn't that why you came here, boy? To know what the future holds?"

"Yes," said Yann through gritted teeth.

Orlenda took a deep breath as if going underwater.

There were three things she told Yann that foggy afternoon, and it was the third one that shocked Yann to the core, as she had known it would. It made him feel as if he were standing on the edge of a ravine, looking down into nothingness. It was an abyss that he had seen before.

"You have survived one bullet, but another is waiting for you in the city over the water."

Yann had gotten up without saying a word and started to walk away.

Tobias called after him. "I will be here when you come back."

By then he was running, feeling as if he were suffocating.

In Covent Garden Piazza, totally out of breath, he had bent over to take in huge gulps of soupy air. What a fool he had been. Did he truly believe in all that hocus-pocus? He laughed out loud, a hard, bitter sound. This much he knew: He was done with trying to find out Têtu's secret. Magic belonged to a world he wanted nothing more to do with. If he was ever to take revenge on Kalliovski he would use a pistol, as any rational man would.

This was the moment when Yann decided to turn his back on notions of sorcery. He would concentrate on the opportunities given to him, and live like a gentleman. No one would ever take him for a Gypsy again; no one would ever know where he had come from.

Two years has passed since that momentous day. It was now the summer of 1792, and Yann was now seventeen years old.

He had never told a soul what had happened at the Gypsy camp, and he had long given up the idea of revenge. The burning flame of grief had lost its urgency: There was so much more he wanted to do. He had worked hard at his studies, acquitted himself well, and was a credit to the Laxtons and to Mr. Trippen. A future he couldn't have envisaged a few years ago was his for the taking—a place at Cambridge University, the possibility of becoming a lawyer. London suddenly seemed to be filled with pretty, flirtatious girls whom he met at private balls and public dances. He had made the pleasing discovery that young ladies liked his company, would giggle, flounce their curls, pout, and generally look charming to get his attention.

"It's because you dance so well, Mr. Margoza," Sophie Padden had whispered to him.

The Laxtons' house in Queen Square had become a meeting point for many of the émigrés who now found themselves in London, under what they felt to be gray skies and diminishing circumstances.

Mr. and Mrs. Laxton's parties were renowned for excellent food and talk. The conversation was often heated, and the ideas expressed both radical and conservative.

The distant drum of the Revolution could be heard loud and clear across the water here in London. It had started out as a glimmer of hope for a new generation, when slavery would be no more, when men and women would be equal, and people would be judged, not by their birth, but by who they were, not divided by race, class, or creed. Yann believed passionately in these ideas.

At one supper party he had met Charles Cordell for the first time. Madame Claumont, a lady from Paris, had also been amongst the guests, along with her friend Sir John Randall.

Yann, as he often did, listened intently rather than join in. But then Sir John Randall said, "We have heard everyone else's views round this table except yours, sir. Speak up—they say revolution is a young man's sport. What have you to say for yourself?"

It was not from a lack of opinions that Yann had kept silent. "I thought when the Bastille fell that all men might truly be free," he said. "It struck me as a good enough reason for stopping time and starting the clocks anew: a fresh beginning when all men would be equal. But what I hear and read is that the people of France are no freer than before. A whole lot of wigs, hats, and crowns will have changed heads, but it looks as if the new masters will be as bad as the old."

"Wise words, young man," said Sir John Randall.

"Alas," sighed Mr. Laxton, "what bonfires we make of Utopian dreams."

"I'm sure the poor will forever help the rich become richer," continued Yann. "Whatever flag you fly, whatever song you sing, whatever church you worship in, it will always be the same. What's the point of playing at politics? All that matters is people."

"Steady on, sir, that is going too far!" said Sir John.

Charles Cordell looked with interest at this young man who spoke with such passion, and he asked, "So if you have no alliance to king or country, what does interest you?"

"What it is to be human," said Yann.

"Go on," said Cordell. "I'm listening."

"Well, sir, as far as I see it, we're all housed in the same skin, be it black, white, or brown. The same blood pulses through all our veins, the same heart beats. Yet some men believe that through birth and privilege they stand above everyone else. I don't believe that. I think that kings have had their day, and the future should be in the hands of the people."

"These are revolutionary views indeed," said Sir John Randall, taken aback by Yann's zeal.

"And views I violently disagree with!" exclaimed Madame Claumont. "There must be order, otherwise society will collapse. People only thrive when they know their place. Absolute monarchy is the only possible way to ensure this."

"Too late, my dear madam," said Cordell. "Your good king didn't seize his chance to put down the Revolution. Now it is too late. With Marat as leader, the Revolution has given birth to a reign of terror that is growing in power day by day. I believe that in the end it will rule everything, destroy everything."

It was shortly after this that Madame Claumont disappeared. Her body was retrieved at low tide, half buried in the Thames mud near Cheyne Walk, her little dog whining beside her.

Henry Laxton accompanied Sir John Randall to identify the body. Madame Claumont was wearing a necklace that was caked in mud, like the rest of her. A red garnet caught Mr. Laxton's eye. He took the necklace away with him, washed it until its color was restored, and studied it carefully. It was, as he had suspected, a necklace like those Charles Cordell had described to him, and the sight of it made him feel sick to his stomach. Madame Claumont had been a good client of the bank. What part, he wondered, had Kalliovski played in her murder?

A terrible, undeniable truth struck him. This was the man Sido was to marry. How could he possibly stand by, knowing what he did, and let her be sacrificed to this monster? Something must be done before it was too late.

chapter twenty

*T*hese days Yann was feeling that the past was well behind him. Then, with three simple words, the world that he thought was his to inherit slipped through his fingers like sand. It was what Orlenda had predicted, and what Yann had chosen to bury somewhere deep in his unconscious mind: His destiny and his fate lay across the water.

On a hot summer's evening, with the study door open to the garden, Mr. Laxton had read him a letter he had just received from Cordell. The three words that stood out, illuminated diamond-bright, were: "Têtu is alive."

It seemed that Têtu, after three years working in provincial theaters where he knew Kalliovski would not find him, had returned to Paris, confident that with all his other activities the count's interest in him had waned. He had been to see Cordell, and was proud and delighted to hear how well Yann had acquitted himself.

Cordell had asked Têtu if he knew anyone who could be trusted to get Sido de Villeduval safely to England, and Têtu had suggested Yann. If Sido refused to abandon her father, then the last resort would be to try to get them both out. For that they would need papers and passports.

As Yann listened, he knew that his future lay not here, but in France; and he remembered with a shudder Orlenda's three predictions and realized that one, if not two, had already come true. Orlenda had told him that he was to take comfort that Têtu was still alive. The next thing she had predicted puzzled him greatly and made him sure that she must be wrong about the dwarf. She told him he had already met the only person he would ever love.

"What is her name?" Yann had asked.

"It begins with S."

All he could think to ask was, "Will we be happy?"

"This love could be the death of both of you," said Orlenda.

Only now could he acknowledge that she had meant Sido— not Sophie Padden. Perhaps, if he was honest with himself, he had always known it, even from the very first moment he had seen her.

The last of Orlenda's three predictions had been the one that had terrified him the most and made him run away. It had been the reason he had wanted no more to do with magic. Finally he realized that there was no more running to be done; he would have to go back and face the bullet. Perhaps, like the magician, this time he would be able to catch it.

Mr. Laxton put down the letter and said firmly, "These are very dangerous times. You don't have to do this."

"But I do," said Yann. "I can't explain why. All I can tell you is that I have known this day was coming. I have been waiting a long time for that letter to arrive."

His determination to give up all that he had earned took Henry Laxton completely by surprise.

"What about university?"

"It can wait. But Sido can't."

Mr. Laxton paused. "Yann, as I said, this is not going to be easy. Kalliovski will not take kindly to anyone trying to steal away what belongs to him. You are dealing with a very dangerous man."

"That makes it all the more important that we succeed."

"In that case I will need a couple of weeks to get all the papers in order; then you can go."

Mr. Trippen sat back at the table after a good Sunday lunch and listened to all Yann had to say about his decision.

"Well," he said, "if the fates are calling you, then go you must. 'There is a tide in the affairs of men . . .'"

"Do you think," interrupted Yann, well-versed in his tutor's love of Shakespearean quotes, "we're simply puppets in the hands of destiny, or do we have the power to change our fate?"

Mr. Trippen contemplated the question, while the youngest

of the Trippens played on the floor with a ball Yann had bought him. His sisters sat listening, looking adoringly at the young man in his fashionable coat, each one wishing that his black eyes would rest on her and twinkle, if only for a moment.

"It is a question," replied Mr. Trippen, "that philosophers, playwrights, poets, and artists will go on asking until the world stops spinning and the sun is snuffed out like a candle. A question, my dear sir, that your Mr. Trippen has struggled with and has no answer for. Though I did once know a man in the Queen Anne Tavern who claimed he had the solution, if not the answer."

"What was it?" asked Yann.

"Aha!" laughed Mr. Trippen. "It lay, according to him, at the bottom of a good tankard of port wine. In other words, my young sir, the question is king, and the answers are different for all men."

"Why don't you do magic tricks anymore, Yann?" said the eldest girl impatiently. "You used to be able to make apples appear from nowhere and do card tricks. Now all you do is talk like Papa and use long words."

"My pudding blossom," said her father, "you have a very good point. Well, young sir, we are all ears."

"I stopped believing in magic," said Yann softly.

Mrs. Trippen came into the room, gathering up the children to take them to visit her mother.

"Don't be long," called Mr. Trippen, "oh flower of my life, apple of my eye, the reason my heart keeps on beating!"

Mrs. Trippen smiled cheerfully. She enjoyed owning furniture weighted down with the gravity of a healthy income. Life was good.

The front door closed and the babbling-brook voices of the children disappeared, leaving only the muted sounds of horses' hooves outside, and inside, the ticking of a clock and the chirping of the two canaries whose cages hung in the window. Mr. Trippen brought out his snuffbox.

"Many men," said Mr. Trippen, taking a large pinch of snuff, which immediately brought on a bout of sneezing, "spend their lives living in the wrong corner of their souls, mainly out of fear of what they might find on the other side."

He took out his handkerchief and blew his nose.

"When I first met you, I would say that you were the most mysterious, magical young man I had ever had the privilege to run into. In the last couple of years it has struck me that you have been merrily trying to board up that side of yourself, close the shop, put up the shutters, so to speak, and old Trippen has noticed the effect it has had on his young Hamlet's countenance. The 'To be or not to be' question has brought about a lopsided quality to your gait. Instead of standing up straight, your right shoulder slopes as if one part of you is in constant disagreement with the other half."

"Yes," said Yann, "I recognize that. What should I do?"

"Whether 'tis nobler in the mind to suffer being ordinary or take arms against a sea of troubles, and by opposing them . . .

except that you are *extraordinary*. Celebrate the magic that you have at your fingertips. Stand up straight, put your head above the parapet."

"Aren't you disappointed that I won't go to Cambridge?"

"No," said Mr. Trippen. "I never thought you would. Doesn't mean I didn't think you could. My advice, for what it is worth, is this: Face your demons."

chapter twenty-one

*Y*ann knew what Mr. Trippen meant. While there was still time, he must go back and find the Gypsies.

Early the next day he took his black horse and rode out to Hainault Forest, to the Fairlop Fair. Here, each year, Gypsies from all over the country gathered under a huge oak tree, making the most of the chance to gossip and trade in the horses and ponies penned in a hastily erected corral. Beneath its canopy of leaves they set up stalls selling trinkets, food, and drink, and the local farmers and their families crowded the little booths to see the puppet shows, to watch the boxing matches, bear-dancing, and sword-throwing, to bob for apples, and have their fortunes told.

Yann arrived in the morning, but it was evening by the time

he found out where Tobias Cooper was. He had to ride some three miles before he smelled the woodsmoke and saw the camp nestled at the edge of the forest.

Tobias walked down the green grassy path to meet him as the sun, round and red, was going down behind the trees in a burst of color. He embraced Yann.

"I knew you would return," he said, "and I know we have not much time, because you are going back across the water."

He took Yann to his tent and they sat down together in front of the fire, where the kettle bubbled away.

"Now let us try again," said Tobias, as if no time had passed. A cup rose into the air and the kettle tipped and poured tea into it, without the help of a human hand. Yann had seen Têtu do this many times.

"What do you see?" asked Tobias.

"A cup having tea poured into it by an invisible hand."

"I did not ask you to look," said Tobias. "Looking is what all fools do. I asked you to see. That is the difference. Now try again. Look at the spaces in between the objects, then tell me what you see."

This time a burning stick was lifted from the fire and stood on end like a torch.

"A burning stick," said Yann, completely at a loss. "What else is there to see?"

"Everything. You see with your eyes. I am asking you to see from here."

He pressed his thumb hard in the middle of Yann's forehead. "This is how you must learn to see. Not with your eyes. They will only deceive you, as I told you before. They are so easily tricked. Now drink."

Yann held the cup tight. He needed the warmth of the tea for comfort. He said, "I stopped believing."

"That goes without saying," said Tobias.

It was not until the moon had taken sovereignty over the night sky that Tobias and Yann left the camp and started to walk through the forest, where the trees stood like sentinels watching for intruders.

Yann kept tripping up; he had lost the basic skills that he once took for granted. Tobias, on the other hand, walked on as if it were broad daylight. At last they came to a clearing, an eerie place surrounded by oak trees on top of which the moon seemed to be balancing. It was a circular clearing, off which led seven paths. Yann had the sensation of walking not on the mossy ground but on a membrane that divided two worlds.

Tobias sat down in the middle of the clearing, Yann beside him, and started to play a penny whistle. It made no sound, or at least none that Yann could hear. After a while, lights began to appear down each path. Phantomlike figures came into focus from nowhere. They seemed no more substantial than mist. Yann watched, hypnotized, as on the path directly in front of him stood a wizened woman.

"Who called for me?" she asked.

Tobias stood up and gave a deep bow. "I did. I have brought the young man as I promised I would."

Yann watched as she seemed to fade and then become whole again.

"Come here," she called out to him.

Then the strangest thing happened. Without moving, without taking a step, he left his body. He could see himself still standing next to Tobias. The old woman held her hands out and he took them. He was being lifted off his feet, up into the night sky, whirling around and around, higher and higher until he was above the treetops, almost touching the moon.

Then, without a word, the old woman let go of his hands and he fell back down to earth. He felt the two parts of himself collide, become one again. So great was the blow that he remembered nothing more.

He woke the next day to find Tobias Cooper sitting at the opening of his tent, filling his clay pipe, talking to Orlenda and Talo. They greeted Yann with warm smiles, Orlenda showing him her little baby before they set off to the fair.

Had last night been a dream? Yann wondered.

"I have been thinking. Have you a talisman?" asked Tobias.

"No," said Yann, feeling strangely different, as if some great burden had been lifted from him.

"Every tawny boy needs a talisman. You need one more than most," said Tobias, and he took from his pocket a small bag and brought out a perfect seashell.

"*Baro seroeske sharkuni*, the very shell of the shells," he said, handing it to Yann. Yann examined it closely. He had never seen one like it.

"It is the shell of a sea snail, and holds great magic. I have been waiting a long time to hand on this talisman. It is meant for you."

"No," said Yann firmly. "It is too precious. I cannot take it."

"You must, for you are alone. But you have a friend, Têtu, and I believe he meant you to find us. He wouldn't have wanted you to return until you had learned to accept your powers without fear, until you stopped hiding from what Orlenda saw in your hand."

Yann knew then how foolish he had been. "I had hoped that the *S* might have stood for Sophie Padden."

"And it didn't, did it?" chuckled Tobias.

"No. No, indeed, it did not. Nor did it stand for Sarah Hinds."

"Though both, no doubt, taught you a lot."

"Maybe," said Yann with a mischievous smile.

"You are a king amongst the Gypsies, Yann Margoza. Take the talisman, wear it with pride and it will keep you safe."

That night they returned to the heart of the forest. This time the old woman was seated in the middle of the clearing. A fire was now burning away with a kettle above it. In amongst the trees hovered the ghostlike figures Yann had seen earlier.

"Go to her," said Tobias, standing on the edge of the clearing.

The old woman patted the ground next to her and Yann sat down.

Close up, her face looked as wise as the earth is broad. In her eyes he could see all that was known and all that was still to be learned. It felt as though she were looking straight through him. A pain struck him in the middle of his forehead as if she were pressing a finger through his skull.

"Give me your hand," said the old woman. Yann felt her papery skin. Her fingers looked like twigs, all twisted and gnarled, her nails like seashells. He flinched, for there was such power in her grip, and suddenly everything disappeared and he was walking across a field, toward a road lined with tall poplars. He could see the wheels of an upturned carriage spinning around and around in a ditch, and started to run toward it. The wind rustled in the trees. A young woman was lying by the roadside, all broken like a china doll. A man was holding her, his horse grazing a little way off; a flurry of autumn leaves swept across the field and there, in a furrow, he could see an infant, her leg broken, her little face contorted with pain. He knelt down beside her, wondering if she too was dead.

With a jolt he was aware of being back in the clearing. The fire and the old woman had disappeared. Yann looked around and for the first time he saw spider threads of light streaming from all the ghostly figures, over-arching him like a huge cat's cradle, until with the sound of a violin string snapping they were gone.

Yann turned to look at Tobias. He too had threads of light

coming from his fingers. And he watched, astounded, as the old man flicked them as a fisherman might cast his line to catch a fish.

"I can see," shouted Yann, "I can see!"

"At last," said Tobias. "Now we can start."

It was a week later, early on a bright and sunny morning, that Yann, having made his farewells to the Laxtons and the Trippens, caught the Paris-bound coach from the strand, the perfect picture of a young English gentleman misguidedly off to visit Paris for the first time. On him were papers and passports and enough money to get out the Marquis de Villeduval and his daughter, Sido.

chapter twenty-two

*O*n the eleventh of August, the Duchesse de Lamantes, worried for the Marquis de Villeduval's safety, sent a messenger to inform the marquis of the serious situation in Paris, and to tell him that the throne of France had been demolished, the Swiss Guards massacred, and the royal family arrested. It was the Duchesse de Lamantes's opinion that they were no longer safe. She also thought the marquis should know that Count Kalliovski was calling for the execution of the king.

In the light of all these developments, the Duchesse de Lamantes was sure that her friend could not now countenance his daughter marrying such a man, and she advised him to leave France at the first possible opportunity.

The Marquis de Villeduval refused to receive the duchess's messenger. He no longer trusted the written word, for he saw it as the sword of Damocles hanging over him. The trouble was that since Kalliovski's last visit, reality had become a stranger to him. While the frayed edges of his sanity daily unwound, he chose to remain locked away in his suite of rooms studying his collection of shoe buckles and remembering which balls, banquets, and fêtes they had been worn at. Nightly now, he walked through the château's empty salons while ghosts danced before him, dressed in all their finery and tall powdered wigs.

It was left to Sido to read the letter, and after that she knew that it was all too late for herself and her father. France, like a pan of milk left too long on a hot stove, was about to boil over.

She slipped downstairs to join the servants in the kitchen, where they crowded around the duchess's messenger. He was a man with things to tell.

"I've never seen anything like it. Why, the very air in the city was electric! At midnight the church bells rang out from steeple to steeple—that's the tocsin that alerts you to danger—followed by a thousand drums and the boom of guns. I'll wager not one person slept, for the terror those bells awoke in them."

"Oh dear Lord, what will become of us?" said Agathe.

"Quiet," said Jean. "Go on. What happened then?"

"Yesterday morning, at dawn, the citizens rose up and marched to the Tuileries Gardens. They were shouting, 'Down with the veto, down with the tyrant.' The troops from the south sang the Marseillaise. They were armed to the teeth—guns, knives, bayonets, swords, you name it. They hacked the Swiss Guard to death. They didn't stand a chance—the king just abandoned them. Only interested in his own skin."

"Oh, lordy Lord!" wept Agathe.

Jean sighed. "A bonfire of hate has been ignited. God alone knows what earthly force can put it out now."

"Did you see anything else?" asked Luc, putting his arm around Lucille's waist.

"Did I see anything else? What these eyes didn't see! All the waters of France won't wash these images away. They're burned into me with a red-hot branding iron."

"Tell us, then."

"Well, when I arrived at the Tuileries by the Palais Royal entrance, the walls were pockmarked with gun- and cannon-fire. I could hear the sound of crashing plates and dishes coming from the royal kitchens—pots and pans thrown all over the place, everybody snatching what they could, either to break or more likely to keep as souvenirs. In the wine cellars I saw a sea of outstretched hands, all fumbling in the sand to pull out bottles of the king's fine wine. They broke the bottles open in their haste to drink and the wine spilled on the floor, mingling with the blood of the corpses. What a shambles! In the chapel, oh Lord, what I saw! All that blood, all them bodies, all them flies, and the smell! The sound of the rabble as it trampled on thousands of fragments of priceless porcelain."

Sido listened silently. Lucille began to weep.

"And the rest of Paris?" asked Bernard.

"There are fires burning all over the city. The citizens are breaking into the aristocrats' houses, looting, killing their servants, smashing their furniture, and burning and destroying anything of value."

"Will they do the same here?" asked Lucille. She was almost beside herself with fear.

"Who knows? When I left they were calling for the blood of the nobility to wash the streets of Paris clean, and they'd started to tear down buildings where aristocrats had taken refuge."

"Enough," interrupted Jean. "You're frightening everyone."

"Well, you asked. I'm only telling you how things stand."

By the time the messenger had left, Sido could see what would happen next.

"I have a wife and children," said Michel Floret, the gardener. "I'm afraid to be found here."

This seemed to go for all the servants, who sorrowfully and apologetically made their excuses and filed out of the kitchen. Even Lucille, who, clasping Sido's hands and with tears rolling down her face, said, "I'm so sorry to leave you, I really am sorry, but I can't stay. I don't want to die. I'm too young."

"I know," said Sido. "Don't worry. You go home with Luc."

Only two stayed sitting at the kitchen table, Jean and Bernard.

"*Eh bien*," said Jean, getting out a bottle of wine. "There is nothing more for it. We'll just have to sit it out and make plans for our escape if the château is attacked."

"I agree," said Bernard.

"No," said Sido, "you must go too. I shall stay with my father."

"But mademoiselle, it's not safe for you here. You must get him to understand."

Sido tried to look calm. "As you know, the marquis has put all his hope for our survival in the wall. He will not leave."

Bernard raised his hands to the air and let out a whistle. "That wall is a farce," he said.

"What do you mean?" asked Sido.

"His laborers hated him for putting the rents so high and taking them away from the land. Their revenge was to use more sand in the mix than they should have."

"I don't understand," said Sido.

"It means the wall will collapse if it's attacked," said Bernard.

Sido felt weak and sat down. "Even more reason for you to go, then."

"No," said Jean firmly, "we're not leaving you. Someone has to stay and help." He poured her a glass of wine. "Though I think I speak for both of us when I say that we are staying out of respect for the late and great marquis, your uncle Armand de Villeduval, and your beloved mother."

Bernard lifted his glass. "Tell you this much—if your uncle were still here, his servants would have fought to the bitter end to protect you all."

"I thank you," said Sido.

That evening the marquis, unaware that anything was wrong, sat down as usual to supper. Annoyed to find that it was late, he rang the bell angrily.

With a heavy heart, Sido opened the door to the dining chamber.

"It is quite intolerable to be kept waiting at my own table," he snapped. "I have guests."

"Papa, all but two of your servants left this morning."

"Did I give you permission to speak?" asked the marquis.

"No, Papa, but I think it might be wise to make plans just—"

"You think," he interrupted sarcastically. "You think? And of what significance are your miserable thoughts? You are just about bearable when silent. When you speak I find your presence quite insupportable."

Sido could take it no longer. She felt overwhelmed by all that she had been told, and by the knowledge that the wall, like her father's mind, appeared to be crumbling. Tears welled up, and the color rushed to her face.

"What have I done that you should hate me so much?" she cried.

The marquis looked up at an invisible point just above her head and rang the bell again with force.

"Please tell me," said Sido.

He still refused to look at her. "Been born, and once born, been a mere girl."

"Is that my only crime?"

"How dare you ask such impertinent questions in front of such distinguished company? Leave the room. I wish to see no more of you."

"Why?" said Sido. "Why, when we should stand together, do you treat me so?"

"Be quiet. I will not be spoken to in this way. You moan and groan like some peasant."

The marquis got up and walked toward the door. "Tell my valet that I shall be dining in my apartment."

"He has left, like the rest of the servants," said Sido.

"Out of my way," said the marquis as he pushed past her, his head held high. "My guests are waiting."

After he had gone Sido slid miserably down onto the floor. Who could save them now? Kalliovski?

She went back down to the kitchen to find Jean still sitting at the table.

"I take it he didn't like what he was told?"

"He wouldn't listen. He loathes me. He said it would have been better if I'd never been born. I should have died along with my mother, then he would have been rid of me."

"Don't say that, mademoiselle. It would have been a terrible waste."

"If I had been a son, would he have loved me? And if I didn't limp? Everything I do is wrong."

Jean looked at Sido. "If it is of any comfort, mademoiselle,

I don't think the marquis cares for anyone or anything, apart from his possessions. He is like an actor who needs the whole stage to himself. There is no room for anyone else, not even his daughter."

"But what can I do?" said Sido.

"Nothing. No matter how much you try to please him, even if, God forbid, you lay down your life for him, he will never love you. It would be best just to accept this, and let acceptance make you stronger. I am sorry to speak out of turn, mademoiselle, but that's how I see it. Is there no other family you can turn to?"

"There's my mother's sister in London. She is married to an Englishman, a Mr. Laxton."

"Well, then," said Jean, "what's the sad face for? At least you know there's someone who will be pleased to see you."

"Yes, but how would I ever get to England?" said Sido.

"Goodness knows, but if things carry on as they are, you may be glad to have relatives there. If it is of any comfort, Bernard and I have worked out an escape route from the château in case the mob should come. Shall I show you?"

He took a lantern from the dresser and guided her out of the kitchen and down the steps that led to the wine cellar. "Follow me," he said, pushing back a small wooden door and lifting the lantern high to show her a long tunnel.

"Where does that go?" asked Sido with surprise.

"To the stables. It was built so that your father would not

have to see any tradesmen unloading wagons. You never know, his vanity may yet save us."

Sido smiled.

"That's better. Bernard is going to keep a carriage ready night and day. Does that make you feel a little less fearful?"

For the next two nights Sido hardly slept. Certain that they would be attacked at any moment, she watched from her window, looking for lights and figures amongst the dark shadows. Only as dawn broke did she allow herself to lie down.

A week later, what Sido had been dreading finally happened. At two o'clock in the morning there was a sudden terrible sound that broke the stillness of the night. She looked into the garden and saw a small army of people advancing on the château, carrying torches and singing loudly, emboldened by wine.

Quickly she dressed and ran to the marquis's bedchamber, just as Jean burst through the door. The marquis was standing by the window in his robe, looking in disbelief at the crowd down below.

"Who let them in?"

"No one did, Papa. They stormed the wall."

"Impossible."

At that moment the window broke. A burning torch landed on the floor and rolled toward the four-poster bed, setting the drapery alight. Sido grabbed a jug and threw water on the flames, while Jean seized the hangings and tried to smother them. It was no use. No sooner had he done so than another torch was thrown in. Downstairs they could hear the sound of breaking glass and hammering on the front door.

"We must leave," said Jean. "They'll be in the house at any moment."

"Not without my buckles," said the marquis. "I won't leave without them."

He pushed open the door to the antechamber. The room was ablaze and he staggered back from the billowing smoke.

"Hurry!" shouted Jean as the marquis desperately tried to beat out the flames to get to his beloved buckles. "If you don't come now, we're leaving you."

The front door gave way and a sound like a wave came crashing into the hall.

In desperation, the marquis grabbed a red-hot buckle and let out a piercing scream as the burning silver branded his hand. Like a wounded child he allowed Jean to lead him down the secret passages, while all around them they could hear the sounds of furniture being broken, ornaments destroyed, and the roar of the fire about to engulf the château.

They rushed down to the cellar, closing the door behind them and stacking baskets of bottles against it in the hope of delaying the mob. Jean went ahead as they groped their way along the dark musty corridor that led to the stables.

Bernard was waiting, trying to calm the two terrified horses that he had harnessed to a carriage. The other horses he had let run wild.

The marquis, on seeing that it was not his finest carriage, demanded that the horses be unharnessed immediately and his gilded coach used instead.

"Get in!" shouted Bernard, losing his patience.

"Surely you don't expect me to travel in a carriage intended for the use of servants?"

"Please, Papa," implored Sido, who was already inside. She looked back and saw the château lit red against the sky as the mob began to move toward the stables.

With great presence of mind, Bernard and Jean pushed the marquis into the carriage and set off at full speed. The mob ran after them, throwing stones that ricocheted off the coach, one breaking the back window and hitting the marquis on the head. They were all thrown across the carriage as it swayed dangerously from side to side, bumping over stones from the fallen wall.

There was no choice as to direction. An angry crowd of peasants was waiting, blocking the road leading to Versailles and Normandy.

The marquis, stunned, sat in the corner of the carriage. Blood trickled down his forehead as he looked back at his beloved château, now consumed by flames.

They reached Paris just as the gates were opening. The gatekeeper, who was more used to seeing people trying to leave than entering, opened the carriage door and sniffed at the all too familiar smell of burned clothes and hair.

He smiled at the marquis, who was sitting in his dressing robe, without his wig, and said with relish, "Now you're one of us. No more the great man, eh, citizen?"

The marquis, who had appeared to be in a trance for most of the journey, looked at the gatekeeper, astonished.

"You are without doubt the ugliest man I have ever had the misfortune to encounter," he said in a dismissive tone.

"What's that?" said the gatekeeper, leaping inside the carriage and grabbing hold of him. "You say that again if you dare."

"Please," begged Sido, "my father is not himself. He has lost his mind. Surely you can see that?"

The gatekeeper looked at her and then threw the marquis back onto the seat of the carriage like a sack of flour.

"Are you here by appointment, my man?" asked the marquis.

"Am I what, citizen?"

"You see," said Sido, "he is not well."

The gatekeeper brushed himself down and looked at Jean. "And who are you, citizen?"

"This is a friend of the family," said Sido quickly. "He is helping me take my father to the nuns at the Hôtel-Dieu. They will care for him there."

Jean took the basket that he had had foresight to bring with him and handed it to the gatekeeper. "It must be hungry work, checking all these coaches for traitors to the Revolution. I admire your dedication, citizen."

The gatekeeper's mouth began to water as he pulled back the

cloth and looked hungrily at the pâté, bread, and cheese. His face was so thin that his cheekbones made a bridge across the flat planes of his features. He took the basket. "Away with you, and don't let me see him come this way again. Is that understood?"

Early as it was, the heat of the city wrapped itself around them as they made their way through the eerie, deserted streets.

Sido had asked Bernard to drive to the Duchesse de Lamantes's town house on the Place Royale, which was the only address she knew. They arrived to find it full of packing cases and the duchess preparing to leave. The marquis sat down on a crate, staring before him like a statue, while the duchess, in dismay, addressed herself to Sido.

"My dear child, why on earth did you come to Paris? It's not safe here. I am leaving, going abroad. Did your father not read my letter?"

"No," said Sido.

"Oh dear." Almost in a whisper, she asked, "And have you seen Kalliovski?"

"No."

The duchess looked around, terrified, as if she expected him to be standing nearby listening, like a cat waiting for a mouse to move.

"I have found someone who will help me to escape. I advise you to do the same. You won't be able to leave without a passport, though, and they are like gold dust. Have you any money?"

"No," said Sido, "we have nothing."

"Oh dear, oh dear, did the marquis not make any arrangements?"

"No."

The marquis, his hand held out before him, muttered, "My collection of buckles was even more valuable than the king's."

"I do advise you," said the duchess, ignoring him, "to leave here as soon as you can. They are arresting all aristocrats as traitors. The prisons are full. It will end in a bloodbath." She went over to her desk and scribbled something on a piece of paper. "By all means stay, but I beg of you, if Kalliovski does come looking for you, not to tell him where I've gone. This is the person you should use to get you out of Paris. I will tell him you need help." She glanced at the marquis. "I will pay him to get you both out."

"Thank you," said Sido, "oh, thank you for your kindness."

"In these troubled times we must support each other," said the duchess, kissing Sido. "Good-bye. I hope we will all meet again in London."

The marquis looked very grave and replied, "I knew, of course, the minute whalebone corsets went out of fashion that things were coming to a pretty pass."

Sido watched as the duchess left and then looked at the piece of paper she had been given. On it was written the name of a Mr. Tull.

chapter twenty-three

*T*he gates to Paris were now barricaded, for there was a tangible fear that the enemies of France were poised to take the city. Everyone coming or going was a potential spy, or a counterrevolutionary trying to escape, every coach suspected of carrying an aristocrat or a member of the clergy. Papers were lingered over and bribes given.

Yann and his fellow passengers stood in a line. A lady from their party became quite alarmed to see her portmanteau opened and her garments sniggered over by the National Guard.

Lefort the gatekeeper, whose domain this was, looked on like a small king of his castle. He had a squint, and dark bushy eyebrows that dominated his face and made up for the lack of expression in his eyes. He was proud of his work, showed no mercy on man or priest, let no one slip through his iron grip. He walked to and fro in his own bilious cloud of tobacco smoke, occasionally spitting out large yellowish gobbets of saliva.

They all heard the mob before they saw what had brought it tearing onto the street. A large coach painted yellow, not unlike the one the king and queen had used for their failed flight to Varennes, was waiting to leave the city. Its grandeur was causing quite a lot of commotion.

"It's the king trying to escape again," jeered one of the onlookers.

Lefort quickly lost interest in the passengers from London and was walking over to the yellow coach when out of nowhere came a group of angry men and women, all wearing the red bonnet of liberty, armed with pitchforks, their sleeves rolled up, ready for action. Yann had never seen such hatred as he saw now, etched upon their faces.

The coachman looked terrified as one of the men leaped at the yellow door, forcing it open with animal ferocity so that it fell off its hinges.

"Shame on you," he shouted at the occupants, "trying to smuggle out the wealth that belongs to France! You're traitors to the Revolution! The enemy within, that's what you be. Well, you'll soon see how we deal with the likes of you."

The husband and wife and their two terrified children were unceremoniously dragged out, screaming. Yann, who had a sudden urge to help them, moved forward. He was stopped immediately by the hand of a fellow passenger who whispered urgently to him, "It isn't worth it, sir. They'll have you thrown in prison for your efforts. Believe me, there's nothing we can do. Just thank the Lord you're not a Frenchman."

Lefort waved away the cloud of tobacco smoke. Seeing that he had caught himself a mighty catch, he had no interest whatsoever in the London stagecoach. Without so much as a second glance, he let it go.

Yann sat back in his seat. From the window he caught a last glimpse of a child's frightened face. What had happened to this city, to its citizens, that they should have so much hatred for their fellow men?

The gentleman whose hand had restrained Yann said, "This is a godless city. I get my business done as fast I can and get out again. Wouldn't catch me staying here any longer than necessary. It's a tinderbox that will self-ignite and go up in flames."

"What will happen to those poor people?" asked the woman whose clothes the National Guard had found so amusing.

"They'll be arrested and sent to prison as cattle fodder for the masses."

The coach rumbled on over the Pont Neuf, where the statue of Louis the Sun King had been torn down. In the distance Yann could see bonfires still burning.

So this is Paris, thought Yann. He felt a thrill of excitement. For better or worse he was back home at long last.

Monsieur Aulard had been well served by the Revolution. For the time being at least, all theaters were free to put on whatever plays they chose as long as they supported the Revolution, made fun of the clergy, and mocked the greed of the aristocrats.

Wisely, seeing which way the wind was blowing, Monsieur Aulard had renamed his small theater the Theater of Liberty. In so doing, he had won the approval of no less a figure than Citizen Danton, one of the most influential men in the National Assembly. With such patronage the theater manager no longer needed to hire magicians to perform cheap fairground tricks to a half-empty auditorium. He now put on productions full of spectacular effects, filled with revolutionary zeal. There was never an empty seat or a dry eye in the house. The only other time the takings had been this good was in the old days of Topolain.

Success had brought sobriety. He treated wine like medicine, doctoring himself with a certain amount each day and not one drop more. In times like these, a man needed his wits about him if he were to survive, for politicians, like audiences, are a fickle lot. What worked well today could be the end of him tomorrow.

This self-imposed regime suited him. He looked younger. He had thrown out his ill-fitting wig and now, in the fashion of the moment, had the air of a man who didn't spend too long worrying at the mirror. His clothes were new, but not flashy. Like an actor, he had reinvented himself for his role as a man of the people. A cockade was securely fastened to every one of his many jackets lest he should absentmindedly forget and find himself mistaken for an aristocrat.

It was well over three years since Jacques Topolain's body had been left sitting in his office chair, holding the sawn-off head of the wooden Pierrot. It was a memory that continued to haunt Monsieur Aulard. So terrified was he of Kalliovski paying him another visit that he had taken the precaution of promoting Didier from caretaker to bodyguard. It was Didier's job to follow Monsieur Aulard wherever he went and to check that nothing and no one was waiting for him in his office.

This morning Monsieur Aulard was more jumpy than he had been in a long while. Last night amongst the audience he could have sworn that he saw Kalliovski; but then again, he seemed to see the man waiting for him on every street corner.

Yann stood in the rue du Temple and wondered if this could possibly be the building he remembered, for it had undergone a huge change. It no longer looked as if it was about to topple into the street but stood upright and proud, with *Théâtre de la Liberté* painted large and bold across its front. A revolutionary flag was draped across its façade like a badge of honor.

He walked around to the stage door and stepped inside, reassured to find that here at least little had changed. It smelled, as it always had, of stale tobacco, wine, and slapstick makeup. Madame Manou was sitting as usual in her sentry box, lit by a single candle.

Yann's eyes took a moment to adjust to the dark. He smiled when he recognized Madame Manou.

"May I see Monsieur Aulard?" he asked.

"Not another," sighed Madame Manou. "What are you? A writer? An actor? A musician?" She peered out at him. "You must be an actor, by the looks of you."

Yann was about to contradict her, but she went on, "I don't know what this city is coming to, theaters popping up everywhere, actors on every street corner, musicians in every basement, writers in every attic. And you know what? They all want to work here." She lifted her shoulders in disgust. "Have you any idea how many stairs there are up to Monsieur Aulard's office?"

"Eighty-two," said Yann.

"*Hein?* How do you know that?" said Madame Manou, quite taken aback.

"I used to work here. You probably don't remember me. My name is Yann Margoza . . ."

Madame Manou leaned out of the box for a closer look. "No, never! Get away with you! You, that street urchin? The Revolution is working miracles." She peered around the side, looking for Didier, and then remembered that the old bear had gone out for a loaf of bread. She had not the slightest intention of walking up all those stairs herself, no matter what that fool Aulard had to say about it.

"Don't need me to show you the way, then, dear, do you?"

Yann went up the wooden spiral staircase two steps at a time, smiling at the memory of a younger version of himself running up. He stopped at the door and knocked.

"Come in," said a familiar voice.

Yann entered to see Monsieur Aulard sitting at a desk piled high with manuscripts. Pieces of paper littered the floor like autumn leaves.

Monsieur Aulard looked shocked. "How the hell were you allowed up?" he said angrily. "Where's that fool Didier? What do I employ him for—"

"Don't you remember me?" interrupted Yann.

"I'm sorry, I don't. Are you an actor?"

"No."

The theater manager pushed his chair back. "Then you *want* to be an actor," he said. "You and the rest of Paris, my friend."

"I was Têtu's assistant. I worked with the magician Topolain. I have been away in England and have just returned."

Monsieur Aulard stood up. "You're Yann Margoza? Is it possible? My word, yes, I can see it now. It *is* you!" He laughed. "Your eyes should have told me. You always had the most extraordinary eyes." He seized Yann's hand. "Who'd have thought you'd turn out such a handsome fellow!"

Yann smiled. "Who'd have thought to see you so sober and successful, Monsieur Aulard!"

"The cure, my son, is the Revolution," said Monsieur Aulard proudly. "Never in all my life have I done so well."

"I've come to see Têtu."

"Hush," said the theater manager nervously, looking around him as if he half expected the door to be flung open and Kalliovski to be standing there, pistol in hand. "Walls have ears," he said. Taking Yann by the arm he whispered, "Come with me."

Yann followed him down the stairs toward the stage door, where Didier was just coming in with his bread.

"Do you need me?" asked Didier.

"No, no, just be outside my apartment in an hour's time."

"Wait!" called Didier as they left. "Aren't you Yann?"

"Not now!" said Monsieur Aulard firmly, as if he were directing the scene.

"But—but—" said Didier.

Yann turned and mouthed, "Good to see you too."

Monsieur Aulard set off up the boulevard and led Yann into the maze of streets that he knew so well. He walked at a brisk pace, checking behind and in front of him at every corner to be sure that they were not being followed.

"How is Têtu?" asked Yann.

"He's all right. It's good to see him again, after all this time. He turned up the other day, just like that, as if nothing had happened."

"What *did* happen?" asked Yann. "I've only just heard that he's still alive."

"Didier found him bleeding to death in the courtyard of the Hôtel d'Angleterre, and carried him back to the theater. You know, he never said a word. I wasn't even aware that Didier was living in the theater, right up in the attic. He carried Têtu up there, removed the bullet and nursed him back to health. There was Têtu, right under my nose, and I knew nothing!"

"When did you find out?"

"Like you, only recently. He left the theater as soon as he was better, and went to work in the provinces. More than that, I can't tell you."

They stopped next to a battered wooden door. Monsieur Aulard produced a key and opened it, holding on to the iron handle and leaning out slightly to see if they were being watched.

"He's staying with me now. I still feel very worried about the whole thing."

"I can see that," said Yann, smiling.

The street was all but deserted. Satisfied that they were not observed, Monsieur Aulard hurried Yann into a wide courtyard. They walked up the stone stairs to the first floor and entered a much larger apartment than the one Yann remembered. Iago the parrot still sat on his perch, looking, like his owner, in better health.

Monsieur Aulard went over and opened the shutters, peering out to check that there was no one down below. Sunlight flooded the room. Yann could tell by the state of the apartment that Têtu was around. He couldn't imagine the theater manager keeping it this neat and tidy. As if to prove the point, Monsieur Aulard threw down his hat, and then he disappeared into the next room.

Yann stood looking down through the windows to the cobbled courtyard. It was overgrown and unkempt, plant pots lay neglected, and a cat, long and lazy, had spread itself, asleep, across the step, warming its belly in the sun.

"Yannick, is that really you?" It was the high-pitched voice he knew so well.

Yann rushed toward Têtu, lifting him off his feet and hugging him tight as tears rolled down Têtu's cheeks. "Oh, it is so, so good to see you!"

"Put me down and let me get a proper look at you," said Têtu, wiping his eyes and walking around Yann, studying him carefully. "Well, what a fine gentleman you've turned out to be. Look at your clothes! Can you speak English? Oh my word, what your mother would have given to see her handsome son all grown up. Tell me, can you read and write?"

"I can," laughed Yann, "and I speak English like a gentleman, without even a trace of an accent."

Têtu clapped his hands and danced with joy. "Well, well, who would have thought it!" He paused, his face suddenly solemn. "Do you forgive me, Yannick, for letting you believe I was dead?"

"There's nothing to forgive. I have so much to thank you for, Têtu. Never once have I felt unloved or unwanted. Without you, I would have been left to die. You have been both mother and father to me."

"No, no, Yann, stop it, there's no need to say all that. Love needs no justification. You were always wanted, right from the very beginning. Whatever happens, don't forget that."

"You've been incredibly brave," said Yann.

"Rubbish. You know, it was never my intention to get shot. Finding myself in that strange predicament, I felt fate had intervened. I tell you this, Yannick, it was the hardest thing I have ever done, not to let you know I was all right."

By now Têtu had brought out some bread and cheese and put them on the table. He sat down and looked at Yann, who was still standing, the sunlight illuminating his face.

"Those things I used to be able to do—read minds, read the future," said Yann, "those gifts left me the night Topolain was killed, the night the Pierrot said, 'I see you all drowning in a sea of blood.' I still have no idea why I said it." He stopped and sighed. "For a long time I felt responsible for what had happened. If I had kept quiet . . .'"

"Yann, it had nothing to do with that. It would have happened whatever you said. Remember the red necklace that you found?"

"And you took."

"Yes, but that's not important. I've been making a few inquires. Did you know that a red necklace just like it was found round the neck of a Madame Perrien, a friend of Kalliovski's?"

"And a similar one was found in London, round the neck of a Madame Claumont," said Yann. "Mr. Laxton believed it had something to do with Kalliovski." He thought back to his vision of the woman lying in a field. Try as he might, he couldn't remember if she too was wearing a red necklace.

Têtu interrupted his thoughts. "Cordell told me about Sido de Villeduval and her forthcoming marriage. A terrible business. There is no question we must try and rescue her. I would do it myself, but my size is against me; once I've been seen, once I've been heard, I'm hard to forget. I didn't want you to come back to Paris and put yourself in danger, but when Cordell told me how you'd turned out, it seemed to me you would be the person to rescue the girl. Cordell thinks you're very clever. I know you're very clever, but I also know you're better suited to adventure than to studying."

"You're right."

"A pity, though, your gifts leaving you like that. You were quite remarkable when you were younger. So, what can you do now?"

Yann sat down at the table and cut a thick slice of bread. "Throw my voice, ride, fence, read, write . . . oh, and . . ."

Over on the shelf opposite he saw a bottle of brandy and two glasses. He pulled at the threads of light.

Monsieur Aulard entered the room and stood there dumbstruck to see a bottle suspended in midair. The cork was removed and the bottle tipped up, filling two glasses, before all four objects landed on the table without a drop being spilled.

Têtu's face broke into the widest grin. "Why didn't you tell me you could see?" He leaped up and flung his arms around Yann.

"How fortunate that you have returned to us with such magic

in your fingers," said Monsieur Aulard, putting on his hat. "If they ever tire of revolutionary zeal I am going to give them magic the like of which Paris has never seen."

"No," said Têtu firmly, "you are going to do no such thing, is that understood?"

Monsieur Aulard shrugged his shoulders. "Understood," he said sadly, opening the front door. "Maybe when the Revolution is over . . ."

"If we live that long," said Têtu.

After Monsieur Aulard had gone Têtu began to talk about the situation in Paris.

"Things are very bad indeed, and getting worse each day. The National Guard have started doing nightly raids to smoke out aristocrats, or priests who haven't sworn allegiance to the Revolution, breaking down doors, pulling up floorboards. The jails are full to bursting."

Yann and Têtu sat talking till late. Yann told Têtu about Tobias Cooper, and about his life in London with the Laxtons, and Têtu told him a little about his three years living and working in the provinces.

At last Yann said, "I've told you everything, and as usual, Têtu, you've told me nothing about yourself. I'm glad to see you haven't changed one bit. You're still the same mysterious person you've always been."

"Now," said Têtu, changing the subject, "let's talk about how we're going to get Sido de Villeduval out. This is going to be difficult and dangerous, Yann. We'll have to plan very carefully. We just might be able to save the girl on her own, but I can't see how we'll ever get the marquis out undetected."

"But I've brought papers for both of them," said Yann.

"It makes no difference," said Têtu. "We have Kalliovski to reckon with, and he has a razor-sharp mind. He has spies. Nothing escapes his attention."

Yann got up and went over to the window. The cat, now awake, one leg pointed skyward, was balancing precariously on the narrow windowsill, busy cleaning its sleek fur.

"I had a letter this morning from the marquis's lawyer, Maître Tardieu," Têtu went on. "It's addressed to Cordell, but as he is away he had it forwarded to me." He handed a sheet of paper to Yann.

"There's nothing on it. It's blank."

"In times such as these, when wise men fear even their shadows, it is prudent to take precautions. It has been written with sympathetic ink."

He lit a candle, and as he held the letter up to the flame the words began to appear.

Yann read it carefully. "What do you think Maître Tardieu is so desperate to tell us?"

"I don't know. I'll arrange for us to see him tomorrow."

Outside there was the sound of a pot breaking on the ground. Red geraniums lay scattered; the cat had vanished.

If only, thought Yann, I could do the same for Sido.

chapter twenty-four

It was a stiflingly hot morning when Yann left the lodgings he had taken in the Marais to go and meet Têtu. He was now dressed in the French mode, wearing a long sky-blue coat with the revolutionary cockade pinned to the lapel, over a red-striped calico waistcoat, under which he wore a shirt of fine cotton, his cravat tied high around his neck. To finish his dashing outfit he wore breeches and riding boots, so that no one seeing him would think him any different from any other fashionable young man of this city, filled no doubt with the same fashionable revolutionary zeal as all other patriotic young men of his time.

Têtu was seated in his usual place at the Café Godet, a corner table facing the street, from which he had a perfect view of all the comings and goings.

"Good!" he said, seeing Yann. "Maître Tardieu will see us at three o'clock this afternoon."

He turned and tried to catch the waiter's eye. The man steadfastly ignored him.

"Never can get served here," said Têtu tetchily. "Listen, I sent Didier out to do some snooping for us yesterday, instead of sitting cooped up in the theater. He's perfect for the task. No one will think he's up to anything, other than occupying vacant space."

"I thought he only worked for Monsieur Aulard."

Têtu huffed and raised his hands. "His talents are wasted there. Didier's no fool. He might well possess the face of a mooncalf but, as I've told him, in times like these his looks could be his fortune; for this is soon to be a city of idiots, where clever men will need to hold tight to their heads if they wish to keep them."

Yann looked around the café. It was as busy as it had always been. At the next table, an argument broke out as to what should be done with the royal family.

"Kill them! They're traitors, the lot of them," said a burly man with a red face. "That's what I'd do with them. Know what he said the day we dethroned him, when he was taken through the Tuileries Gardens to the National Assembly? He said, 'There are a great many leaves: They fall early this year.'"

His companions burst out laughing.

"Good Frenchmen being slaughtered, and all the idiot can talk about is leaves!" said the burly man. "Would you credit it?"

Didier pushed his way into the café. He was still wearing the tiny red liberty cap, which looked ridiculous on his huge head, and sweat was pouring down his face. He pulled out a chair next to Têtu. "It's too hot, too hot by half, and it ain't even midday."

Têtu stretched up and pulled the cap from his head. "Take care, my friend. With a cap that ill-fitting, you might be seen to be mocking the cause."

"It's the biggest I could find," said Didier, offended.

Yann laughed. "Better get someone at the theater to make you one that fits, in that case."

"Have you any news?" asked Têtu.

Didier turned around and looked longingly at the counter, where waiters were busy pouring wine into pitchers.

"At least let me have a drink, will you? It's thirsty work finding out what people are doing in this weather, I can tell you."

"*Garçon*, a jug of coffee and some bread," shouted Têtu.

"I've only got one pair of hands," the man snapped.

"Anyone would think he was doing us a favor, instead of serving up stale bread and watered-down coffee," said Têtu.

Yann got up and elbowed his way through to the counter, where the proprietor's wife sat knitting and keeping a beady eye on the customers. She looked up from her stitches, about to say, "Wait your turn like everyone else," but seeing Yann said instead, "What can I do for you, my lovely?"

"How do you do it?" asked Didier as the woman brought over their order, smiling at Yann.

"By being a proper gentleman, with manners," said the woman with emphasis. "They're rare in this dog kennel of a city, I can tell you." She ruffled Yann's hair and walked away, swinging her hips.

Têtu stared at him through narrowed eyes.

Yann laughed.

Didier didn't wait to be asked. He went straight for the bread and then started to speak with his mouth full, spitting out food in the process. He wiped his mouth on his cap.

"I've been making inquiries about the marquis."

"Yes, and what have you discovered?"

"His château was torched three days ago. There's nothing left of the place."

"Was anyone hurt?" asked Yann quickly.

"No. From what I gather, all the servants had already scarpered, except two, who helped get the marquis and his daughter out. They're now staying near you in the Duchesse de Lamantes's old residence in the Place Royale. She's left for Jersey."

"What about the marquis and his daughter?" asked Yann.

"Give us a chance," said Didier, mopping his face. "You're getting me all flustered. Where was I? Oh yes, I've seen a girl with a limp. The servants—a chef and a coachman—don't get out much because the master can't be left alone, so the girl goes to the market, that's what I was told. I followed her down the rue des Francs-Bourgeois. She don't spend much."

"Was anyone else watching the place?" asked Têtu. "Any of Kalliovski's men?"

"Not that I could see," said Didier. He was about to cram another huge mouthful of bread into his mouth when Yann snatched it away.

"What do you think you're doing?" growled Didier.

"Finish your story and I'll buy you a jug of wine," said Yann.

"Oh, so that's it. You want to know about the young lady, what she looks like. I got your ticket. Well, she's pretty. Looks like a ripe cherry waiting to be plucked from the tree, if you get my meaning."

"We do, and most of your crumbs too," said Têtu sharply.

"I'm impressed that you managed to find out so much," said Yann.

"I have my sources," said Didier.

"Which house is it?" demanded Yann. He got up. "I'll go and see if I can talk to her."

"Good," said Têtu. "Try and get her to agree to leave her father."

Yann went up to the counter and ordered wine and more bread for Didier.

"I'll see you at the theater," he said over the heads of the customers, and slipped out of the door and down the Boulevard du Temple.

It did not take him long to walk to the Place Royale. Its arcade gave welcome shelter from the blistering sun. On the corner was a café, and along the inner wall stalls had been set up by women selling an odd variety of wares. Yann took his time to work out the best place to stand so that he had a clear view of the main door to the duchess's residence.

He waited, leaning against the cool stone.

From his vantage point at the corner of the square he was able to observe Sido before she saw him. Her mass of dark hair was tied up with a crimson ribbon, her face porcelain pale. She was dressed in a white muslin gown and carrying a basket, limping slightly as she walked toward him. Only when he said her name did she stop.

"Mademoiselle Sido. Do you remember me?"

She looked at him, her head to one side, wondering for a moment if hunger had made her hallucinate or whether it was just an incredible longing to see him again that had conjured up this apparition that stood before her.

"Yann Margoza," she said softly, as if the words were stepping-stones across an unknown river. She wanted to touch him, just to reassure herself that he was made of flesh and blood rather than dreams and desires.

"Yes."

Her face lit up.

Oh, yes, thought Yann, I always knew you were going to be lovely.

"What are you doing in Paris?" she asked.

"What is anyone doing in Paris? Trying to survive," he answered. "Would you like to eat?"

"I have to go and get food for my father."

"We can do that later. Why don't we eat first? I would like to talk to you."

They walked together to the Café des Bains Chinois on the rue des Rosiers. Yann asked for a table at the back, where he hoped they would not be observed.

The smell of food was like an intoxicating perfume that made Sido feel faint.

Can this be happening? she thought. "He looks even more handsome than I ever dreamed he would."

Yann turned to look at her, startled. What an unguarded thing to say, he thought.

"I am very flattered that you—" He stopped abruptly, realizing with a shock that Sido was not talking, yet he could hear what she was thinking. Had his gift come back? Could he once more read people's minds? He turned to look at the other customers in the café, wondering if he could hear what they where thinking as well. Nothing. Not a word, only the chitter-chatter of voices, the clinking of glasses, the clicking of cutlery. Only Sido's thoughts rushed in upon him.

"You look well," she managed to say. "When I last saw you . . ." Here she stopped herself, suddenly aware of his dark eyes on her. It was as if he had walked inside her head and could see for himself just how much and how often she had thought of him since they last met.

The meal arrived. Yann was glad of the interruption. It gave him time to try to think straight, as Sido's thoughts flooded his mind.

"Eat it slowly," said Yann kindly. "If you eat too fast you'll be sick. Take some bread first."

"How do you know I haven't eaten?"

"Because I do."

She was quiet, savoring the food in her mouth as if she were eating life itself. She remembered how she had felt when she had first seen him three years ago at her father's château. The sense of being in church, that her soul was visible, that there was nowhere to hide from him.

"I've been staying with some people called Laxton," said Yann, pleased to be talking aloud.

Sido stopped eating and looked up at him, shocked. "Did you say Laxton?"

"Yes," he said, studying her. She had sapphire-blue eyes, and a long elegant neck down which an endearing curl of dark hair had fallen. *Lovely* was the wrong word to describe her. *Lovely* didn't do her justice. No, Sido was beautiful.

"You know my aunt? Can this be true? Tell me . . ." Once again she checked herself. She felt her emotions were about to spill over, like water in a glass. She feared she would say too much. Best to keep these thoughts to herself, so she asked, "But how?"

"Têtu. Do you remember the dwarf?" And he told her as much of the story as he dared, leaving out the bullet.

"They want you to come to London. That's why I'm here."

"I must be dreaming," said Sido. "You have come back to take me to London?" The idea seemed, in this terrifying city, nothing more than a chariot of clouds.

She was quiet for a moment. "I fear it's too late," she said at last. "I can't leave. Earlier this year I was formally betrothed to Count Kalliovski. He came down from Paris with my father's lawyer, Maître Tardieu, and papers were signed."

What she didn't say, and what Yann could hear loud and clear, was that she had felt like a piece of unwanted furniture, to be sold for the right price.

"How is the marquis's health?" asked Yann.

"He's not well. He burned his hand badly in the fire." She paused. "It's not just that. It is in his mind that he is most disturbed. My father has become obsessed with Count Kalliovski, convinced that he ordered the burning of the château. He believes him to be the devil, come to tempt virtuous men to tread the path to hell."

"And this is the man you are betrothed to?" Yann exclaimed, almost shaking with rage.

"I am uncertain now. My father has written to Maître Tardieu instructing him to inform Count Kalliovski that the marriage is off."

"When did he do that?"

"He wrote the letter the day after the fire. There are fleeting moments when his mind becomes clear."

"Do you have anyone to help you?"

"Jean Rollet, my father's chef, has stayed with us; Bernard the coachman too, but he has family in the city. His wife is worried that he will be sent to prison if he is seen to be still working for an aristocrat." She stopped talking and bit her lip, trying her best not to cry.

It was what she was not saying, more than what she said, that struck Yann powerfully: The marquis was haunted by visions of his dead wife, who stood before him; the present was only a fleeting stranger, the past took up most of his quarrelsome days.

Sido didn't want to cry, but still she could not prevent tears welling up in her eyes as she said quietly, "Such is the state of my father's mind that I can now hardly be in the same room with him before he takes to shouting and demanding of invisible footmen that I be removed. In truth, he frightens me."

Yann then reached out and touched her hand. Her skin was rose-petal soft.

Sido wiped her eyes. "What will people think of us?"

"That we are lovers having a quarrel."

Sido's face turned deep crimson.

"Leave your father, let me get you out. I can do it, I have the papers and the money," said Yann. "There is a new life waiting for you in London."

For all his passionate words he could hear her thoughts and could see all the knots, the longing to be loved by a father who would never love her. He said in desperation, "He has never cared for you. What do you owe him?"

Sido looked bewildered. Had she said these things out loud?

"Come away with me today," begged Yann.

"I cannot. I couldn't live with myself if I did."

He sighed, and pushed back his chair. "I knew you would say that. Is your father willing to go to England?"

"Yes. The Duchesse de Lamantes, who took us in, has recommended a man who will help us escape, once my father is well enough to travel."

"How are you going to pay him?"

"The duchess very kindly said she would loan us the money, and that she would pay this Mr. Tull for us."

"Mr. Tull, did you say?"

Sido nodded. "Do you know of him?"

Yann remembered Mr. Tull only too well. How was it, he wondered, that he was in Paris helping émigrés escape?

"Have you met him yet?"

"No, but we've had a message telling us to contact him when we're ready."

Yann said earnestly, "Please don't. Let me get you out instead of Mr. Tull. After all, that's what I'm here for."

"I don't think my father would consider it. The duchess suggested Mr. Tull, and so Mr. Tull it has to be."

In spite of the clamor in the café, they could hear the church bell chiming the hour.

Sido wished, as they shopped together for food, that she had the power to slow down time, even to stop it altogether, or at least never to forget each passing moment. They walked back slowly toward the Place Royale. With every step that took them nearer to her front door she wondered if she would ever see Yann again.

As they parted Yann said, "I will be here at the same time tomorrow."

He walked back to the theater floating on air. The colors all around him looked brighter than they had two hours ago. Never could he remember feeling so alive. Why should that be? he wondered. He smiled at himself. As if he didn't know! It was because she had been thinking about him all this time.

He jumped up in the air, hit the sky with his fist, and laughed out loud. She loved him. It was so simple. At that moment he realized something that he hadn't dared whisper even to himself, something that Orlenda had seen so clearly in the palm of his hand: There was only one person for him, and that was, and always would be, Sido de Villeduval.

The gravity of this realization made him once more aware of his feet upon the street, Didier's words a pebble in his happy thoughts: "Like a ripe cherry waiting to be plucked from the tree." A sudden and terrible dread overcame him. He was now certain that the involvement of Mr. Tull did not bode well.

chapter twenty-five

$\mathcal{T}$êtu was waiting impatiently in the wings of the theater, watching a couple of tumblers practice their moves and a juggler throw his unlit torches up into the air.

"Where is Yann? Curse the boy," he said under his breath.

On stage Monsieur Aulard was shouting loudly and without much effect at a singer whose rendition of the Marseillaise left a lot to be desired.

"No, no, mademoiselle," Monsieur Aulard bellowed. "We want to stir the audience to a patriotic fervor, not send them screaming from the theater."

Têtu turned around to see Yann slip through the shadows.

"At last!" he hissed. "I thought you'd forgotten our appointment with the lawyer."

"Quiet!" shouted Monsieur Aulard. "How's one expected to work when there's bedlam going on backstage?"

"I saw her," said Yann.

Têtu took his arm. "Come on, you can tell me about it on the way there."

Once out of the theater they set off toward the Left Bank.

"Well," said Têtu as they walked along, "did you tell her our plan?"

"Yes."

"Good. And did she agree?"

"No. She told me that they had made a previous arrangement. The Duchesse de Lamantes had recommended that they use Mr. Tull."

"Mr. Tull," said Têtu. "Why Mr. Tull?"

"He was the one the duchess had employed to take her to London. She left disguised as a governess."

"Now that's interesting. I'd heard that Mr. Tull was working in Paris. By all accounts he's doing good business."

"He speaks terrible French, and he's not very bright. I have a feeling he must be working with someone here."

"Maybe," said Têtu. "But he has done this many times before."

Yann kicked at a stone. "I don't like the idea of Mr. Tull being involved."

"If it is of any comfort, it was Mr. Tull who took you safely to London. Why should he not do the same for Mademoiselle Sido and her father?"

"I don't know."

"He must have gotten the necessary papers. Anyway, I can tell you this much: We would never have been able to get both of them out. The girl, maybe; the marquis, impossible."

"I still feel uneasy."

"Tell you what we'll do. The minute we're finished here I'll get Didier to make inquiries for us as to Tull's credentials, so that when you see Mademoiselle Sido tomorrow you can advise her what to do for the best." He stopped walking and looked at Yann. "You will be seeing her tomorrow, I take it?"

"Yes."

"Good, very good. You never know, by then she may have changed her mind and decided to go with you by herself."

"I doubt it," said Yann.

The lawyer's house was near the Sorbonne, down a dingy covered passage off the rue St. Jacques. It was so dark that the lanterns hanging in the niches were all lit. Yann and Têtu stood there waiting in the gloom for the door to open, sensing eyes peeking out of all the buildings, spying on them. In the window of the shop opposite, a solitary candle dimly illuminated its macabre contents, waxwork heads stuck on pikes. One was of Louis XVI, another was of Marie Antoinette. Yann felt a shiver go down his spine.

"My word," said Têtu. "A glimpse of what is to come."

"Yes?" said the maid, opening the door.

"We have an appointment to see Maître Tardieu."

The girl took them up a narrow, dark staircase that led to a room of miserable proportions. Lit only with a few candles, so used was this room to the perpetual gloom of twilight that the outside world seemed almost divorced from it.

The lawyer reminded Yann of a mole. He was dressed in a worn-out black velvet coat, his face gravestone gray, worry etched into every feature, thick heavy spectacles stuck firmly on the bridge of his nose. He did not look a well man. He was sitting at a table piled high with papers. Next to him stood an inkstand and a stone jar of quills, beside which were the remains of an unfinished meal. He seemed lost for words as they entered the room, not knowing what to make of this pair, while the maid fussed with the plate and straightened a forlorn-looking chair.

"That's all, thank you," said Maître Tardieu firmly, and the door clicked shut behind her. Never for a moment had he imagined Cordell sending him a mere youth and a dwarf, apparently from the circus. He had been expecting two serious and well-connected gentlemen to help him. Had Cordell no idea of the urgency of the situation?

"We live in strange times indeed, sir," said Têtu, reading the lawyer's thoughts.

"No, we live in terrible times," said Maître Tardieu. "Who would think that I would live so long as to be rewarded in my old age with such times as these." He took off his glasses and nervously wiped them on his sleeve, with the effect of evenly coating the already smeared lenses with more grime. "I take it you've heard about the marquis's château?"

"About the fire?"

"Yes. What a dreadful business. The last of the marquis's great fortune gone up in flames." The lawyer sighed. "He wrote to me a few days ago instructing me to break off Mademoiselle Sido's betrothal, said she wouldn't be marrying the devil."

"Have you informed Kalliovski?"

Tardieu mopped his forehead. "I have, sir."

"Have you had a reply?"

"None," he said, absentmindedly moving papers from one pile to another for want of something to do.

"I am aware, sir," said Têtu kindly, "that we are not what you had in mind when you asked Monsieur Cordell for help."

"Quite," said Maître Tardieu. "Quite."

"But whatever else you may think of us, we are to be trusted, of that I can give you my word."

"Yes, Cordell wrote and told me as much . . ." He stopped, then started again. "But sir," said the lawyer, standing up, "I didn't expect—"

"A dwarf," interrupted Têtu.

"Quite, quite."

"My size, sir, is of no importance to me, though I see it more often than not reflected badly back at me in the eyes of my fellow man."

"This, sir, is a most sensitive matter. I am afraid it is for Monsieur Cordell alone."

"That is not possible," said Yann. "He is away in Coblenz."

For a while the silence in the room felt almost tangible. Then Maître Tardieu said, "This goes against my better judgment, but I see there is nothing else to be done." He put his hand under his chin as if to prop up the weight of his head, and lowered his voice. "Something very distressing has come to light. Oh dear me, yes, very distressing indeed. I have received a packet from a Monsieur Giraud, a lawyer of my acquaintance who lives in Normandy. He was called in to help identify the remains of a body found on the marquis's estate, near where Mademoiselle Sido's mother was killed. Monsieur Giraud concludes that this ring, found amongst the bones, was the property of the marquis's half brother, Armand de Villeduval, who disappeared about the time of the accident, and that the remains were his."

He tipped the contents of the packet onto the table. Out fell a ring and seven bloodred garnets.

"The ring," continued Maître Tardieu, "bears, as you can see, the coat of arms of the Villeduval family. I remember that Armand de Villeduval used to wear it on his left hand. The garnets . . ." He paused. "Will you wait here? There is something else I must show you."

When he left the room, Têtu picked up one of the garnets and studied it.

"Does it remind you of anything?"

"Yes. The red necklace I found in Kalliovski's room."

Upstairs they could hear the lawyer shuffle across the floor-boards as the ceiling creaked above them.

"How can anyone live in this place?" said Yann.

"Moles like the dark."

The lawyer came back carrying a velvet drawstring bag.

"This," he said, "belonged to Mademoiselle Sido's mother. She instructed her maid that if anything happened to her she was to give the purse to me."

He emptied it onto the table. The brightness of the jewels that fell out shone even in the darkness of the gloomy room. In amongst them lay a red ribbon studded with seven garnets.

Maître Tardieu brought out his handkerchief and mopped his brow again, the heat a sticky, unwelcome visitor.

Têtu picked up the red necklace. "How did this get in amongst such valuable jewels?" he asked.

"The maid told me that she had taken the necklace off her dead mistress, along with her rings. She had no idea if it was valuable or not, and just added them to the other jewels. Does it signify anything?"

"The seven garnets found with Armand de Villeduval's ring were once attached to a red ribbon identical to this," said Têtu. "It is the signature that is left on every one of his victims."

"Sir," said Maître Tardieu, "you are alarming me greatly. Please, in heaven's name, explain yourself. Whose victims?"

"Kalliovski's. I think it proves that Armand de Villeduval and Madame Isabelle de Villeduval were murdered, but the question—and one you might have the answer to—is why?"

"We must call for the police," said the lawyer.

"That would be unwise," said Yann. "It would be as good as signing your own death warrant."

"Oh dear, oh dear, what is to be done?"

"What we want to do is get Mademoiselle Sido to London, where she has family and will be out of Kalliovski's reach."

"I agree that would be best. If Kalliovski were to marry Mademoiselle Sido, he would be in control of her inheritance. Can I ask—how do you plan to get her out?"

"We have been told that a Mr. Tull is to take her and the marquis to England," said Têtu.

"Not the marquis. The man, you know, is quite mad. If anything will scupper the plan, he will. Do you really believe this Mr. Tull is up to the job?"

"That's what we're going to find out," said Yann.

"But, young man, I don't want anyone but yourself taking these jewels back to London, is that understood?"

"Yes," said Yann. "I will make sure that Mademoiselle Sido receives them safely."

"I can't tell you how delighted I shall be to see them with their rightful owner at last. I am an old man: I don't like keeping such valuables in my house, not in times like these."

"Then, sir," said Têtu, "we will make the necessary arrangements to relieve you of the jewels."

They left the lawyer's house with two vital questions still unanswered. If Kalliovski had murdered both Sido's mother and Armand de Villeduval, what was his motive? And what part had the marquis played? The questions hovered there angrily, like stormclouds in search of thunder.

The next morning Yann was back at the Place Royale, eager to tell Sido of her unexpected good fortune. He took up his position as before, not wanting to draw attention to himself. There were spies all over Paris, looking out for potential émigrés.

By half past one, Yann had to acknowledge that something was wrong, and the unpleasant image of Mr. Tull came back to haunt him.

Yann moved nearer to the door, wondering if he could have missed her, hoping beyond hope that she would still come down. As he leaned against the wall, he could hear the women nearby gossiping.

"That poor girl! There she was, trying to stop him from shouting, and he kicked her in front of everybody." The woman folded her arms and huffed. "Most probably that's how she got that limp in the first place."

"Well, he's not right in the head, is he?" said her friend. "You could see that. Mad, like the lot of them. Too much inbreeding, I say. That's what's wrong with all these stinking aristocrats."

At that all three women chuckled.

"He was a sight for sore eyes, wasn't he? Did you notice that one side of his powdered hair was stuck to his head, as if he'd been sleeping on it?"

"Telling us all to keep away because he was a marquis and

shouting out at the top of his voice that the devil was coming to get them! I thought the National Guard would come and arrest him, the noise he was making."

"It took two strong men to get him into that carriage, didn't it?"

"You had to feel sorry for the girl, though. She was in tears by the time they took off."

Yann had heard enough. A wave of panic flooded through him as he walked past the women and toward the door. He knocked hard, but he knew it was hopeless. He should have gotten her out when he had the chance. Now he hated to think of the danger she was in.

By the time Yann returned to the Theater of Liberty it was early evening. The curtain was due to go up shortly, and crowds were lining up outside, eager to see the show, and being entertained by musicians and tumblers. Yann went through the stage door and up the stairs to Monsieur Aulard's office.

Têtu was in the middle of a terrible argument with the theater manager. Didier, his great arms folded across his chest, stood watching his boss and the dwarf bellow at each other. Têtu had his sleeves rolled up as if ready to start fighting.

"He is here to protect me, not to run errands for you," Monsieur Aulard was shouting.

"You don't need protection. You're not in any danger. We, on the other hand, need vital information, and that old mooncalf of yours is the one for the job."

"Don't keep calling me a mooncalf!" snapped Didier. "You're always doing that. It's irritating me."

"Stop it!" shouted Yann. They turned to look at him. "Stop it! Sido's gone. Tull came last night. She's left with the marquis."

"Well, that was fast," said Têtu, out of breath. "With luck she'll be well on her way to England by now."

"No, something's wrong. When the carriage came last night the marquis kept screaming and wouldn't get in. A crowd gathered and he kicked Sido in front of them and insulted them all."

"He is deranged," said Monsieur Aulard. "What do you expect?"

"If he was making that much of a din, then their attempt to escape must have been obvious," said Têtu. "Why wasn't he arrested?"

"They probably thought he was being taken to the asylum," said Monsieur Aulard helpfully.

The implication of Têtu's question suddenly hit them all like a hammer blow. Têtu rolled down his shirtsleeves and pulled at his jacket, all notion of fighting gone.

"That scoundrel," he said. "We need to make immediate inquiries about Tull. I take it you don't mind if I use Didier?"

"Of course not. Did I ever say I did?" said Monsieur Aulard.

"Don't worry," said Didier, shoving his red cap onto his head. "I'll be back in time to take you home after the show."

"Thank you," said Monsieur Aulard, taking hold of Didier's hand. "You are a good man." He went back to his desk. "But Didier, for pity's sake go down to wardrobe and get a hat that fits."

Têtu and Didier set off toward the cafés on the rue du Temple. Yann decided to take the maze of small streets that led off the rue des Francs-Bourgeois in search of anyone who had information about the coach or its driver that might lead him to Tull.

It was well past midnight when he gave up. By then the streets were deserted. Occasionally he would come across groups of sans-culottes swaying as if the city were at sea, singing patriotic songs.

"Good night to you, citizen," they would call drunkenly.

Suddenly an idea came to him. He remembered how partial Mr. Tull was to his beer. Where in the city, he wondered, was a café that sold beer to tempt an Englishman? Of course, the café in the Palais-Royal!

By the time he arrived, most of the clientele was emptying lazily out onto the street. The few customers remaining looked as though they were glued to their chairs. The place smelled of stale wine and beer, and was filled with the smoke from too many pipes. The barman looked up when he saw Yann enter.

"We're closed, citizen."

"I haven't come for a drink. I'm looking for an Englishman by the name of Tull. Does he come in here?"

"What's that to you?" said the bartender, putting down the glass he was rubbing with a dirty cloth.

"I need to speak to him," said Yann. "It's urgent."

The bartender grabbed him by the lapels of his sky-blue coat.

"Beat it. As I said, we're closed. Now, you wouldn't want me spoiling those good looks of yours, would you?"

He let him go. Yann felt a surge of ice-cold fury rush in upon him. He lifted his head slowly to see threads of light coming from everything and everyone in the café. Yann stood there like a puppet-master, feeling in complete control. Instinctively he put out his hand, pulling at the threads, so that first one glass and then another fell, smashing all around the startled bartender, who stood petrified as he watched the young man orchestrating objects to move at his will.

The last customers ran from the café as chairs went flying across the room. Yann slammed the door behind them. He laughed. He was enjoying himself. He turned back to the bartender.

"Let me ask you again. Does a Mr. Tull drink here?"

"Yes, yes," said the bartender anxiously.

"And do you know who he works for?"

The bartender beckoned him closer.

"You promise you won't say anything?" he whispered into his ear. "I'm a dead man if you do."

Exhausted, Yann walked back to his lodgings. The performance in the café had taken all his strength. Now, more than anything, he needed to sleep. Suddenly he understood why Têtu had always looked so ashen after working the Pierrot.

He dragged his way up to his room to find Têtu sitting on the stairs waiting for him.

"Where have you been?" he asked.

"Trying to find out who Mr. Tull works for," said Yann, opening his door. Even though it was nearly dawn, the air hadn't cooled down. There was no wind, not even a breeze, just insufferable heat. He sat down heavily on the bed.

"The Duchesse de Lamantes was brought back to Paris two nights ago under the arrest of the National Guard," said Têtu. "Apparently Tull has a lucrative trade in double-dealing his customers."

Yann lay down on the bed. "Tull," he said, looking up at the skylight, "works for Kalliovski. I'm sorry, Têtu, I need to sleep."

Têtu got up to leave. "There is one last thing you should know. Two more prisoners were delivered to the Abbaye last night. The Marquis de Villeduval and his daughter."

$\mathcal{M}$r. Tull felt that he had earned his money good and proper. The night before last had been hard work indeed. It had taken him longer than he had expected to get that lunatic of a marquis into the coach. The noise the man had made was enough to wake the dead, blast his blue blood! He attracted unwelcome attention. Mr. Tull had had to bang loudly on the roof of the coach.

"Bloody well shut up! If you don't, I'll come and deal with you."

The sound of Mr. Tull's large fist and rasping voice reverberated around the inside of the coach. It made Sido jump, but it had the desired effect. The marquis stopped banging on the windows. He looked at Sido, aghast.

"Hear that? The devil is up there and he's coming to get you. As far as I'm concerned he can have you, wretched cripple that you are."

Sido sat huddled in the corner. She felt vulnerable. Her leg hurt from where her father had kicked her, and there was no Jean Rollet to protect her if he decided to attack again. She just hoped that Jean would be all right. He had told her he had relatives he could stay with for a while, that she was not to worry. Seeing him disappear had been hard indeed, as if the last brick in the ruins of this life had come tumbling down. She didn't like Mr. Tull, and she didn't trust him.

Since Sido spoke hardly any English, and Mr. Tull's French was so bad that she had trouble working out what he was saying, there was no way of discovering whether she had reason to be concerned. All she knew was that they were leaving behind everything that was familiar.

"Well," said the marquis as the coach made its way through the darkened streets, "what is it you want from me?"

"For you to calm down," replied Sido.

"And if I do, will you and the devil disappear?"

Sido turned away from him and looked longingly out of the grimy window. She thought of Yann and wondered what he was doing. This Revolution should have been so glorious, she thought. It should have been her salvation, yet here she was, tied by birth to one of the pillars of the old regime. Everything her father stood for she loathed, yet she felt that the word *liberty*, a word that was used so often and with such passion, would never apply to her.

At St. Germain the carriage slowed down and then came to

a sudden stop. She could hear people speaking outside, and dimly through the grubby windows she saw that Mr. Tull was not alone.

Suddenly she realized what was happening. A feeling of suffocating panic overtook her. She tried desperately to open the carriage doors and gave up, defeated. They had been tricked. They were not going to England. They were being taken to prison.

"Sit down," said her father sharply. "It is not your place to open the door. Leave that to the footman."

Mr. Tull unlocked the carriage and stood aside as one prison guard took charge of Sido and two others dragged the marquis out, taking the precaution of tying his hands behind his back. Mr. Tull stood there looking unconcerned. He couldn't care less. They were just another pair of lost sheep rounded up for the slaughter. He would get a good purse for the marquis and his daughter, more than enough to settle his bills and allow him to forget his cares in this stinking sewer of a city. It was another night's work successfully done, though it hadn't been as much fun as duping the old duchess. He chuckled at the memory of seeing her dressed up as a governess. He had heartily enjoyed her humiliation. Still, the girl stuck in his gullet a little. She didn't deserve her fate, but orders were orders, and who was he to judge the right and the wrong of it.

"Anyway, money's money," he said under his breath as he climbed back up onto the coach. "They've brought it on themselves, all these lords and ladies. Let *them* eat cake."

The marquis entered the prison of L'Abbaye as if going to stay at a grand château. He did not notice the dirtiness of his surroundings, nor did he hear the growls of the jailers' dogs. He stood there tall and proud, a man to be reckoned with.

"What is your name?" the clerk at the desk asked.

"I am the Marquis de Villeduval of the Château de Rochefort des Champs."

The clerk smiled. "You don't say, citizen."

The gatekeeper, an ugly, bad-tempered man with a paper-cut for a mouth and an all too generous helping of teeth, stood swaying back and forth and smelling strongly of liquor. At his side were two ferocious hounds that looked more than a little hungry and saw all new prisoners as potential dog meat.

"And your name, citizeness?"

"Sido," she said quietly. She did not give her surname. It seemed pointless. What did any of it matter anymore?

"Which would you prefer, citizen, a cell with two beds or one?"

"I need an apartment to myself," said the marquis imperiously, "and I shall need a room for my valet."

"And what about the young lady, citizen?"

The marquis looked around the room and, appearing to see no one, lowered his voice. "She hasn't followed me, has she? Been trying to shake her off, you know. If you see her, don't let her in. Demand to see her papers. She's in the employment of the devil and I know for certain that she's dead."

The clerk looked at him, puzzled. "You're a strange one, you are. Well, I take it you want two single cells? That will be thirty livres a month, not counting your meals, which are extra, as is water and a glass. We aim to provide the highest service here."

The marquis appeared not to have heard a word; he stood with his eyes fixed at some invisible point before him.

"Show me to my apartment," he demanded.

"Not so fast, citizen, payment up front. Nothing on the slate. We don't know how long your stay is likely to be."

The guard standing behind him started to laugh.

"Do I know you, sir?" asked the marquis.

The guard directed a great gobbet of spit onto the stone floor.

"I don't think I've had the pleasure," he smirked.

"We have no money," said Sido quickly. "We have nothing."

"No money!" snarled the turnkey. He laughed disdainfully.

"Then you will both be living in the banqueting hall," said the clerk. He called to another guard to take the marquis to the men's quarters.

"Which cell for her?" asked the turnkey.

"The one for nonpaying guests."

"My pleasure," said the turnkey. "This way."

"Papa!" cried Sido as the marquis was led away. He did not turn around.

"Friendly kind of man, ain't he?" said the turnkey. "This way, citizeness."

The dogs were now pulling so hard that Sido thought at any moment the turnkey would topple over. He yanked the dogs back, holding on tight to a rail with his other hand.

"These are the women's quarters." He held up the lantern to reveal a row of doors, each with a small barred window. In one of them the face of the duchess appeared. Sido could hardly believe that it was only a week since she had seen her, so altered was her appearance.

"Oh no," she called out, seeing Sido, "not you as well. I am so sorry, I didn't . . ." Her voice trailed off, lost as the turnkey prodded Sido down the long dark corridor.

If there is a hell, thought Sido, this must be how it would look, how it would smell. She wished she had had a drink of water before she'd gotten into the coach. She felt so unbearably hot and thirsty.

"This," said the turnkey, opening a door, "is for lady customers who can't pay for their board and lodging." He pushed Sido inside. "Sweet dreams, citizeness."

Sido stood with her back against the heavy door, in a soup of thick darkness, unable to see a thing. The key turned noisily in the lock.

It took a while for her eyes to adjust. She was in a long dormitory with two rows of beds, one to each side. There was a narrow table down the center. It was stiflingly hot, the air heavy with the smell of unwashed flesh and urine.

"There's one free at the end."

Sido jumped, not sure where the voice had come from.

With her hands out before her she made her way slowly down the dormitory, at last finding the free bed. It was no more than a wooden board. Never in all her life had she felt more wretched than she did now. She started as something brushed past her ankles, and quickly pulled her feet up onto the plank. She could just make out the shape of a large rat sitting up and twitching its whiskers before scurrying away. She put her shawl into her mouth to stifle a sob. Was it really only yesterday that she had seen Yann, sat in a café with him? Had he truly said that he would take her to London? Here in the stinking darkness it seemed as if it must all have happened in a dream, in another life, a long time ago.

In the morning, Sido's rowdy companions were all curious to know what such a sweet innocent was doing sharing their dormitory.

"This 'ere, *chérie*, is for those who ain't got a sou to their name."

Sido said nothing. The women looked to her like brightly colored parrots, their haggard faces painted with rouge, their hair tangled and matted with grime.

"Look what the dog brought in last night," said one of them, laughing. "She would have made you a bit in your house of sin, eh, Madeleine?"

"Ain't she sweet, soft to the touch like fresh-baked bread. What d'you bet she's never lain with a man?"

Sido put her hands over her ears and tried to block out the comments and catcalls.

"Leave her alone," came a voice she recognized from the previous night. An amazon of a woman came forward. "Go on, shut up the lot of you. She don't need to hear your vulgar tongues."

At once all the women fell away.

Sido said quietly, "Thank you, madame."

"They call me La Veuve Joyeuse, the merry widow, on account of my late husband. They accused me of murder. Self-defense, more like it. Does that shock you, my pretty?"

"No," said Sido, "nothing seems to do that anymore."

The woman laughed. "Stay close by me and I'll make sure those hyenas leave you be."

"Who are they?"

"Riffraff, my dear. Not to be trusted. They'll sell their lousy bodies for whatever they can get."

The cell door opened and the turnkey stood aside as a guard brought in a pail and a basket of bread, which was put on the table.

"Well," said the guard, grinning at Sido. "How do you find our citizens of the night? Sweet and innocent just like you? I think not!"

The food was handed out, beans and hard, stale black bread. Tepid water, brown in color, was all there was to drink.

"It's the Café Royal," said one of the young women, grinning at Sido through broken teeth. "Eat up, citizeness, and welcome to hell."

Sido felt so desperate for a drink that she gulped down the water. It tasted revolting.

"Easy now," said her new friend.

She bit into the stale bread. It was so hard that it was impossible to chew. The beans made her gag.

"If you don't eat, my pretty, you'll get ill and die," said the widow.

Sido tried again. Her stomach registered its protest and she was violently sick. She lay on her plank, longing to be able to wash, not to be this filthy, to smell this rotten. When the turnkey came back she still felt so unwell that she could hardly get off her bed.

"Didn't the maggots agree with you, then?" sneered the turnkey.

His dogs growled at her, showing off their fangs, and Sido, without being able to help herself, was sick on the turnkey's shoes. "You little hussy, you did that on purpose!" He lifted his hand to slap her.

La Veuve Joyeuse stepped forward.

"She's not well. Can't you see that?" And so tight was her grip on the turnkey's arm that he started to whine and call out for help.

"Anyway," said the widow, "your dogs have cleaned it up for you, so there's no cause for complaint, is there?"

That night Sido lay on her wooden board, her stomach still heaving, feeling that death would be preferable to this. She finally fell asleep, but at around three in the morning she was roughly woken by a guard. He grabbed hold of her arm and dragged her through the dormitory.

The women, disturbed by the noise, sat up. "Where are you taking her?" shouted the widow.

"None of your bleeding business."

Sido felt giddy from having been woken so abruptly, and she couldn't help stumbling. Her leg hurt. Her head ached.

The guard locked the door behind him.

"So you've been royally looked after, I see."

Sido said nothing.

"Do you know how she got her name, that friend of yours, La Veuve Joyeuse? Shall I tell you?"

Still Sido said nothing.

"She tore her husband limb from limb, because he betrayed her, turned her in as the leader of a gang of brigands. Now there's one to tell your children—if you live that long."

Sido was taken back the same way she had been brought the previous night, then up some stone stairs to another smaller door.

The guard knocked and pushed her inside, closing the door behind her.

It was dark in the room but she knew instantly that she was

not alone. There was a smell of expensive cologne that she recognized.

"We meet again."

The voice seemed so close to her that it made her jump, as in the darkness a light was struck and a candle lit. There before her stood Citizen Kalliovski.

chapter twenty-seven

Sido looked completely broken, her face pale, her dress filthy. On seeing her, Kalliovski was in no doubt that she would be his, regardless of the marquis's objections. The game was all but won.

Only two women in his life had ever had the wit to resist him. One would have nothing to do with him, and the other . . . the other . . . had revealed in him a weakness that no true gambler can afford. Weakness was what he looked for in others; to detect it in himself was unforgivable. His strength was to know that every man had a flaw, every soul its price. Just once had he been powerless against passion, defeated by the Queen of Hearts. Never again.

He dusted down his tailored coat. "How do you find your new home?" he asked as a thin smile curled across his lips. Sido averted her eyes. He repulsed her, his face waxwork-smooth, a mask that hid the beast within. Through waves of nausea she now saw him as a large black cat, playing with its prey, waiting to pounce.

"You wouldn't be in this situation if your papa had been wiser. Such an ill-advised escape. Leaving France in its hour of need is, mademoiselle, in case you didn't know, a criminal offense."

Sido said nothing. All she had to protect herself against him was silence, the one skill in which she had become an expert. It comforted her to see a flicker of irritation cross his emotionless face.

"I have seen your father. He is not himself. He believes me to be Lucifer, the all-powerful. In the circumstances, I have to take it as a compliment."

He stopped, observing beads of sweat on her forehead. How pale she looked.

"You will be glad to know that when your father wrote to me saying he wished to end the betrothal, I saw it as no more than a symptom of the madness that now afflicts him. I am a generous man and my offer of marriage still stands. If you agree I will make sure that the charges against you are dropped and that you are both freed. I see no reason why your father should not live out his days at the château in Normandy."

Sido began to feel icy cold, even though the room was hot and stuffy. She could hardly breathe for lack of air. Still she remained silent.

Kalliovski let out a mirthless laugh as he remembered the way her mother had stood before him all those years ago when she had refused to become his mistress. She had paid a high price for that mistake.

"I need a reply," he said.

Sido felt as if the walls were slowly moving in on her as he came closer.

Don't flinch, she told herself desperately. Stand tall, think of Yann. She suddenly had a vision of him waiting for her in the Place Royale. Tomorrow, or was it today? She had lost all sense of time. She held her breath as Kalliovski stroked the side of her face, then her neck, pressing his thumb and forefinger into her soft flesh, feeling for her pulse. She knew from the power of his grip that he could strangle her with ease. Still she stood silent, shivering as his hand moved slowly down toward her breast, her heart beating like a caged bird's. She looked at the floor, feeling she was going to vomit as once again a wave of nausea overtook her.

Her quiet resistance was beginning to fascinate him. It seemed that he might have been wrong about her; maybe she would turn out to be a worthy opponent after all. If she had fallen on her knees and begged for mercy he would have despised her. That was the usual way with women, whining and weeping, saying they would do anything as long as they weren't ruined. How bored he was by charms so easily won.

Could it be that this docile girl was a more serious-minded

version of her mother? That would be something to savor, and the thought thrilled him. Oh yes, she was proving herself to be a prize worth waiting for.

Instinctively Sido turned her face away and tried to free herself. He took hold of her arms, pinning them behind her back so that she could not move.

He said in a whisper, his lips brushing against her neck, "There may be a way out of this prison, but there is no escape from me. I will be the first man to kiss you, to bed you. Whether you come willingly or not, you will be mine and mine alone. Do you understand?"

Sido could hardly hear the words above the whirling sound in her head, the throbbing of the blood in her veins, which was drumming to a frantic beat. A wave of heaviness swept over her.

She hoped that she had said, "I would rather die than marry you." She could not be sure, for all there was turned black.

Sido woke to find herself not back in the dormitory on her wooden board but in a proper bed in a small room with the luxury of sheets. There was a window, high and barred, and a chair on which was placed a vase of bright bloodred roses, their petals lush and out of keeping with their gray surroundings. She sat up as the door opened, expecting to see Kalliovski. Much to her relief a plainly dressed woman with a bunch of keys at her waist entered, carrying a tray.

Citizeness Villon was a buxom woman, the wife of the prison

governor. Carefully she set down the tray with its bowl of soup and freshly cut bread.

"You gave us quite a scare," she said, handing Sido a spoon. The soup, chicken broth with herbs and potatoes, tasted delicious. She sipped it, savoring its rich flavor.

"It's good to see you looking better. Citizen Kalliovski has undertaken to pay for all the little extras too. What a charming, thoughtful man! You're lucky to be under his protection, if I may say so. Why, he's even gone to the trouble of ordering you a new dress."

"How long have I been here?"

"Several days. Prison fever. Now, eat up. Have a little more soup and bread."

"Do you know where my father is?"

"He's been moved to a cell of his own. Citizen Kalliovski has been good enough to have a bed brought in for him to make his stay comfortable."

Later that morning Citizeness Villon returned with two warders who brought in a tub of water. Sido bathed herself and washed her hair, beginning slowly to feel more human. Cleanliness, she thought, stands for hope, dirt for despair. She dried herself and dressed in her new gown. It smelled of lavender, reminding her of the château garden where she used to walk on sunny afternoons.

Citizeness Villon inspected her charge.

"You must go back to the main prison now," she said, handing her over to the turnkey. "But don't you worry. I'll bring all your meals as well as your clean laundry."

"I see you've been promoted to your own cell," said the turnkey as he walked her back along the corridor. He leered at her. His breath stank of stale tobacco and rotten teeth. "You smell nice. I like it when young ladies smell nice."

He unlocked a door. "Well, here it is. Versailles itself can't compare." He chuckled as he bolted and locked the door behind him.

The cell had nothing in it apart from a bed, a bucket, and high up in the wall, a small window. At least, Sido thought, I don't have to share it.

She slept badly that night, disturbed by screams and sobs from down the corridor. She lay looking up at the window, watching the moon as its large round face peeked in through the darkness, asking her what she was going to do.

She had no answer to that question. It seemed there was nothing she could do, other than accept Kalliovski. There was, as he had said, really no choice. It was a *fait accompli*. The thought of him touching her again made her shiver, and tears rolled down her face onto the lumpy mattress.

The next morning Sido woke to the sound of the bolts to her door being pulled back.

"You're a popular couple of high-ups, ain't you?" said the turnkey. "Get up, your lawyer wants to see you. Look lively."

He led her to a whitewashed room with a table and four chairs, and closed the door behind him. Next to enter was her father, followed by Maître Tardieu and a clerk.

Her father appeared quite altered. His hair had turned completely white and his skin seemed to have fallen from him like the tide pulling away from a pebbled beach. All that remained was the haunted, frightened look in his eyes.

He turned on Maître Tardieu. "I won't read the will. I refuse. You shouldn't have let him change a word. I hold you responsible for this outrage, sir."

"Please, Papa, Maître Tardieu is here to help us."

The marquis's voice rose, as did the state of his agitation. "Be silent, madame. Where are my servants? Take me back to my room this instant."

"Please calm yourself."

Her father lashed out at her, hitting her hard across the face. She stumbled, to be caught by Maître Tardieu's clerk.

"Are you all right?" he asked softly.

For a moment Sido thought she was dreaming, for it was Yann who had caught her.

Putting his finger to his lips, he helped her to a chair. "Don't say anything," he whispered.

"It's the only way to deal with ghosts, thrash them!" shouted the marquis at the top of his voice.

The turnkey, hearing the commotion, came rushing back into the room.

"What's going on here?"

"That man," said the marquis, pointing at the lawyer, "is no more than dog muck on my shoe. I will not speak to him."

"Then hold your tongue," said the turnkey. "You've ten minutes here and then I'll be back for the pair of you."

"No," shouted the marquis. "Take me away now. Keep her from me. I've had enough of that dead woman. I say again, you can both rot in hell."

"Better take him then. I'll be as quick as I can," said Maître Tardieu, looking despairingly at the turnkey and rubbing his aching temples. The heat and the smell were overpowering. He sat down at the table.

The door closed with a loud thud. Maître Tardieu looked around nervously and put a finger to his lips. He spoke almost in a whisper.

"Mademoiselle Sido, I tried to get to see you earlier this week, but it was impossible because you were ill. I think you should know that Kalliovski is applying to have you released as long as you agree to marry him. Is that what you want?"

"No, no. I honestly thought—"

"That Mr. Tull would get you to England," interrupted Yann. "He was working for Kalliovski. You didn't stand a chance."

Maître Tardieu coughed. "May I continue? Time is of the essence. Your case comes up before the tribunal in less than two days. You and your father are accused of being counterrevolutionaries and of trying to escape from France, taking with you a vast fortune."

"But that's nonsense. We have nothing. You know we have nothing."

"It matters not." He let out a heavy sigh. "I am an old man, and there is much still on my mind and much that is unresolved. I want to rest easy in my grave."

"I am sure you will," said Sido kindly. "You have been very good to our family."

"No, I feel that I have failed you and your grandfather, to whom I was devoted."

"No, sir, you are too hard on yourself—"

"Please, mademoiselle," Maître Tardieu broke in. He leaned toward Sido and whispered, "Put your trust in Yann Margoza. It is your only chance of escape."

"But sir, I can't leave my father here."

Yann was concentrating so hard on Sido that he didn't notice the look of anguish that crossed the lawyer's face at these words.

"Sir," said Sido, rising, "are you ill?"

"It is nothing." He clasped his chest. "My heart is not as strong as it used to be." Yann helped him to a chair. "Please, mademoiselle, think of yourself. Unlike others, you have family in England waiting for you—"

Yann, now almost desperate, interrupted. "Danton is stirring people into a fever of hatred against all those held in the prisons. It will explode and you will be caught in it unless we do something."

Along the corridor they could hear the sound of boots and the click-clack of dogs' claws against stone.

"I am going to come for you," said Yann. "When I do, you must be ready."

The turnkey opened the door. "Well, old lawyer, is she going to plead innocence? That the horse had a mind of its own and took off to see an old mare in England?" He laughed heartily at his own joke.

Outside the prison, Maître Tardieu gulped desperately at the fresh air, his hand holding the railing tight. Overcome by the heat, he felt unsteady on his feet. Yann led him into a nearby café and ordered him a drink.

"What can we do?" asked Yann, looking at the gray face of the lawyer. "She's not going to leave him and I can't see any way of getting that madman out."

"I can assure you he isn't worth it. Mademoiselle Sido, though, is a different matter; she has courage and dignity. She is a true de Villeduval—takes after her uncle and grandfather. The late marquis's first wife, you know, was just like her son, a weak-minded woman who ended her days in an asylum."

He picked up his glass and drank. "Oh dear, oh dear," he continued. "I wanted to say something in the prison, but I couldn't bring myself to voice it. After all, it is only rumor and hearsay. I deal in proof, in evidence: That is the *raison d'être* of a lawyer. Gossip is not to be trusted—it could not be upheld in any court of law. All the same, there is Mademoiselle Sido left to rot in hell's waiting room. How did it come to this?"

Yann was barely listening. He pushed his hand through his hair. "There must be a way of getting her out."

"I debated with myself about telling her," said Maître Tardieu. "Maybe I should have. It might have helped."

"What might have helped?" said Yann, turning to look at the lawyer.

"It was rumored that Armand de Villeduval and Mademoiselle Sido's mother were lovers, and that they were planning to flee to England, taking the child with them. My late master told me on his deathbed that in the portmanteau that had gone missing were letters that led him to believe . . ."

Yann sat bolt upright. He finished what the lawyer was about to say. "That Armand de Villeduval was Sido's father?"

"Precisely. Find the letters and you may well have enough evidence to make her change her mind about leaving the marquis, for I believe there is blood on those pampered pink hands of his."

"Where do you think those letters are, sir?" asked Yann.

"The first place I would look is in Kalliovski's apartment."

On the wall opposite the café, scribbled in dripping red paint, were the words *Kill the enemy within.*

Yann knew there was hardly any time. The only way to get her out was to be bold—and bolder.

chapter twenty-eight

*T*he letter that Monsieur Aulard had just signed sat worryingly on his desk. Never had a piece of paper frightened him so much. He knew it held the power to snuff out life itself. More to the point, his life.

What was that children's game, he thought bitterly to himself, the one with paper, stone, and scissors? Which one was it that won over paper? With a shudder, the answer came to him. Scissors—the guillotine! Yes, his neck was on the block. He was about to send two tickets to Citizen Kalliovski inviting him to bring one of his famed automata to the theater that very night. The letter said that an old friend of Topolain's wanted to talk to him about the threads of light, and it was signed, "From a well-wisher."

This hadn't been Monsieur Aulard's idea; far from it. He

could not imagine what the threads of light were. It was part of Têtu's master plan to get Kalliovski away from his apartment so that Yann could break in and search for Armand's letters.

"Do you really think Kalliovski will take the bait?" he asked.

"He won't be able to resist," replied Têtu.

Monsieur Aulard stared transfixed at the letter, remembering only too clearly the Pierrot's head sitting in the lap of the dead Topolain.

"I still don't understand why Kalliovski killed Topolain," he said.

"It was because Topolain let slip that they'd met before in St. Petersburg. Topolain used to do card tricks to entertain the gamblers. The man who was later to take the name Kalliovski was there."

"Why didn't Topolain just keep quiet?"

"Why indeed? He wasn't thinking straight. He was trying to impress and said the first foolish thing that came into his head. Kalliovski didn't want his cover blown. He couldn't be sure that one day Topolain wouldn't remember the exact circumstances of their meeting. He could not allow anyone to have that power over him."

"Why? What would it matter?"

Têtu sighed. "Is your knowledge box not working? Has your brain shut up shop?"

"I just want to be clear," said Aulard, offended.

"It was in the gambling dens of St. Petersburg that the self-styled Count Kalliovski started his meteoric rise to fame and fortune."

Yann heard with a start the word that Têtu was thinking but not saying. Usually Têtu's mind was shut to him, but one word had slipped under the barricades. A word that sparkled like a diamond in the mud, too bright to be missed. Gypsy.

What Têtu was really saying was: "He was a Gypsy we used to know."

"A Gypsy," said Yann out loud.

Têtu spun around. "I never said that."

"You thought it."

"It's a figure of speech, that's all."

"Not one that you would ever use."

"Yann, forget it, I didn't mean anything by it."

"What does it matter?" said Monsieur Aulard. "What's wrong with you both, that we're now arguing over a word that Têtu never said?" He threw his hands in the air. "*Mort bleu*, my life is on the line and you . . . are beyond belief!"

Têtu looked closely at Yann. "That is the first time you've been able to do that. You're getting good."

"When you've both finished talking, could we get back to the matter at hand? I have invited Kalliovski to the theater. Why would he come here?"

"For the same reason he wanted us to perform at the marquis's château. He wanted to see if we could work the threads of light."

"I'm lost. Threads of light? What are they? No, on second thought, I don't want to know. In case you haven't noticed, Paris is nearly under siege, the enemy is only miles away, men are going off to fight, and we will have an empty house tonight. No one will come, especially not Kalliovski." Monsieur Aulard was struggling to keep his composure.

"In that you are very wrong," said Têtu. "Your theater will be full and Kalliovski, I can assure you, wouldn't miss it for the world."

Perspiration now dripped down Monsieur Aulard's forehead and his hands were shaking. He was trying to stop himself from crumpling up the paper before him. He wanted to refuse to have anything more to do with this foolhardy plan.

"Are these letters really so important?" he said pathetically. "Why don't you just get the girl out? Leave Kalliovski alone."

"I could, if she would leave her father. But she won't," said Yann flatly. "I need to be able to show her some evidence that her father was involved in the death of her mother, and maybe prove who her real father is."

"Wait, wait, not so fast. Didier, my medicine!"

"No," said Têtu firmly. "You need your wits about you."

"*Mort bleu!* Are you telling me you don't believe the marquis is her father?"

"Yes," said Têtu. "We think it was his half brother, Armand. And we are sure that the marquis, with Kalliovski's help, had something to do with their murders."

"Murder? This gets worse with every word! We should report it to the authorities and let them deal with it. For goodness' sake, you are magicians! I run a theater! This is out of our field."

"We are the only people who can save Sido," said Yann, "and if we can do this well, then maybe we can get other people out and save them from the guillotine."

"Tell me I'm not hearing this. Have you lost your mind? That's a criminal offense! We could be accused of counterrevolutionary activities, of being spies. I can see it now, your heads not on the poster outside my theater but on pikes with pretty ribbons of blue, white, and red."

"So we just do nothing?" said Yann. "We sit back and let the slaughter begin? Should we be glad to be part of it? I love France, but I'm not going to join those who think that slaughtering French citizens will do any good. All I want to do is to try and stop this insanity."

Monsieur Aulard swallowed. "Spoken like a true hero! But do we have to stick our heads above the parapet?"

"Spoken like a true coward," said Têtu.

"Listen," said Yann, "none of us can afford to turn our backs on what's going on. There are spies everywhere in Paris. The press has been shut down. Free speech does not exist—speak out of line and see where you end up. So much for liberty! Look how many people have been rounded up in midnight raids, and not just aristocrats and priests. The prisons are full to bursting. Don't you want to help us?"

"It's still better than the old regime," said Monsieur Aulard weakly.

"It won't be if the leaders of the Revolution have their way. They're calling for all the prisoners to be killed, talking about tearing them limb from limb, ruling by terror and terror alone."

"They don't mean it literally, I'm sure," said Monsieur Aulard.

Yann threw his head back and burst out laughing. "Oh, I see, so we're expected to be able to tell the difference. A man will stand there reading the poster and saying to his friends, 'Good old Marat, the people's friend, uses such fine and descriptive words. What he meant to say was . . .'"

Monsieur Aulard sat back in his chair, defeated. He had no idea how he had managed to let himself be hoodwinked into this mess. If he was caught, dear Lord . . . Couldn't he just go back to the good old days? To yesterday, even, when all he'd had to concentrate on was giving the public what they wanted, a show full of patriotic drivel and heads on pikes, a pantomime of folly.

He was so busy making up his own epitaph that he hardly heard what was being said. He looked up wearily as Didier started talking. That was another thing. Didier, yes, Didier, whom he employed to protect him, now seemed to be working full-time for Têtu. Oh, he thought miserably, for what I am about to receive, may someone help me.

"Well, Didier, did you find out how we could get into Kalliovski's apartment?" asked Yann.

"Yes, yes, I did," said Didier. "Citizen Kalliovski has one servant whom he leaves to guard his apartment. His sole task is to make sure that no one enters while his master is away."

"How do you know?" asked Monsieur Aulard. Despite his anxieties, he was impressed with Didier's skill. Who would have thought the old mooncalf had so much going for him in the upstairs department?

"I've become friendly with the concierge of the building where he lives, on the rue Payenne." Didier blushed. "She's called Jeanne."

"How long has this fellow been with Kalliovski?" asked Yann.

"She says he's been with him the longest of all his servants. Got a funny eye."

"Milkeye," said Yann.

"Do you think she'd let Yann deliver a basket to Kalliovski?" asked Têtu.

"If we went in by the side entrance, I don't think she'd mind."

"Tomorrow," said a mournful Monsieur Aulard, "is the second of September, my birthday, if any of you are interested. My last birthday, no doubt, for as sure as there is a sun in the day and a moon in the night, I shall be murdered by Kalliovski. When I am dead, and if you haven't been guillotined, Didier, would you be so kind as to put lilies on my grave?"

Têtu jumped up from his seat and turned on him furiously.

"This is not about you! This is about an innocent girl who will be killed if we don't act. This is about saving lives. This is about Yann. He is the one you should be worrying about. If you don't wish to be involved, go home and put your head under a pillow. But if you want to try and find some semblance of bravery, you could pull yourself together and stop being a big girl's bonnet."

Monsieur Aulard looked crushed by the impact of the dwarf's words. It was true he was a mouse of a man when it came to bravery; still, he was doing his best.

"Take this and put it on," said Têtu, pulling out a black cap from his jacket pocket.

Monsieur Aulard looked at it. All the questions he wanted to ask and dare not sat heavily on his bushy eyebrows.

"Well?" said Têtu. His voice hadn't softened at all. "What are you waiting for? Just put it on. Don't make such a drama out of everything."

Timidly, as if it were a candle-snuffer, Monsieur Aulard put the cap on his head. "It doesn't fit!" he complained.

"Where has he gone? What've you done with him? He's disappeared!" shouted Didier. "What a good trick!"

Such was his relief that Monsieur Aulard suddenly felt liberated from his worries. He was surprised not to find himself floating up to the ceiling with relief.

"This is wonderful, Têtu," he said, putting his two very visible hands on either side of the dwarf's face and kissing him loudly. Forgetting his fear of Citizen Kalliovski, he said with the excitement of a child, "I'm going to find out if anyone else can see me. Wait here."

"If you see your reflection, don't worry. No one else will," Didier called after him.

They waited until he had gone.

"I told everyone at the theater to pretend he was invisible if they saw him wearing the black cap," said Didier seriously.

Yann chuckled.

"Yann, it's not funny," snapped Têtu. "If this fails he'll be a gibbering wreck and useless to us. If it works, he might find the courage he needs."

"How did you get everybody to agree to it, Didier?" asked Yann.

"Simple," said Didier. "I told them they wouldn't get paid if they let the cat out of the bag."

"Brilliant. Masterly," said Têtu with a sudden laugh.

"It works!" said Monsieur Aulard, rushing back into the room. "We could make our fortune with this."

"No," said Têtu, bringing him down to earth with a bang. "If we manage to stay alive, that will be fortune enough."

Before he left that night for Kalliovski's, Yann went down and stood in the center of the empty stage. There was no one around. The wings were dark, as was the auditorium. A workman's lamp hung down from the fly tower, casting a faint light upon him in the gloom all around. He looked out over the shadowy shoreline of empty seats. It seemed to him there was no lonelier place to stand than here on the empty stage, the home of illusion with its haunting dread of failure.

In the silence, in the darkness of the wings, he could almost see Topolain and the wooden Pierrot walk onto the stage, hear the magician call out to the audience, "No bullet can harm me! I am invincible, I have drunk from the cup of everlasting life!"

Yann knew then that he had come back to Paris to face the pistol, to catch the bullet. If he survived, Sido too would be free.

As he stood there he heard a voice he recognized from a long time ago. It came from the stalls. He didn't call out, or ask who was there; he knew enough now not to question what the spirit said.

The voice was gentle.

"There is nothing to fear except the power you give to your own demons."

chapter twenty-nine

$\mathscr{I}$t was a warm evening as Didier and Yann made their way toward the rue Payenne. The news on the street was not good. The Duke of Brunswick's army was advancing steadily toward the capital. There was a crackle to the atmosphere, like the forewarning of a terrible storm.

Still, for tonight at least the sky was clear, with a tinge of watercolor rose spilling into the darkening clouds. By dawn those with an appetite for violence would take over the city and change the course of the Revolution forever. For the time being, liberty still wore its bridal gown, a bright promise in the hearts of its citizens. Tomorrow it would lose its innocence, be drowned in blood.

The mansion where Citizen Kalliovski lived was home to members of the revolutionary council, just as once it had been home to the great and the good of Parisian society. Its new clientele enjoyed exactly the same privileges as the previous residents; only the banner that flew from the ornate balcony was different.

Yann and Didier were watching as, on the dot of seven, Kalliovski's beetle-black carriage pulled up outside the building. Two servants came out, supporting a woman between them, and lifted her into the carriage. The only hint that she was not human was that her feet never touched the ground. Shortly afterward, Kalliovski and his hound Balthazar climbed into the carriage, and it set off in the direction of the theater.

Yann smiled to himself. The man had taken the bait.

At the side entrance, Didier knocked three times. The door was opened and the beaming rosy face of Jeanne appeared. She stood on tiptoe and threw her arms around Didier's neck, planting kisses on his face.

"What kept you, my old bear?" She stopped, seeing Yann. "Who's this?"

"He's a friend. He has to deliver something to Citizen Kalliovski and, well, as I was seeing you I thought I would bring him with me." Didier leaned forward and kissed her. "You don't mind if he goes up the back way, do you?"

"His apartment's one flight up," whispered Jeanne, looking around anxiously.

"Is there anyone else who might demand your attention this evening, apart from me?" asked Didier.

She giggled, and he squeezed her tight.

"No, they've all gone off to a meeting somewhere. They tell me it's going to be a long night, and I need protection. I'm all alone, my old bear, with only your strong arms to keep the enemy from charging in on your sweet little Jeanne."

Yann left them to it and quickly moved up the stairs that led to the main part of the house. Here all was quiet. The silence had a strange, eerie quality to it, as if the house had become detached from the rest of the world.

On the second floor was the apartment he was looking for. Taking a deep breath, he knocked on the door. It was opened by Milkeye.

"This is for Citizen Kalliovski," said Yann.

"He's not in," said Milkeye hoarsely, moving as if to close the door.

"Will you at least take the basket?"

Yann pulled back the cloth to reveal a round cheese, a loaf of bread, and a bottle of red wine. The smell was pungent and tempting. Milkeye grabbed the basket.

"My master doesn't like cheese," he said.

Yann shrugged his shoulders and reached to take back the gift. With his outstretched palm Milkeye pushed him so hard that he landed with a thud on the opposite wall, with the door slammed firmly in his face.

Ten minutes was what Têtu had reckoned before the wine and cheese worked their magic and Milkeye would be fast asleep. Yann gave it fifteen to make sure before gently trying the door.

To his relief, it opened easily and he found himself in the dark empty hall.

There was just enough light for him to make his way cautiously into the salon. It was an enormous room and furnished on a grand scale. He looked around, half expecting to see Milkeye felled like a tree on the floor.

There was no sign of him, just the basket on the side table. The bottle of wine was missing but the cheese was untouched. This was not a good sign. It would take both to knock him out completely. Yann wondered why he could hear the beating of a drum; then he realized it was his own heart. He spun around, fearing to see Milkeye in the long shadows. But the room was empty.

Guardedly he went through the interconnecting doors to the next salon. Surely he must be here somewhere—behind this door maybe? Every sound echoed cannonball loud in his head. Something was very wrong. Yann felt his mind whirling. He walked through to the third salon. The door was ajar and he pushed it open, to be greeted by a blast of cold air.

Yann stopped, hearing voices. Jeanne had told Didier that no one was allowed into the apartment while Kalliovski was out. He listened intently.

"*Velvet and violence.*
Brocade and blood.
Damask and death."

There were several voices, none of them Milkeye's. The words came in a high moan, sharp and urgent to his ear, as if some bizarre game was being played. But by whom? Didier must have been wrongly informed.

> "Fur and fury.
> Calico and corpses,"

came the whispered words. Yann felt every sense in him alert as he pushed the door further open. The room was in total darkness, the shutters closed tight against the light. He felt his breath coming fast, as if he had been running to get here.

Calm down, calm down, he said to himself, waiting for his eyes to get used to the darkness. He lit a candle, and immediately the voices stopped and everything went deathly still.

The room had been made into a workshop with a bench and a long table; in the half-light he could see shelves filled with glass jars. What was inside them he couldn't make out. Books were piled high, charts and maps of the heavens were scattered about, and there were burners, jars, and surgical instruments on the workbench.

He heard something rustle and spun around, expecting to see Milkeye behind him. There was nobody there. He was slowly moving the candle to look more closely at what was in the glass jars when he heard the whispering voices say, "Calico and corpses."

Yann stopped, transfixed to the spot. The sight in front of him nearly caused him to drop the candle, for ranged along the back wall of the chamber stood six automata, their eyes shut, only their ruby wax mouths moving.

The thing Yann despised in others he now saw clearly in himself. Fear had wrapped itself around his heart. If he were to let it get the better of him he would be dead; that much his reason knew. The other part of him just wanted to get the hell out of there. The battle inside him was won when he saw the dull threads of light coming from the automata and he realized with a shudder that someone had already pulled them tight as violin strings. Tight enough to keep the six automata whispering all night long.

Yann set to work to loosen the threads of light and as he did so, he heard the automata calling to him with their songs of sorrow that seemed to come from a dark place indeed and to have little to do with the living. He watched almost hypnotized as six pairs of glass eyes opened and stared at him. Now he noticed that they all wore identical red necklaces. The hairs on the back of his neck tingled, and in that moment everything slowed down as if time itself were yawning.

"You think I'd fall for such a cheap trick?" said a voice from behind him. Milkeye was standing in the doorway, a pistol in his hand. "I've waited a long time for this."

All Yann could think was, I should run, but he couldn't. He was paralyzed by the knowledge of what was coming next, the inevitability of it. He had the insane desire to burst out laughing, for this moment was what he had been dreading. Here it was in all its glory, and it seemed almost nothing, compared to the long endless terror of waiting.

The pistol went off, the noise surprisingly shocking. He saw the flame from the gunpowder, the bullet graceful in its slow arc across the room toward him, trailing smoke as it went.

It had taken years for this bullet to find him. He reached out for it with his mind, tried to catch it in his hand. It scorched his flesh before piercing through his skin and lodging in his shoulder. Pain flooded him like water from a dam; the impact of it knocked him off his feet. He slumped down by the workbench. Milkeye was now coming toward him, the pistol reloaded, his finger on the trigger.

Yann fought not to lose consciousness. He pushed himself back toward the automata and felt the folds of a taffeta skirt fall around him as one of them bent over to take the bullet in her back. Yann couldn't see where Milkeye was, for her stiff and dusty hair had fallen in his face. Her blazing eyes looked straight at him.

"We," she said, "are the Seven Sisters Macabre. One of our party is missing. What is your name?"

"Yann Margoza," he managed to say, as blood-black curtains threatened to close in front of him.

"Calico and corpses," she said, and her graveyard breath brought him to his senses.

Once more he experienced the feeling of leaving his body, as he had done before in the forest. Now he stood in the middle of the room, a puppet-master of the threads of light.

At his command, the Sisters Macabre began to walk toward Milkeye, the dusty taffeta of their skirts trailing behind them like waves upon a shore. Milkeye loaded his pistol for the third time and fired at the oncoming automata. It did not stop them.

Yann felt the two parts of himself collide once again. The pain brought with it crystal vision. He dragged himself up near the workbench, feeling that he was ten feet tall and invincible. He pulled at the threads of light, lifted a chair, and brought it down on Milkeye's head, then picked up another chair and another, until Milkeye let out a grunt and collapsed on the floor.

The room and its occupants began to spin around and around. For a moment Yann couldn't remember why he was there. Then he felt a cold wax hand touch his face, and with a start became conscious of one of the Sisters Macabre standing next to him.

"We are his experiments. He believes that in us he can find the secret of perpetual youth. He believes he can hold time back for himself. We have been robbed of our lives. We have been robbed of our rest. What is it you want of us?"

"Letters, love letters written by Armand . . ." The name, what was the name? Why couldn't he remember . . . "de . . ."

"Villeduval," said all the Sisters together. "All you had to do was ask."

Yann leaned lopsidedly on the workbench, trying to find his balance.

"Velvet and violence.
Taffeta and terror,"

said the Sisters Macabre as Milkeye writhed on the floor, his legs twitching.

If only the pain would stop, thought Yann, I could think straight. I would know what to do. All his thoughts now were consumed by the burning ache in his shoulder. There, he could hear it again, that sound of the distant drum fading away as his strength ebbed from him.

"Is this what you came for?" asked a Sister.

He heard a ripping sound as the fabric of her dress tore apart, and where the womb should have been two doors sprang open to reveal a bloodred empty chamber. She reached in with her white wax hands and handed Yann a bundle of letters.

A second Sister pulled out a bloodred drawer from where her stomach should have been, and handed him a black book.

"This is for you. It is the Book of Tears. It is bound with our flesh."

"He stole our lives.
He stole our hearts.
He stole our deaths,"

whispered the Sisters Macabre together as they gathered around Yann, making sure that the letters and the book were safely in his coat pocket before they lined up once more against the back wall, their eyes closing, their mouths whispering.

> *"Velvet and violence.*
> *Brocade and blood.*
> *Damask and death."*

Yann was still clinging to the bench when he became aware of the grisly contents of the jars. They were filled with parts of bodies: in one, a head; in another, limbs; in another, a stack of hearts.

> *"Calico and corpses.*
> *Satin and suffering,"*

whispered the Sisters Macabre.

Yann's shirt was wet and he wondered why it was red.

The room was spinning again and into this unsettling scene came Milkeye. Like some monster he had grown more arms and legs, all trying to get him. Yann kicked out desperately, but still those hands kept coming.

He staggered and sank to his knees. Someone should warn Têtu that Kalliovski can work the threads of light, he thought, as the curtains of his mind, blood-black, treacle-thick, came down for good: the show well and truly over, the end of the performance.

chapter thirty

"*Nom de dieu!*" said Monsieur Aulard, entering his apartment with Têtu to see Yann stretched out on his kitchen table and Didier, his shirtsleeves rolled up, washing blood from his hands in a basin. "Is he dead?"

"No," said Didier. "Luckily the bullet didn't go into the bone and the wound is clean. He should be all right."

Têtu climbed up onto a chair to take a closer look at Yann.

"What happened?" he asked, cautiously inspecting Didier's work.

"To tell the truth, I'm not sure. I didn't hear the gun go off, but I was worried because he'd been so long. I rushed into the apartment to see Milkeye with his hands around Yann's legs. He'd been shot. I thought he was dead. There was blood all over the floor."

Têtu felt Yann's forehead. "At least he has no fever. That's something." Seeing the bullet sitting in the basin, he picked it up and examined it. "As always, you've done well, Didier."

Didier gently lifted Yann up and took him through to the next room. "I'll put him in your bed," he told Monsieur Aulard.

"Can't he sleep somewhere else?" asked Monsieur Aulard.

Didier looked disgusted. "No," he said, "not after I've cleaned up that tip of a room of yours and put fresh linen on the bed. He needs to rest."

Clean linen too, thought Monsieur Aulard. Do they think I'm made of money? Have I nothing left to call my own?

Didier came back into the room with a fresh basin of water and scrubbed the table clean. Then he went over to the cupboard, brought out a bottle of Monsieur Aulard's best brandy and three glasses, and rolled down his sleeves.

"I don't know about you two, but I need a drink and no mistake. How did your evening go?"

"Tricky. Tiring," answered Têtu.

"And nothing to show for it but a bullet," said Monsieur Aulard.

Didier said nothing.

Kalliovski had arrived at the Theater of Liberty, causing quite a sensation with his automaton, which looked as though it was modeled on that poor woman Madame Perrien. Monsieur Aulard had once seen her at the theater and remembered her as being pretty, with an infectious laugh. The automaton was a hideous mockery of what she had once been.

Though the audience had clapped when she walked unaided to her seat, her movements were jerkier than Kalliovski would have liked. To a perfectionist such as he was, it was one of the many flaws that needed ironing out. After tonight, with Têtu working for him, everything would be different.

He sat himself down in the front row next to his automaton, with Balthazar at his feet, and stretched out his legs. He all but had Têtu within his grasp, for he was certain that it was the dwarf who had sent the invitation. With the coming of the Terror, Têtu would need protection. Together, what couldn't they do! Yes, it was worth coming for that alone.

He took out his watch. It was a beautiful piece of craftsmanship, the face showing an image of the Grim Reaper. If he left at the intermission he would get to the meeting on time. He smiled to himself.

From the prompter's desk, Monsieur Aulard dared himself to look into the face of his demon, for the man sitting in the front row had haunted him ever since that terrible day when Topolain's body had been found in his office, and here he was, not ten feet from him. He held on tight to the black cap in his pocket. The feel of it comforted him and calmed his shredded nerves.

"Are we ready?" he asked Têtu nervously.

"Oh yes, my friend, and I think you are going to enjoy seeing a true master at work." Têtu flexed his fingers as if about to play a piano. "Bring up the curtain."

Kalliovski appeared to take little pleasure in what was happening on stage. The show itself was an affront to his intellect. It was just a cacophony of patriotic songs, drivel for the masses that fed into the fever of the moment.

Têtu was interested to see how tightly Kalliovski controlled his automaton. No wonder she had moved so stiffly. He started gently to play with her threads of light, expecting at any moment that Kalliovski would become aware of what he was doing, for a true shaman would know instinctively when someone else was interfering. It didn't take him long to discover that Kalliovski was a mere amateur, with no natural gift.

Têtu stood the automaton up. Standing next to Kalliovski, she started to sing the Marseilleise. In the flicker of the oil lamps, the audience and the actors on stage whose performance had nothing to do with magic were taken aback by this creature and her ethereal voice.

A shout went up from the audience. "Bring up the lights! Let's have a proper look."

As if on cue, the automaton turned to bow at them. Try as he might, Kalliovski could not regain control of the threads of light; his mind did not have the strength. He could do nothing but sit there and envy the brilliance of such sorcery.

The audience were soon out of their seats and singing along with the automaton, tears rolling down their faces.

Kalliovski was caught, and he knew it. He was forced to take unwarranted credit for his patriotic creation. By the time the curtain came down, the applause was deafening. He was unable to leave his seat as members of the audience came to stare at the automaton and ask him questions about it.

He hissed to one of his henchmen, "Fetch me the theater manager."

At this point Monsieur Aulard broke into Têtu's story of the evening's events.

"Go on, tell Didier what I did."

And Têtu, who generally declined on principle to give credit to anyone, softened slightly and said, "There is no doubt that without our friend's bravery, Kalliovski would have left the theater long before the final curtain call."

Monsieur Aulard had refused to be hurried down the gangway, no matter how many times Kalliovski's henchman prodded him in the back. He insisted on stopping and talking to the odd patron who would jokingly ask whether he was going to offer Kalliovski's automaton a job in his theater. He walked toward Kalliovski as if toward the guillotine itself. With every measured step, he felt a little braver. At last he reached the front row. Kalliovski had a look that said: "You will be dead unless you can explain this." He nodded at one of his men, who handed him the invitation.

"Are you responsible for sending me two tickets to your

wretched fleapit of a theater to see this travesty of a show?"

Monsieur Aulard held tight to the black cap in his pocket; just to know it was there gave him courage. He leaned toward Kalliovski, a smile stuck fast to his face. "I don't think the rest of the audience find it a travesty."

Kalliovski stood up. He towered above Monsieur Aulard, who instinctively took a step backward as his stomach lurched forward. He had forgotten quite how frightening the man was. It was something about his face and those eyes that burned straight through you like drops of acid.

Monsieur Aulard kept talking. "Why, citizen, I thought by the reaction to your remarkable automaton that you were enjoying the performance."

"The dwarf is in the theater, I know it," hissed Kalliovski.

"You mean Têtu?"

"You know I do," spat Kalliovski.

"I don't know if he is here tonight or not. I will make inquiries, but first I must congratulate you, citizen, and ask you how such magic is accomplished."

He knew he had him. Kalliovski's pride was such that he was not going to admit that the automaton's performance had little or nothing to do with him.

"If he's here, shall I say you would like to see him after the show?"

"No, I will see him now." Kalliovski nodded toward his two henchmen as each took an arm of the automaton.

Monsieur Aulard handed back the invitation. "Forgive me, but won't you stay to see the end of—"

He never finished what he was saying, for the automaton said loudly, "I don't want to go home. Don't take me home. I want to stay."

The audience started to clap. "That's it, citizen, you tell him!" shouted someone. "Sing us some more songs!"

"If you wish," said the automaton.

"We do!" shouted the audience.

Kalliovski shot a murderous look at the theater manager.

The bell rang for the second half to begin, and the little band started to play. Monsieur Aulard bowed and took his leave, saying he hoped Citizen Kalliovski would enjoy the rest of the show. He returned backstage, still stroking the black cap in his pocket as the curtain came up.

Just after the first song was over, one of Kalliovski's men came in to give him a message. Once again it looked as if he was about to leave. Têtu acted quickly. He made the automaton rise into the air so that she hung there, hovering above the seats. The audience gasped in amazement. "She's floating!" cried someone.

It was then that Têtu became aware that he had an invisible helper. Often when he played with the threads of light he had found that spirits would interfere. He had been concentrating so hard that he hadn't realized there was someone else out there. As the automaton floated above the audience, out of it emerged a phantom in the shape of a beautiful woman, a spirit made of light that illuminated the auditorium.

Balthazar hid under the seat, his ears pinned back, whining miserably. A stunned silence broke over the audience.

"Who are you?" someone called out at last.

The spirit said nothing.

"Are you alive?" shouted another.

"I was alive once. I was murdered."

At these words Kalliovski leaped up from his seat and backed away toward the wall of the auditorium where his two henchmen stood, terrified.

The apparition hovered above the seats, her dress flowing behind her, moving ever closer to him. Then, with a sudden wild laugh, she vanished. The audience, silent for a moment, started clapping and cheering, shouting for more.

Kalliovski, recovering himself, stared piercingly into the wings, wishing now that he could pull the theater down brick by brick until he found what he was looking for—the dwarf. What he would give to have that power! And he *would* have it. He would become master of the dark arts; nothing was going to stop him.

The final curtain came down. He clicked open his watch. He was late. He started for the door, leaving his automaton behind, nodding to his henchmen to bring her. But before they could reach her she called out, "Sweetie, wait for me," and Kalliovski turned to see his waxwork lady gliding up behind him, all stiffness gone. As she reached the doors to the auditorium Têtu let go of the threads of light, and she collapsed lifeless on the floor, leaving Kalliovski's men to pick her up.

Têtu was exhausted. Sleep, he knew of old, was the only cure for his state. Still, he waited until the last of the audience had left, for he was curious to know the identity of the spirit that had come to his aid. Once more the darkened, empty stage was filled with light, and he saw her standing before him. There was no mistaking who she was. No wonder Kalliovski had been so frightened. She was even more beautiful than he remembered: the only woman the dwarf had ever loved.

"Anis," he said softly, "so it was you. I should have known you would have been here for him." He held out his hand toward her and felt something brush softly against his cheek, smelled for a moment her intoxicating perfume.

"Be careful," she whispered as she faded away. "You are not out of danger yet."

"Anis, Anis," said Têtu longingly into the impenetrable darkness. But she was gone.

He wiped his eyes. Was he becoming a sentimental old fool? He told himself it was just tiredness as, tears running down his face, he walked back into the wings. Grief once more had made the world seem unbearable.

"You should have lived," he said quietly. "You should have raised your own son. You would have been so proud of Yann."

Monsieur Aulard caught up with Kalliovski at the main door of the theater.

"Têtu would be delighted to see you," he said, still holding tightly on to his black cap. "He is backstage. He was most impressed by your abilities with the automaton, and so was I. I hope that if you ever need employment, you will remember my humble theater."

Kalliovski grabbed hold of Monsieur Aulard by the lapels of his coat.

"Tell him I will see him later, and as for you—the guillotine is a hungry lady. Be careful." He let the theater manager go, and Monsieur Aulard stood there mopping his brow as he watched the driver flick the horses' flanks with his whip, reassured to see that Kalliovski was not heading toward his mansion. Finishing his story, he told Didier and Têtu with pride, "I wasn't scared, because I had my black cap."

Têtu stayed quiet. He had said nothing about knowing who the spirit was. Some things, he thought, do not belong here. They live in the hinterland between this world and another.

"Still, for all our grand gestures and daring deeds, this is a disaster. We have failed dismally in our task," said Monsieur Aulard dramatically.

"Don't be so hasty," said Didier, bringing out Yann's coat and taking from it the packet of letters and the leather-bound black book. Têtu grabbed them, and nearly dropped the book when he realized what the binding was made of.

"Why didn't you tell me you'd gotten the letters?" he cried.

"But Yann was shot! How did you get hold of these?" asked Monsieur Aulard.

"You shouldn't have taken it for granted that because he was shot, he failed," said Didier. "There's more to that boy than meets the eye."

"You're brilliant," said Têtu.

"I didn't do it. It was Yann."

The two men stopped as Yann came shakily into the room. Didier rushed forward to help him to a chair.

"What are you doing up?" asked Monsieur Aulard.

"I'm feeling better," said Yann. He looked as white as snow.

"You've done very well to have gotten all this," said Têtu.

Yann smiled. "The letters were hidden inside one of the Sisters Macabre."

"Sisters Macabre?"

"They are automata. One had a red chamber in her stomach, containing the letters. Another gave me this. She called it the Book of Tears."

"Wonderful!" said Monsieur Aulard.

Têtu rummaged about until he found a little bag of herbs. He put it in a jug with some boiling water, strained it into a bowl, and handed it to Yann.

"Here, drink this."

It smelled and tasted so revolting that Yann spat it out immediately.

"What are you trying to do, Têtu? Poison me? Give me some water. That is the most disgusting thing I've ever tasted."

"It will do you good, make you heal quickly. Come on now, drink it up."

Yann did as he was told, and shortly afterward his eyelids began to close and Didier carried him back to bed.

That night only Didier and Yann slept. Monsieur Aulard and Têtu sat up reading the love letters of Armand de Villeduval and Isabelle Gautier.

"It breaks your heart to read of such great love. And that poor little daughter of theirs, lost and neglected! To think that she's to be given to that monster Kalliovski! We have to save her!" said Monsieur Aulard passionately.

"We must get back to the prison," said Têtu. He picked up the Book of Tears and started to look through it. "What's this?"

"Just blank paper," said Monsieur Aulard.

"I think not," said Têtu. As he held it up to the heat of the candle flame, page after page of writing appeared. "You see? It's sympathetic ink that can only be seen once it's been heated."

On the title page were the words *The Red Necklace*, and the following pages listed the names of all those who had borrowed money from Kalliovski, how much they owed, and what secrets they had given up for the loan.

"So much blackmail! Is there anyone he hasn't bought?" mused Monsieur Aulard.

"There may be a few who were not blinded by his wealth and connections, but only a few, I'd say," replied Têtu.

The dawn chorus had started when Monsieur Aulard at last put the book down. As he did so, a sheet of thin folded paper fell out, covered in elaborate flowery handwriting. He pored over it.

"Têtu, this is what we've been looking for!" he exclaimed. "If Sido is in any doubt about leaving her father, this will not fail to convince her."

It was a letter from the present Marquis de Villeduval, addressed to Count Kalliovski, asking him to arrange the deaths of his wife and his half brother and of their daughter, Sido.

chapter thirty-one

Citizen Kalliovski's carriage made its way slowly through the busy streets toward the Tuileries Palace. It was a warm night, the buildings still retaining the heat of the hot summer. Nothing had cooled down, not the temperature, not the citizens, not the Revolution, not the war. The gated city felt like a vast witch's cauldron, the flotsam and jetsam of its population slowly rising to the top, ready to boil over with frustration, hatred, and murder.

Kalliovski had not yet been home. There had been no time. The note that had been delivered to him at the theater was from Citizen Danton, telling him of a meeting that he should attend if he wanted Sido de Villeduval's release papers signed. He sat cursing the fact that he was already late, angry with himself for having stayed so long at the theater, and wondering why Têtu had brought back Anis's ghost. He raised his gloved hand and brought it down hard on the side of the carriage. Damn it, tonight of all nights. He didn't need to think of her. He had sworn he would never think of her again.

He took out his pocket watch. He was now over an hour late. The carriage edged along, slower than a funeral march. He banged loudly on the ceiling with its painted cherubs.

"Can't you go any faster?"

"No, sir," the coachman called down. "Too many people."

Kalliovski thought angrily that Danton would not have the manners to wait for him. No, they would all have conveniently forgotten just how much he had helped by supplying the money to buy extra pikes and arms. It was all well and good, wanting the citizens of Paris to put an end to the traitors in their midst, but bare hands and fine words weren't enough. They needed weapons to be successful.

Tonight's meeting was unofficial, by invitation only. It would be the last chance for Danton, Marat, and their cronies to trawl through the prison registers and to make quite sure that no one important had been rounded up by mistake, for tomorrow the killing would begin. Justice, for what little it was worth, would then be in the hands of the people: sheep, the lot of them, led by Marat, a leader of sheep who had ignited their imaginations with his clever words. What use was it, Marat argued, for a man to go off to fight for his country when the prisons were full of counterrevolutionaries? They would break out at the first opportunity and kill the innocents at home while the men of Paris were away fighting.

Kalliovski gave a thin smile as he thought, Oh world, beware of clever sheep. They are the truly dangerous ones, for they understand the stupidity of the flock, know just how easy it is to lead the people to slaughter.

At last the carriage stopped at the palace and Kalliovski made his way through the ill-lit entrance hall and down the forsaken corridors. Portraits of solemn, stiff-looking men in powdered wigs still hung on the walls in their gilt frames. How horrified they would be if they knew what was being discussed behind closed doors tonight! Not long ago the place had bristled with footmen and attendants, with dukes and princesses, with gossip and rumor and tittle-tattle. How many times had he been called upon to help some distressed viscount or embarrassed prince out of a difficulty? He had made a great deal of money from their follies. Now he saw no one, heard no one, just the click-clack of his own boots, and the scratching of Balthazar's sharp claws, upon the marbled floors.

Whom did he prefer? This bunch, with their bull-like orators and clever sheep, rich in words but not much else? Or the king and the aristocracy, foolish, narcissistic people who could hardly babble out a sentence without tripping over their own protocol, but whose pockets were lined with gold, ready for the taking?

The question remained unanswered as Kalliovski entered the large antechamber adjoining the room where the meeting was being held. The imposing double doors were firmly closed. He was surprised to find so many people waiting, a motley group who must all, like him, have paid handsomely for release papers to be stamped.

Kalliovski walked past all of them and knocked loudly at the main door. It was opened by a lizard of a man with hooded eyes.

"I have a note from Citizen Danton summoning me here," said Kalliovski. He was about to walk straight past, but the man put out a firm hand to stop him.

"Not so fast, citizen."

"Do you know who I am?"

The lizard-man studied him carefully, from his immaculate black coat and high necktie right down to his shiny black boots.

"Well-heeled," he said, slamming the door.

Kalliovski did not take kindly to such treatment. His blood boiled at the injustice of it. After all he had done for this miserable crew, he had no intention of waiting. Carefully brushing off any trace of the hand on his coat, he knocked again loudly. The same man opened the door.

"I have come for the release papers for Sidonie de Villeduval. I was told that they would be ready by now."

"Then you have been misinformed, citizen. Look around you. You're going to have to wait like everyone else. You're no bleeding different. Equality, remember? That's what it's all about." And once again the door was slammed shut.

Kalliovski was outraged. Such rudeness would not have been tolerated under the old regime. The man would have found himself in the Bastille for his impertinence. He went to knock on the door a third time. No one dismissed him like that.

"Sir, I wouldn't do that if I were you," said a thin, anxious-looking man, getting up from his chair. "They've already arrested one person for being impatient. I am hoping to get my son out of prison. They took him in the middle of the night—for what, we haven't been told. My wife . . ."

He stopped, seeing the look of indifference on Kalliovski's face, and quickly returned to the safety of his chair.

Once more Kalliovski took out his pocket watch to check the time. His well-constructed plan must not fail at this last important stage. As soon as he had Sido's release papers, he would go straight to the prison and have her freed, and then without further delay they would be married. He had even found himself a Catholic priest, one of the very few who was not languishing in prison, to carry out the deed. He wasn't going to risk having a revolutionary wedding, not with the Duke of Brunswick so close to victory. He wanted the certificate to be aboveboard, to hold Papal weight, for then and only then would the considerable fortune finally be his. He might not have had the mother, but fate would give him the daughter and her inheritance. Revenge becomes all the sweeter, he thought, when it has been ripened by misfortune and then served cold, icy cold.

He smiled to himself. If the Duke of Brunswick were to

invade Paris, he would have no hesitation in changing sides again. He was well aware that to have allegiances, to take a stand, to hold a firm political view, was the recipe for a short life. When the winds are liable to change quickly, it is best to be a reed and know how to bend. He had one motto, and it had not failed him yet. Have no mercy, show no mercy.

He walked back and forth, Balthazar by his side. Still the door remained closed. He had not bargained on this delay. He had planned to have Sido out of prison by now.

Time was dragging its feet, refusing to go any faster, as if it were hoping to keep night pinned to the stars. At last it let go and the inky dark sky gave way to the bloodred dawn.

The door of the antechamber opened. Everyone turned to see who the new visitor was. One of Kalliovski's henchmen entered the room.

"What is it?" Kalliovski asked brusquely.

"I'm sorry to report, sir, that there's been a break-in at your apartment."

"You must be mistaken. Milkeye wouldn't have let anyone get past him."

"I am afraid I'm not, sir."

"Where is Milkeye?"

"Out cold, sir. We can't wake him."

"Anything taken?" Kalliovski's voice was like the hiss of a viper.

"No, sir. Milkeye must have shot the intruder. There's blood all over the place."

"Any sign of a body?"

"No."

"Anything else?"

"Not that we can see."

Kalliovski felt a warm rush of relief. Now, if the Book of Tears were to have gone, that would be a different matter. At least the Sisters Macabre wouldn't give up their secret so easily.

"There is one other thing, sir, but it's not important."

"What?"

"It's the automata, sir."

"What about it? Speak, man."

"Two of them have been opened."

"Did you look inside?" asked Kalliovski in a menacing whisper.

The man trembled. "Yes, sir. They were empty."

Kalliovski brought his fist down hard into his gloved hand. He paced back and forth, his eyes wild. He knew that only someone who could work the threads of light would have been able to open the secret chambers, but Têtu had been at the theater and there was no one else capable of doing such a thing.

"Are you sure?" His hands automatically went toward the man's throat and he began to strangle the life out of him.

The people in the room, shaken from fitful sleep, now did their best to separate the pair. Kalliovski shook himself free and looked down at the man on the floor, who was crimson in the face and gasping for air. Terrified, he pulled away from his master.

Kalliovski's eyes sparked with flashes of pure rage. He kicked hard at the wall.

"Go and wake Milkeye. I want to know who did this, and I want them found and brought to me alive. Everything must be returned to me. Do I make myself clear?"

At that moment the door to the meeting room was opened. "Wait!" said Kalliovski. White with anger, he pushed his way to the front of the line to ask for his document.

"There's no one by the name of Sidonie de Villeduval on the list," said the lizard-man, with some relish.

Kalliovski scribbled a note and handed it to him.

"This is for Citizen Danton, and if you value your life you will give it to him."

"Are you threatening me?"

"Yes," said Kalliovski, "and if you don't do as I ask, I will kill you and take pleasure in it."

"A good joke, citizen," said the man, blowing smoke through his nose like a dragon. But a shiver went down his spine, and he took the note and closed the door behind him.

All those waiting shifted uneasily on their feet. Only a few had left with the documents they needed.

Church bells rang the tocsin and in the distance, cannons boomed.

Kalliovski was left wondering if it was possible that Têtu had tricked him. Had he set up that charade at the theater in order to keep him there while someone broke in? But who? No, that couldn't be . . . they would never have known where to look unless . . . He stopped. Unless . . . whoever it was had been able to make the Sisters Macabre talk, and only a powerful shaman could do that.

He supposed Têtu might have broken in earlier. No, on second thought that was unlikely.

Then it came to him, a moment of realization just as the day was dawning. "Of course!" he shouted out. "The boy!"

Why hadn't he put the pieces together before? The boy, the one who got away, was back in Paris. Why had he been so slow?

Anis had had a child!

That night, all those years ago, after she had run away from him, when he had found her working with Têtu and Topolain in the circus: That night, he had begged her to be his wife, promised he would change. She had refused . . . stood there, her dark hair, her eyes blazing, so mysterious in all her beauty . . . If he couldn't have her, then he was determined no one else would . . .

He remembered the delicious softness of her neck, how he had put his hand around her throat and she had smiled at him, showing no fear. Her eyes, flecked with gold, had stared into his soul and saw who he was, what he would be capable of. He hadn't meant to harm her; he just wanted her to close her eyes, not to look at him like that. He had pressed his hands tighter and tighter around her neck. The sense of power tingled within him; he was walking on the edge. He had shaken her like a doll, felt the flutter of her heart as it ceased beating beneath his hand.

In the silence that followed, before regret threatened to break him in two, in the last moment he had ever allowed himself to feel anything for anyone, he had heard the soft sound of a baby crying.

Only much later—too late—had he found out that she had had a child. What had happened to it he never knew. He had put it from his mind.

Now he realized, of course, of course, Têtu had taken the child, brought him up. The boy at the château on the night of the marquis's party—that was him!

He could still hear Anis laughing from beyond the grave.

$\mathcal{S}$ido had been awake most of the night. She had lain there trying to remember how long she had been in prison, and failing. Time had become a blank, possessing no marked features. Each day was the same, played out to the background noise of weeping, clanging doors, and barking dogs. She felt that she had always been in jail, and that life outside was no more than a passing interlude.

She had seen her father only once since Yann and Maître Tardieu had come. She had gone to sit with him in the large hall that had once been a chapel. The minute she had spoken, he had exploded with rage.

"Dying was the only good thing you ever did, you wretched woman!" He was shouting so loudly that the guards had come running, and had to restrain him from attacking Sido. "Away with you and your bastard!" he yelled. "I will have no more to do with you."

Sido had stood transfixed, watching the guards wrestling to control him. She said under her breath, "I have a right to my life. It was given to me. It is mine to cherish. It is mine to claim. To throw it away is a sin."

She said it aloud to cut out all the vile things he was shouting. Once back in her cell it finally struck her that there was no point in trying to help a man who had always hated her. Sane or insane, his sentiments had never altered. Only when she was silent had he shown the slightest regard for her. Why? Because then she could be anything he wanted.

She let out a sigh as the moon made a welcome appearance at the bars of her window, its sad face frowning.

"What do you want?" it seemed to ask.

"Why, what everyone wants," she replied. "To be loved for being myself rather than what someone wants me to be."

Was that such a bad thing? With Yann she had simply been Sido and she had felt so free, as if she had feathers as white and wide as swans' wings, ready for the wind to lift her up, to fly, to float, weightless, between the clouds.

She sat up knowing that she had arrived at a decision. If Yann came for her, she would go.

"I have a right to my life, it was given to me, and it is mine to cherish. It is mine to claim. To throw it away is a sin." Saying it made her feel stronger. She wanted nothing more to do with the name de Villeduval. If ever she was free again, she would call herself by her mother's name. She at least had loved her.

Just before dawn, the church bells started to ring all over the city. This was no pleasant Sunday sound, the gentle call to prayer. In the frenzy of their chimes, loud enough to wake the dead, the bells sounded a warning of oncoming danger, their clamor heightened by the barking of the prison dogs.

The bells were still ringing and the dogs still barking by the time the sun was up. This was unusual, for the dogs were normally released by this time, to do the rounds with the guards.

Normal, she thought, was such an ordinary little word. It was only when normality was gone that you realized how much you missed its presence. What would she give to see the turnkey this morning, arriving as he usually did, his voice as rough as gravel, fighting a hangover and leering into the cells, hoping to catch a glimpse of a woman in a state of undress. But this morning the corridor remained empty. And that was not the only thing that was unusual about this day.

Normally, Citizeness Villon brought breakfast to her. Like the guards, she had not turned up. The plate from last night's supper sat on the chair, gravy stains hardened to its surface like glue.

She watched the shadows cast by the sun and thought it must be well past midday, but still no one appeared.

The atmosphere in the prison was electric. Sido could feel frenzied waves of terror rushing through the cells, a sense that something terrible was looming. This nameless fear began to spread like an uncontrollable fever as the prisoners started to bang on the doors of their cells, the sound swiftly reaching a crescendo that in itself would normally have guaranteed the arrival of a guard, furious to have been dragged away from the guardhouse and his card game.

Today, it seemed, nothing was normal. She sat on her bed trying her best to keep calm, staring at the stone wall of her cell in whose uneven surface she could make out a face that reminded her of Yann. It was the memory of that one glorious hour in the café that had kept her from dwelling too much on what was happening in the present. Escaping to this imaginary place had been the only way to block out the atrocities of prison life.

For the past four days, more and more people had been brought here. Some were dragged, others walked with their heads held high. Mothers carried their children, who looked scared and bewildered, their young voices pitiful with their questions of "Why are we here? Where are we going? What have we done wrong?"

Sido's daydream was shattered by the chilling cry that came over from the male prison: "They are going to slaughter us all!"

Now panic was given full reign, with shouting, pleading, and desperate cries for the guard to come. These were silenced by other, more dreadful noises from outside and the groans and screams of the dying at the hands of the bloodthirsty crowd. What the prisoners had feared the most had started. At about four o'clock the iron door at the end of the corridor in the women's section clanked open to admit three persons: two sans-culottes, their sleeves rolled up, hands covered in blood, with the red caps of liberty on their heads, and one jailer who carried a torch to show them the way. They peered in at all the prisoners, their eyes wild, their voices so brutal and their accents so thick that it was hard to tell whose name they were shouting.

At last it became clear that they were calling for the Duchesse de Lamantes.

Sido heard a key turn in the lock, heard the duchess beg to be left in peace, and then a commotion as a chair was knocked over. The men dragged her out into the corridor, calling her every name under the sun, while the duchess wept noisily and screamed, "Where are you taking me?"

"To the jailer's office, citizeness, to be tried before the People's Tribunal as the traitor you are," came the cold reply.

The duchess was dragged down the corridor, making one last desperate grab at the iron bars of Sido's cell as she passed. Her eyes were wide with fright.

"Don't let them do this to me!" she cried as a wooden truncheon hit her hard on the knuckles. Shrieking with pain she let go, to be hauled unceremoniously past the row of cells. The iron door closed with a deadly thud. For a moment all was silence, broken only by the quiet sobbing of the other terrified inmates.

We are like sheep, thought Sido, waiting to be taken to the slaughterhouse.

She slid down the corner of the stone wall, buried her head

in her arms, and tried to take herself back to that magical place where there was just Yann. Only too soon she heard the sound of boots on stone again, advancing down the long corridor and stopping before her cell. She watched as the key turned in the lock.

So this was it. This was her end and she knew it. She didn't even look up to see who had come for her. She felt their strong arms, smelled their unwashed flesh, their sweat. She was not going to let herself be dragged like the duchess. She stood up straight and shook herself free from their clutches. What did any of it matter? She was as good as dead.

"We are all equal, but I, unlike you, am not armed," she said calmly. "Please take your hands off me." The two brutal-looking men, astonished to be spoken to in such a manner, let go of her. Sido took a deep breath and walked down the corridor, trying her best not to limp. She didn't want anyone's pity.

"To La Force," she heard as the duchess came out of another room. Seeing Sido standing on the stairs waiting her turn, she shrugged her shoulders as if to say that it wasn't too bad. Then the street door was thrown open. For a moment Sido was blinded by the light; then she saw all too clearly a sea of swords and pikes. The duchess, realizing what fate held in store for her, tried to pull away from the guards, only to be caught screaming by three men carrying bloodstained sabers. She raised her hands above her head.

Sido saw them lift their swords. She closed her eyes and

tried to shut out the nightmare cries and the loud grunts of the men as they wielded their weapons. Then the street door was slammed, leaving the stone-paved floor splattered with the duchess's blood.

Sido's legs were trembling as she was taken into the jailer's office.

The room was lit by torches and in the shadowy light she could see that it was full of men. Behind a table sat a man called Stanislas Maillard. He was dressed in black, his long lank hair pulled back into a queue at the neck; he had a gaunt face and deep-set eyes. That made Sido think that if death ever had a face to call its own, it would look like his.

Maillard had been elected to carry out the duties of the President of the People's Tribunal, a task he took no pleasure in, yet nevertheless performed meticulously. On the table before him were the prison register, a stack of paper, a bottle of wine, and a glass. Sido could tell from the men's voices that they were from Marseilles and other parts of France, all eager onlookers of the spectacle.

"Name, age, and place of birth?" said Maillard, drawing his bony index finger slowly down the list.

Sido answered the questions clearly.

Having found her name in the register, he glanced over the charges and consulted his grim colleagues. Then he informed her that she was being held for high treason against the nation.

"How do you answer?"

"I support the Revolution and wish its success with all my heart," said Sido. She knew that any other answer would mean death.

"Then why did you try to leave our glorious country?"

"I was born into a family where my wishes and views held no weight." It sounded to her as feeble as it was. She knew it wouldn't save her.

At that moment the door to the makeshift courtroom burst open and another prisoner was dragged in before the judge. His guards pulled back his head.

"Another priest we found hiding in the chapel."

Maillard sighed and methodically checked the prison register to find him. His menacing eyes flickered around the room.

"Did you take the oath?" he asked

"I am not afraid to die," the man said bravely.

"Away with him!" came an angry roar from the men in the room. Death hovered there above the priest's head as Maillard waved him away.

Sido shivered. His shrieks filled the room.

The president refilled his glass and looked again at the papers.

"Put some gunpowder in your wine, citizen," said one of the guards. "That's what we do. It'll put fire in your belly and rage in your heart."

The president shook his head. He looked again at the papers. This one was definitely prettier than any of the others he had gotten rid of this morning, and she had a lovely voice.

"So you say you had no way of stopping your father being a traitor to his country?"

"That is right, sir."

"Enough. How do we find the prisoner?"

"To La Force," came the shout from around the room.

In other words, thought Sido, guilty as charged. The president brought down his hammer and cried, "To La Force! Take her away."

Sido was determined to keep her head up high, to look him straight in the eyes so that he would not forget her. Two guards seized her roughly by the arm as the judge brought down his wooden hammer and shouted, "Next!"

At that moment the door to the office was pushed open and a dreadful apparition charged into the room. The guard, if guard he was, was drenched in blood. He looked exhausted. Furious, he stood in front of Maillard and slammed his bloodied fist on the table.

"What do you think we are?" he shouted. "We've been hacking and killing all day without a stop. We ain't machines, you know. A man needs his rest. A man needs something to eat."

Maillard looked up at the clock and spoke to the two men who were about to take Sido out. "Leave her!"

Sido was shoved forcibly down on a bench.

"What shall we do with her?" said one of the two guards. "We need a break too, you know."

Maillard looked at Sido. There was no getting away from it; she was a problem he didn't want. A pretty problem, and she had nice eyes. He tapped his fingers rhythmically on the table, looking for a way out of his predicament.

Bringing up his hammer, he bashed it upon the table again and proclaimed, "Innocent!"

For a moment Sido wasn't sure if she had heard him right or whether this was a coded message for them to kill her later, but then a shout went up in the jailer's office. *"Vive la Nation!"*

Her guards rushed forward to congratulate her, lifted her up, and carried her out of the street door toward the gate, shouting, "We have one who is innocent."

From her position high up on their shoulders Sido could see every detail of the scene before her. A huge fire had been lit in the prison courtyard, which added an eerie light to the pile of bodies heaped together, many with their limbs hacked off, while around the railings to the prison the faces of the citizens pressed closer, eager to have a look at the new butchers of Paris. The dogs, freed at last, were licking the ground as the men sat by the heaped corpses, eating their lunch and laughing heartily, holding up wine bottles and dipping their bread in the blood.

Sido, still held up high, floated through this unreal world. She fixed her eyes on the gate, sure that if she were to look away for a moment all chance of freedom would vanish. She was set down outside to join the press of onlookers.

Life is mine, she said to herself, and with those words she felt the thrill of freedom.

Suddenly, an arm locked itself tightly around her waist and a hand, a black-gloved hand, covered her face. Her freedom had lasted for less than a minute. She was pushed into Kalliovski's carriage and fell back heavily against the velvet cushions. The feel of the luxurious fabric went through her body like an electric shock. She let out a scream as the automaton slumped forward across her lap. She pushed it back, gasping at the ghostly apparition of Madame Perrien.

"I owe you an apology," said Citizen Kalliovski. "I had hoped to get your release papers signed before this bloodbath began."

She looked at him in horror. Then, remembering the agreement, she asked, "My father, did you get his release papers?"

Kalliovski took a letter from his pocket. He dangled it in front of her.

"I said to you that if you came willingly, your father would be released. Do you come willingly?"

She sat as far away from him as she could, pushing herself into the seat.

"Do you?"

Sido nodded.

"Kiss me then, show me that you mean it."

Sido sat trembling, battling with herself. Finally, taking a deep breath, she bent forward to kiss him on the cheek. He grabbed her, and pressing his thumb and forefinger into her jaw forced her to look at him. His lips, like a blood-filled wound, came closer and without thinking she spat at him.

Kalliovski hit her hard across her cheek, making her eyes smart with pain, and threw her back into the seat. Bringing out a pure white handkerchief he opened it up carefully and wiped his face.

"Who would have thought you had such a wild spirit. It will be a pleasure to break it." He laughed. "And break it I will. Shall I comfort you a little after your ordeal by saying that even if you had come willingly, I would not have had your father freed? I don't like what is happening but there is something inevitable about it, a certain poetry. Your father and all his spoiled and silly kind have brought this upon themselves."

He knocked on the ceiling of the carriage and it started to move slowly away through the crowd.

"Would you like to know what today is?"

Sido turned away and looked out of the darkened windows.

"The day the box of demons was opened," she said quietly, more to herself than to him.

"No, *ma chérie*," he said, smiling. "Today is our wedding day."

chapter thirty-three

*O*ver on rue Barbette, Didier had been woken at noon by the frenzied clang of church bells accompanied by shouts and the sound of boots on cobbles. Wasting no time, he had hurried down to find out what was happening. The clamor of the mob reverberated around the rabbit-warren of shops and apartment buildings as it surged along the street.

Didier rushed to the baker's shop on rue des Rosiers and knocked so hard on the door that the glass panes rattled. The terrified face of the baker, dough-white with fear, peeked out from behind the blind. Seeing it was an old friend, he quickly let him in and double-locked the door behind him. Talking nonstop, he took Didier through to the back room, where his family was sitting around the table eating. They looked as startled as rabbits caught by the sound of a gun.

"What's going on?" asked Didier.

"Haven't you heard? They say Verdun has fallen and that the Prussians are marching this way. They're just a few miles outside the city gates. Notices have been put up on all the street corners, saying that if we don't kill the enemies in our prisons they'll break out and slaughter us all."

"Rubbish," said Didier. "Priests, nuns, children, prostitutes, an assortment of aristocrats and forgers—can you really believe people would kill them?"

"I don't know. I'm only telling you what I've heard. There are calls for all the traitors to be torn limb from limb." He stopped, steadying himself against his oven as if for the first time the true meaning of his words had dawned on him. "It's a terrible day," he said sadly. "Makes you wonder if we're any better than the beasts of the forest."

He handed Didier a loaf of bread. The smell was comforting in a world that suddenly appeared to be made up of jagged edges.

"Thank you," said Didier, thrusting it inside his coat.

"If you don't want to be caught up in a bloodbath," said the baker, "I'd advise you to stay inside." He put an arm around his wife and patted his children's heads. "Call me a coward if you like, but that's what I'm going to do."

He saw Didier to the door. "They say it's going to be a good day for the grave digger. Take care, my friend," he whispered after him.

Didier pushed his way along the street to Monsieur Aulard's apartment to find Têtu up and making coffee and Monsieur Aulard, barely awake, sitting slumped in a chair with his stockings down around his ankles.

"Where's Yann?" asked Didier. "There's not a moment to be lost. I think the massacres are about to start."

"I know," said Têtu. He did not finish what he was saying, for Yann appeared in the doorway.

"What's happening?" asked Yann. "Why have all the bells gone crazy?"

"Something's going on at the prisons," said Didier, taking the warm loaf from his coat and putting it on the table. "It seems that we're about to be invaded."

"Then why did you let me sleep?"

"Because you've been wounded," replied Têtu, bringing a pot of coffee to the table. "I've managed to get a carriage to meet us at the St. Denis gate at seven o'clock, which should give you time to get your strength up for the journey. I've had word from Cordell that he will be in Dieppe, staying at the Hôtel de Paris, so that is where you are to take Kalliovski's Book of Tears."

"I'm going to get Sido out before I go anywhere."

"It may well be too late to save her."

"No, don't say that—it can't be!"

"Yann, I am sorry, the world has gone mad. You would never make it to the prison in time, even without the wound."

"No, no!" shouted Yann angrily. "I haven't come this far to

give up now, just like that." He turned away in disgust. "What do I do? Tell the Laxtons that I was slightly wounded and didn't feel strong enough even to *try* to get Sido out? Still, never mind, they should be pleased I got the Book of Tears! Têtu, I would rather die trying to get her out than do nothing."

He went back into the bedchamber and came out a few moments later already dressed and pulling on his sky-blue coat, wincing as a sharp stab of pain went through his shoulder.

"I was told by a fortune-teller that there was a bullet waiting for me in Paris," he said. "The fear of it nearly stopped me from coming back. Last night the thing I dreaded the most found me, and I survived it. Têtu, I am still alive, more alive than I have ever been. I know I can save Sido, I *know* it."

"Then if you don't want an infection, your wound will need to be rebandaged."

Reluctantly Yann gave in and sat down, fidgeting impatiently while Didier attended to the wound.

"You're not fit to go anywhere, not even Dieppe, rattling about in a bone-shaker of a carriage." Didier bandaged him up again. "Also, you have a slight fever."

"Stop fussing."

"Before you go," said Têtu, "I should tell you that I found out last night that Kalliovski went to get Sido's release papers signed. I don't know if he managed it or not. Your only hope of finding her is to find Kalliovski. If I were you I wouldn't bother with the prison."

"Thank you," said Yann. He leaned down toward Têtu and spoke to him in Romany. "One last thing. Did you know Kalliovski can use the threads of light?"

"Yes, like a feeble child with a puppet. He is an amateur, for the time being at least. Unless . . . "

"Unless what?" asked Yann.

"Unless the devil goes walking."

Yann kissed Têtu on both cheeks. "Don't worry," he said in French. "Today I feel invincible. Today I am ten feet tall and as strong as Hercules."

"Today you have a fever," said Têtu.

"I will be there in time for the coach. You bring the Book of Tears, Sido's papers, and the letters." At the door he turned back. "Wait—the jewels! You must get them from the old lawyer."

"I know," said Têtu. "Now go."

"Oh, *mort bleu!*" said Monsieur Aulard, leaping to his feet in desperation. "No, no, Yann. Can't you see that once Kalliovski finds out what has been stolen, all hell will break loose?"

"Just get the jewels," said Yann, and he left, taking the stairs two at a time.

Têtu looked at Didier, who was clutching a thick slice of bread, knowing full well what was about to be asked of him.

"Get after him and try to stop him being killed."

"I'll do my best," said Didier, picking up his cap and taking a quick swig of coffee.

After he had gone, Têtu grabbed his coat and hat. "What

are you doing just sitting there?" he said to Monsieur Aulard. "Come on, get dressed. We have a lot to do. We've a lawyer to see, jewels to collect, and a carriage to meet."

"Mort bleu!" said Monsieur Aulard. "Will this never end?"

Just as if he knew exactly what Monsieur Aulard was thinking, Têtu said soothingly, "You are doing well, my old friend. You are braver than I ever thought you could be. Now, my size is against me. I need you to help me get through the crowds."

Monsieur Aulard, holding tightly to his black cap, squared his shoulders and sighed. "Then we'd best get going. I will protect you."

It took Didier some time to catch up with Yann, who had managed to weave and duck his way through the back alleys and down less crowded streets. At nearly every turn his way was barred by the sheer volume of people armed with spades, pitchforks, kitchen knives, and rusty swords. It was as if they were welded together like one determined, monstrous body made up of flesh, sinew, teeth and hair. With one purpose, with one mind, with murder beating in their hearts, they moved inexorably forward. They had no past, no future; they were caught in the great unthinking moment, their hearts and minds driven wild by the frenzied ringing of the tocsin, the firing of the cannons. It was as if Paris itself had a voice and howled its terror for all to hear.

It had taken Yann hours to get anywhere. He had made it as far as Kalliovski's apartment, to be told he had not returned. He went back to the Pont Neuf, but here, just as earlier, the press of people made progress almost impossible. Yann felt time slipping through his fingers like sand. Every now and then news would reach his ears of what was happening in the prisons, each report more horrific than the last.

They say the butchers of Paris had to show the sans-culottes how to kill a man.

They say the blood is running down to the Seine.

It's harder to kill a man than you think. Some of them were running around squawking like chickens, with bits missing.

These snippets of conversation made Yann more and more desperate. He climbed up onto the parapet of the bridge to get a better view of how far the masses stretched. On the opposite bank he could see the crowd divided. One half was setting off toward the Champ de Mars, the other making its way toward St. Germain and L'Abbaye.

Yann stood looking over the crowd, his mind whirling, the pain in his shoulder sharp and jagged. He cursed the fact that he had failed to persuade Sido to leave while there was still a chance.

Didier was now able to see Yann standing there in his sky-blue coat like a sailor looking out over an awesome sea of people. What was he searching for? Why was he drawing attention to himself? Didier wanted him to get down before he was pushed into the river.

"We'd best get off this bridge and make for the bridge of Notre Dame," he shouted above the noise.

"Wait," said Yann.

It wasn't the first carriage he had seen that day, but the others had been abandoned, turned over, splintered, many set alight, making the movement of the masses even harder.

As it got closer Yann recognized it as Kalliovski's shiny black coach with six fine white horses, the one in which he and Têtu and Topolain had traveled when they were taken to the Marquis de Villeduval's château. He smiled to himself, for this meant only one thing: Kalliovski had had no time to return home after the meeting. Otherwise he would have chosen to travel in a humbler coach, for this one stood out like a beacon of wealth and privilege as it fought its way against the oncoming tide of people. He must already have been to the prison.

In that moment Yann was certain that Kalliovski had Sido in the coach with him.

"Didier," he shouted, "look!"

Didier too had seen the coach, but unlike Yann the sight of it gave him no cause for joy. It was proof that they needed to get out fast.

"Get down, Yann. If he sees us, he'll kill us. Let's aim for the Palais Royal."

"No," said Yann. "Come on, follow me."

Didier knew he had no choice. Yann was now walking along the parapet, making his way ever closer to the coach. Didier followed, plowing through the crowds until at last he had his hand firmly on the door and his huge face pressed up hard against the darkened glass of the window. He could see Kalliovski, with Balthazar snarling at his feet. An automaton was sitting in the middle, and Sido was hunched in the corner, her hands to her face.

Didier called to Yann, "They're in there all right."

"Get those horses," came a cry from the crowd. "They should be pulling cannons, not carriages."

A man leaped up and the coach driver did his best to push him off, shouting, "I have a member of the Revolutionary Council in here."

For a fleeting moment sanity prevailed. The mob parted as the coach started to lurch forward again.

"Stop them!" shouted Yann as the terrified horses snorted, rearing up and showing the whites of their eyes. The coachman tried to calm them down and made one last frantic attempt to get free of the crowd.

"It's an aristocrat trying to escape, a traitor to the cause!" yelled Didier at the top of his lungs.

The crowd needed to hear no more. That one seed of doubt worked its magic, and they swarmed upon the carriage and cut free the horses. Again the crowds parted, this time to make way for the horses to be taken like trophies won on the field of battle. The coachman slumped over on his seat, clutching a dagger that stuck out of his belly.

From where Yann was standing, he could see people pulling wildly at the doors, rocking them violently from side to side.

The coach looked like a huge black beetle being swarmed over by ants. He could hear Kalliovski shouting that he was a friend of the people. Some men had now climbed on top of the roof and were about to put their axes through it, waiting to make firewood of the coach and its passengers.

He could see the automaton being flung out, ripped limb from waxen limb, as Balthazar snarled, savage and futile. Then he became aware that Sido had been dragged out, her arms pinned behind her and a knife at her throat. Didier was battling to get to her, but Yann knew that he wouldn't be able to make it in time and for a moment he could hardly think straight. Then he realized he could see threads of light surrounding her. He felt his fingers tingle with excitement.

Yann pulled hard at the threads of light. The knife flew free of Sido's throat and stabbed a man some way away. The victim screamed with pain and collapsed, while Sido's captor looked on amazed. In that moment Yann lifted him off his feet and threw him so that he fell backward into a startled and unwelcoming mob.

Those who witnessed these events were convinced that there was an invisible force at play amongst them. They prayed it was on their side.

Sido felt as if she was in a nightmare. She hadn't seen Yann, let alone heard him call out, "Run!"

It was too late. Another man came forward to grab hold of her. Sweat was beginning to roll down Yann's forehead as he pulled once more at the threads of light. The man holding Sido, terrified by this invisible foe, let go of her and started to wield his axe around and around his head. There was a scream of anguish as it flew out of his grasp and landed in the red bonnet of one of his comrades. Before he could do anything, Yann lifted him as high as he could and dropped him onto the crowd below.

Didier now took his chance. He charged toward Sido like a bull and hauled her up on his shoulders.

"It's all right," he said urgently as she tried to resist him, "look," and he pointed at Yann, standing on the parapet of the bridge. To her eyes he looked as an avenging angel might.

By now the crowd was in a fever of rage, like some grotesque creature that had started to feed upon its own flesh. Fighting had broken out, panic had set in. Yann leaped down, and following Didier they wove their way through the mob.

Yann caught a glimpse of Kalliovski, then he was engulfed by the crowd. His gravel-deep voice rose in one last cry.

"You will never get away from me! I will find you!" Then his words were drowned by the shouts of "Kill the traitors to the Revolution!"

When at last they were off the bridge Didier put Sido down. Yann took her hand and they pushed their way through the crowds.

"Where're you taking her? She's an aristo like him," a voice screamed. The woman was an apparition of ghastliness, her teeth black, her hair wild, with the smell of the fish market. She screamed it out again.

"No," shouted Yann, "no, you're wrong. That bastard had snatched her from me. She's my sweetheart."

He didn't wait for a reply. He didn't even turn around to see if they were being followed, and at last they broke free of the mob. Now they were running until all three were completely out of breath. Sido, gasping for air, pulled at Yann's hand.

"I can't go any farther."

There were just forty-five minutes left to get to the meeting point.

They stopped and Didier, leaning his back against a wall, turned his head this way and that. In the distance they could just hear the faint sound of the crowds and of cannons being fired.

Yann, his heart pounding with excitement, could hardly believe what they had done. He laughed out loud and looked at Sido.

"Life is life!" he shouted.

Sido needed no one to tell her what that meant, she who only a few hours ago had narrowly missed death and had now escaped marriage to a man she detested. Instead, by some strange magic she could not understand, she was alive and free and with the person she had dreamed of in those dark hours in her prison cell. Oh yes, life was life, and may it never stop being so.

chapter thirty-four

*I*t was now five minutes past four o'clock. Têtu was sitting in a deserted café near the gate of St. Denis, while the coachman across the road held fast to the horses, frightened more of losing them than of losing the carriage. Horses in a city at war, he knew well, were more valuable than gold.

Monsieur Aulard chewed nervously at his fingers, as he had not done since childhood, wondering what on earth could have happened to Didier and Yann. The street was eerily quiet. Occasionally shutters would be gingerly opened and he would see a frightened face peering out. No doubt the residents were wondering whom the carriage was waiting for and how long it would be before the enemy came marching in through the gates.

Never had the theater manager wished more that horses didn't snort quite so loudly or that their bridles and harnesses didn't sound like alarm bells going off. They were attracting unwanted attention, of that he was certain.

"Where are they?" he said desperately, taking out his pocket watch and opening and closing it for the umpteenth time.

Têtu, despite his earlier concerns, seemed unperturbed by the fact that they hadn't arrived. He had his eyes shut and his feet up on a chair in front of him.

They had both come from Maître Tardieu. The old lawyer looked as if his heart wouldn't hold out much longer.

"This will be the death of me," he had said miserably as he had scurried away to dig out the jewels, terrified that his every movement was being watched by some invisible eye that could see straight into the heart of his molehill house. He had virtually thrown the bag of gems at Têtu, begging him to take them and be gone, relieved that at long last he could be free of this incriminating evidence.

"Think," said Têtu cheerfully to Monsieur Aulard, "you could be sitting in your theater, bored rigid by the patriotic rubbish you have to put on. Instead you're here, center stage in a real life drama for a change."

"*Mort bleu, mort bleu!* Are you trying to be funny?" said poor Monsieur Aulard, pausing from chewing his nails to wipe the beads of sweat from his face.

"They'll be here any minute," said Têtu reassuringly. He stood up and went to pay at the café bar. "Patience, my friend, patience."

Monsieur Aulard followed Têtu as far as the middle of the road, where he stopped, hoping upon hope that Yann and Didier might turn up. But the street remained empty.

Têtu walked past him toward the coachman, who was as jittery as a carpet full of fleas.

"Better get ready. They will be here shortly."

"Where? But where?" said Monsieur Aulard, waving his arms wildly. "There is no sign of them."

Without even turning around Têtu said, "Look again."

Monsieur Aulard was a man who had spent his whole life working in the theater. A man who could boast of having been born in the dressing room between the acts of a Voltaire play, a man who after recent events most sincerely believed that nothing could ever surprise him again, but who was completely taken aback by the sight of Yann, Sido, and Didier suddenly appearing in the road before him like a mirage. So much so that he was stripped of the tools of his trade. Words simply failed him.

"I'm sorry we're late," said Yann. "We had a hell of a time getting here."

"I can imagine," said Têtu, bowing graciously. "My dear young lady, we meet again and it is with great pleasure."

"It is so good to see you too, sir," said Sido.

The driver, relieved at last to have his passengers, climbed down and opened the carriage door.

"Your documents are all in order," said Têtu. "You should have no trouble traveling. You're going as brother and sister,

Sarah and Robert Laxton. You are meeting Charles Cordell in Dieppe, at the Hôtel de Paris. He has chartered a boat. I have already sent a messenger to say that you will be there in the early hours of the—"

Monsieur Aulard interrupted him, anxious to speak to Sido.

"Since your papers state that you are both English, it might be best to let Yann do all the talking. Now, the reason for your stay is that you have been at school here learning French and due to the political unrest your brother has come to take you home. I've packed some clothes from the theater for you—you can't travel in your prison clothes—and enough food for the journey. You will be stopping just outside Paris so that you can change."

While Monsieur Aulard talked away, Têtu took Yann aside and spoke to him in Romany so that they would not be overheard.

"You've done well. I knew you would. What of Kalliovski?"

"The last I saw of him he had been overpowered by the crowd and they were in a murderous mood," said Yann. "I don't see how he can have survived."

Têtu looked relieved. Now Yann would never need to know the truth of who his father was.

"Let's hope you're right. Yann, I'm proud of you. Now hurry, get Sido to Dieppe and come back as soon as you can. This is not over. You promise?"

"I promise."

Earlier that morning, *happy* was not a word Sido imagined she would ever use again, but despite all that had happened, happy was what she felt, unbelievably so, as the carriage made its way through the St. Denis gate and Paris disappeared from sight as the windmills of Montmartre came into view.

Yann, sitting opposite her, smiled, and they both burst out laughing, at what, they didn't know. At the fact that they had done the impossible? At how fate and luck had been with them? What did it matter? They were on the road to Dieppe. They talked of everything and nothing, with the ease of long-lost friends. All Sido's shyness was gone.

The coach stopped at the inn at Pontoise, a low, timbered building that bustled with people and coaches, none heading in the direction of Paris, all relieved to be away from the city and all hoping to reach the coast. Inside, the rooms were packed with customers waiting to be served, elated that they were, so they believed, as good as free. Some spoke loudly and carelessly, their voices betraying their aristocratic roots.

Yann instinctively disliked the place. The innkeeper, a hard-looking man, appeared to be encouraging these unwise fools while others, more timid, stayed quiet, pressing themselves against the walls. All the comings and goings were overseen by the innkeeper's wire-thin wife, whose tiny buttonlike eyes saw everything and missed nothing. The main room had tables and gnarled wooden beams that loomed oppressively over the diners as if they too were keen to hear what secrets were being told.

While Sido went to change her clothes, Yann found a table in the corner by the fireplace, where he could keep an eye on the door.

He looked around him, seeing frightened people who hoped that their passports would be good enough to take them through to London. Some, he was sure, were without even the money for food, having spent all they had just to get out of the city.

At the next table sat a group of men who had drunk more wine than was good for them, all talking loudly. Every time their glasses were empty the innkeeper kindly refilled them. Where was their driver? Yann wondered. He had a strong feeling that the man had taken their money and fled.

One of the men stood up, swaying slightly, and bowed when Sido came back into the room.

"Get up, you libertines," he shouted to his friends. "Can't you tell when a lady of breeding has entered the room?" With a clatter of chairs, all the men rose and bowed, so that those at the other tables looked curiously at her.

Yann whispered urgently to her as she sat down, "Don't speak. We're leaving. Just follow me."

It was too late. At that moment the door to the inn was thrown open and three soldiers in National Guard uniform entered. Yann knew that escape was now impossible. He watched, certain that the innkeeper and his wife were well acquainted with these men. The customers all shifted in their seats like a shoal of fish that know sharks are near.

The man in charge, an officer of sorts, had a face that looked as if it had been chiseled from granite. His nose had a gobbet of snot hanging from it, which he wiped on his sleeve. He looked around the room, inspecting the customers.

"I see before me, if my eyes don't deceive me, which they don't, men who should be doing their duty for France and the Motherland instead of sneaking off to England like the aristocratic rats they are. Your papers, vermin!"

The other two soldiers started to go through the room, pushing and shoving the customers. One of the group at the next table, winking to his companions, held up a bag of coins and whispered something to one of the soldiers, who spat on the floor and slipped the purse into his pocket.

"Another charitable contribution to the war fund!" he shouted out, lifting the man's arm up high above his head. "Thought he could bribe his way out of being a traitor."

No doubt, thought Yann, this and everything else they gathered would be divided among the innkeeper, his wife, and the three soldiers.

The same soldier made a great show of examining the men's passports.

"Look at this," he guffawed. "Forgeries, every one of them." He handed the passports to the officer.

The travelers started to protest. The officer ignored them. "Take them," he ordered. "They'll enjoy a night trip to Paris."

More and more of the customers were dragged out. At last only the regulars and Yann and Sido were left.

Now all eyes turned to watch the last bit of sport until more coaches arrived from Paris and the whole show began over again.

"What have we got here?" said the officer, leering at Sido. "A pretty little aristo if ever I saw one."

"Excuse me, sir," said Yann in broken French. "Where are your manners? This is my sister you are speaking to. We are English."

"English?" said the officer, snatching their passports. "You English? You're too dark to be an Englishman." He sniffed and wiped his nose.

Yann could feel Sido shaking beside him and he put his arm firmly around her.

"Pretty, pretty little bird, what have you to say about your brother?"

Sido said nothing.

"Here to learn French, eh? Bet you can speak it like a native."

The officer studied their papers again, holding them up to the light. He handed them back. "Well, you can go."

Yann felt Sido move but he held her fast, knowing that to do so would give the game away.

"Go then! Don't you understand any French?" bellowed the officer. It wasn't until he had gestured toward the door that Yann and Sido walked out. The sight of all those wretched men and women rounded up, standing roped together on tumbrels, made Sido feel weak-kneed. She knew exactly where they were being taken. Back to the prisons and certain death.

"Stop!" shouted the officer, coming to the door after them and spitting onto the ground. "What did you say your names were?"

Yann carried on walking toward the carriage.

"Hey, you lad," shouted the officer. Yann turned and made a gesture with his hand as if to say: "Is it me you want?"

The officer waved them away and relit his pipe. Ten out of ten stupid fools fall for that one, he thought, saying their names out loud and clear in French, titles and all. Either that young man was honest or he was one of the best actors he'd come across for a long time.

chapter thirty-five

Sido sat back in the carriage, her heart racing.

"All those people, and like us they thought they had escaped," she said. The enormity of what had just happened made her shiver. Then, looking at Yann, she asked, "Do you think my father's been killed?"

Yann nodded.

"I just hope he kept his arms behind him. I could see that those who tried to protect themselves had the slowest of deaths. What am I saying? I'm talking about killing people! Why? What has happened to us?" A tear rolled down her face. "It's madness. I left my father without a second thought because I'd grown tired of his hatred of me. Does that make me as bad as them?"

"No, Sido, it doesn't."

"And Kalliovski?"

"I can't see how he could have survived that mob," said Yann. "And it isn't wrong to hope that today, when so many innocent people have been slaughtered, they might have found one guilty person who deserved it."

"Is anyone truly innocent, I wonder. I thought I was, but look how I abandoned my father. I just left him to his fate."

"Sido," said Yann, "there was nothing you could have done. Today wasn't about choice, it was about luck. You were one of the lucky ones." He brought out a blanket and wrapped it around her. "You need to sleep, and then you'll feel better."

She curled up on the seat beside him with her head in his lap.

Yann sat staring out of the window. The sky was black and starless as they made their way with all haste toward Dieppe.

In the rocking motion of the carriage Sido fell fast asleep. Yann leaned back in the seat, lost in thought. He knew now what he was going to do. All those travelers tonight had needed help to escape. There must be better ways of getting people out of Paris than leaving them to the mercy of two-timing crooks like Mr. Tull and the innkeeper and his wife. The great hope of Liberty, Equality, Fraternity, he thought sadly, that should have meant a better world for all, appeared to have been massacred by man's own worst enemies: Stupidity, Greed, and Terror.

Looking back over the day's events he realized that every time he had worked the threads of light he had become stronger at it, the pain in his head a little more bearable. What was he going to be capable of with practice? There was still so much to learn, so much Têtu had to teach him and tell him. He looked down at Sido and gently brushed a strand of hair from her face, remembering how she had looked when he had first seen her asleep on that huge four-poster bed.

If things were different, if there were no Revolution, no war, no threads of light, if he were rich, would he go back to London with her and ask for her hand in marriage? He smiled, for the answer was simple. Yes, yes, he would.

It was the times they lived in that complicated the matter. "One day I will make my fortune," he said out loud to a silent carriage, "and then . . ."

He stroked Sido's cheek and bent down to kiss her, whispering what his heart had always known, what he had never said before to anyone. "I love you. I always will."

Sido didn't stir. For the first time in days she had felt safe enough to fall into a deep, dreamless sleep.

She woke just as they were coming into Dieppe and sat up dazed for a moment, not knowing where she was; then, remembering, she smiled and straightened herself out.

"You've slept through all the changes of horses and a lot of shouting, and you didn't once stir," said Yann. "Do you feel better?"

"I think so."

Yann handed her a flask and she took a drink. Then he took from his knapsack a small package of letters tied with ribbon, and the letter the marquis had written to Kalliovski.

"What are these?" asked Sido.

"They are for you to read when we get to Dieppe, and then you will understand, and realize that you were very much loved by your mother and your father."

"No," said Sido. "You're wrong, very wrong. My father hated me. He said he would have preferred me dead."

"Why do you think he hated you?"

"How can you say one minute that he loved me and then the next ask me why he hated me? It was because of my limp. He liked things to be perfect."

"It wasn't because of your limp. What if the marquis were not your father?" Sido sat there thinking. It was an idea that had never occurred to her, yet it made more sense than anything else had. It explained her father's hatred of her. It explained why he never mentioned her mother, and why she was not buried in the family tomb.

"Oh dear," she said at last. "I thought it was just to do with his insanity, but I see now why he was bellowing at me. He thought I was my mother. No wonder he told me to take my bastard and be gone."

She was quiet for some time.

"I have a strange memory of him, the only happy one I have," she said at last. "It doesn't fit with anything else. Maybe I dreamt it. I remember we were at the château, and he was with my mother."

"That would have been your real father, Armand de Villeduval, the marquis's younger brother."

Sido gasped. "Are you sure?"

"Certain. When you've read the letters you'll understand. The marquis wrote to Kalliovski, asking him to have you all murdered. Kalliovski obliged—but you survived. Your grandfather suspected foul play. He had his will changed and left you a large proportion of his estate, which will go to your husband on your wedding day. The marquis must have thought he would have control over your money if he chose a suitably stupid husband for you, someone he could manage. What he hadn't bargained for was Kalliovski."

It was very late when they finally arrived, exhausted. They were pleased to find that Charles Cordell had waited up for them.

"You made good time," he said. "I got them to leave some food out."

They sat over their supper talking about what had happened in Paris.

"The messenger from Têtu told me that they hadn't stopped the killing, though they ran out of prisoners at L'Abbaye and made their way to the Conciergerie, among other places," said Cordell.

"There would be no hope for the marquis," said Sido. It was the first time she had not referred to him as her father. It was a great release, a heavy cloud lifted.

"No. I gather his mind had gone. I should think it would have been quick; he wouldn't have been aware of what was happening.

I am most terribly sorry that you have been through such a dreadful ordeal. Tomorrow, if the tide is right, we should be away from France by mid-morning."

Sido said good night. On the stairs she turned and looked back at Yann. "Will you be here tomorrow?"

He said nothing, just smiled.

"Well," said Cordell, "I suppose you are wanting your bed as well. Shall we talk in the morning?"

"No, sir, I shall be leaving early for Paris. Could we talk tonight?"

"How is your shoulder?"

"It throbs, but it is healing."

"I have called for a surgeon to examine it."

"There was no need."

"You might think not, but I can assure you that Têtu would kill me if I didn't ask someone to look at it."

"It won't stop me from going back."

"You are still young and I thought that maybe . . ."

Yann took out Kalliovski's Book of Tears. Cordell looked at it, stunned.

"What is this?"

"Open it and see."

Tentatively Cordell opened it at the first page and read the words *The Red Necklace.*

He sat down, and burst out laughing. "Yann, you are good and no mistake. Where did you find it?"

"Inside one of the automata. Kalliovski has a collection of them, the Sisters Macabre. One of them was the keeper of this book. She called it the Book of Tears."

Cordell flicked through the pages of names. He looked up, and taking off his glasses, rubbed his temples.

"This is beyond anything I thought possible. All these people and the terrible sums they owe him! Many, I may say, the bank's clients. You have indeed turned over a stone and found a deadly viper there. Tell me, has Kalliovski created a near-human machine, as he claimed?"

"No, he was not even halfway there. What knowledge he has he can't use properly. Did you know that Mr. Tull works for him?"

"No, I didn't, but I am afraid it doesn't surprise me."

"There are people out there making money by double-selling their clients. I should think they will make a tidy sum from such unscrupulous work."

"You are right, Yann. After today there will, I believe, be a flood of desperate people who will risk everything to escape from France. I'm not just talking of nobles. I mean anyone who supplied goods to the aristocracy, anyone who looks intelligent enough to ask the unanswerable question: What happened to this great and glorious idea?"

"That's what I think. Têtu and I can help these people. We have the perfect setup in the theater. No one would suspect what we're up to."

"Mr. Laxton and I have been discussing this very matter," said Cordell. "You have already proved that you can get people out of Paris. You and Têtu between you could save a lot of souls. You have unique talents, Yann, which I believe will be much needed in the months to come. Tell me, before we part, are you certain Kalliovski is dead?"

"The last time I saw him he was in the hands of the mob. I am sure they will have murdered him."

"Good," said Cordell. "For all our sakes, I hope so."

The two of them shook hands.

"Have a safe journey back. I will be in touch," said Cordell.

That night in the city of the slaughtered, while the massacres still continued, the devil went walking. He could never resist the call of fresh blood, and now there was a rich harvest amid the blighted victims of the carnage. He was searching as always for one cursed soul into which to breathe his fiery life. He was not to be disappointed, for lying amongst the broken and the near-dead was one Citizen Kalliovski, with his dog, Balthazar.

Kalliovski was raging at his own demise: that he, a gambler, should have been cheated by the Queen of Hearts and her bastard, the Jack of Diamonds. For Anis had had his child, and it was Yann Margoza.

$\mathcal{T}$he next morning Yann woke early. He had told Cordell he intended to leave before anyone was awake, by which he meant before Sido was up, for he had decided in the carriage that he would not trust himself if he were to see her again. His mind, so fixed on returning to Paris, did not need a moment of doubt.

He washed and got dressed. The fever he had had yesterday was gone. Picking up his knapsack, he made his way down to the hotel lobby.

Sido stood waiting for him.

"You were going to leave without saying good-bye," she said.

"I just didn't want to upset you."

"You see, I sometimes know what *you* are thinking too. If you had done that I would never have had a chance to thank you. I read the letters."

"Now you know how much you meant to them."

"Yes, they were going to England to start a new life. I wish . . . I wish . . ."

What she wanted to say she couldn't. Instead she said, "I wish you didn't have to go back."

He took her arm and they walked out into the garden.

An early-morning mist hung over the lawn. The air smelled of sea salt and leaves. Once the sun was up it would be a bright day. They walked on in silence, both lost in their own thoughts.

"The truth is," said Yann after a while, "that if I were to come to London with you, I would find it impossible to say good-bye and return here. But there is so much more that needs to be done, so many people to be saved. And I could do it, Sido, I could do it." He took the shell from around his neck. "This was given to me by a Gypsy called Tobias Cooper. It is a talisman, a lucky charm. It will keep you safe, and one day I will come back to collect it. I promise."

She looked at it carefully. It came from a land she would never know, and yet she understood. Holding it tight, she said, "You must go."

Lifting her face up to his, he kissed her. If a promise had a taste, Sido's sweet mouth would be it. It was a kiss that sealed both their fates, interweaving the threads of light that had bound them together since they had first met.

"Live your life, Sido, whatever happens. Live in the moment, don't live with regret." He took his last kiss.

She stood there for a long time after he was gone, and thinking that he could not hear her, not now, she held the shell to her lips and whispered all that she had felt too shy to tell him. Her words were caught on the breeze and though she did not know it, they would find him, would travel with him, they would haunt him and become the magic charm that one day would call him home to her.

Our story is over, though in its end lies its beginning.

Some Historical Background

The Red Necklace is a work of fiction. I am a storyteller, not a historian; though I have immersed myself in the period, I am aware that some details may not pass the scrutiny of a specialist historian. A vast number of excellent books have been written on the Revolution, and I have consulted a great many of them, as well as eyewitness accounts and letters of the time. Any historical inaccuracies are my own responsibility as storyteller.

While the Revolution is well documented, the history of the Gypsies, whose story is woven into my book, is less so. Their suffering and persecution has continued throughout time and in all countries.

Paris in the eighteenth century was the epicenter of intellectual thinking, of fashion, of taste. While in the countryside feudal lords held sway, the city was the birthplace of the Age of Enlightenment. Meanwhile, the king still ruled by absolute power.

On the world stage France's great enemy was England. Humiliated in 1763 by the English conquest of Canada, the French in the 1770s saw rebellion in America as a chance for revenge. King Louis XVI raised huge loans and sent a fleet out to help the fledgling nation. In 1781 the British surrendered at Yorktown, a victory for the Americans that secured their independence. The French hoped to profit by driving the English out of trade with their newfound friends, but the Americans preferred to do business with their old partners. As the king's loans fell due, the country was plunged into crisis.

France's territories at this time were divided into hostile provinces and its population into rival classes. The nobles and the clergy had all the privileges and paid no taxes. The people possessed no rights and were taxed heavily. The country was now facing bankruptcy. The king, in hope of finding a solution to the worsening crisis, called a meeting of the Estates General. The First Estate was the church, the Second was the nobility, and the Third Estate the peasants and the middle class. It was the Third Estate that paid all the taxes. If anything, it did little but illustrate the injustice of the situation.

As France looked toward the Estates General, in the summer of 1788 there was a terrible hailstorm that flattened the wheat and spoiled the olive and the grape harvest. It was followed in November by one of the worst winters on record. Everything froze; people began to starve. When the people stated their grievances for the Estates General, they looked for sweeping change, but the king and the nobility resisted. The result was the forming of a national assembly by the members of the Third Estate, determined to have power for the people.

Louis XVI, fearing he was losing his grip, gave orders that the hall where the national assembly met should be closed. The assembly moved themselves to a nearby tennis court and swore an oath that they would not be separated until France had a constitution.

The king and his court plotted to defeat the national assembly, beginning by firing Necker, the Swiss banker appointed as Minister of Finance. Necker was wildly popular, and had blocked other attempts to halt the national assembly's work. The people of Paris, seeing their last hope of salvation gone, took matters into their own hands and stormed the Bastille. Three days later the king visited the city, surrendering to the Revolution.

In August 1789 the feudal system was abolished, as were the many privileges given to the nobility and the clergy.

In April of 1791 Louis XVI's true feelings were revealed when the royal family attempted to escape and were brought back to Paris in disgrace.

The following year war was declared on Austria and her allies, who were sheltering noble counterrevolutionaries and plotters.

The monarchy was finally abolished in August 1792, and on September 2 the massacres began. Around 1,500 people were slaughtered, but at the time many believed that tens of thousands had perished.

The guillotine, the symbol of the terror, was modeled on two earlier devices, the Halifax Gibbet and the Scottish Maiden. What made the version that bears the name of Dr. Joseph-Ignace Guillotin unique was the efficiency of his modifications, with the angling of the blade and the head brace.

My story covers the beginning of the French Revolution. It was fired by noble ideals of equality and freedom, from men such as Robespierre, Danton, and Marat, who were frustrated by the injustices of society. Once the terror started, these fine ideas were lost and no one was safe any longer from the insatiable appetite of the guillotine. It was to become a horror story that today still makes us shudder at the cruelty and stupidity of mankind.

As Danton said: "You have seen nothing yet but roses."

Acknowledgments

I would like to start by thanking Jane Fior for all her support and help in getting out a polished first draft; Judith Elliott for her tireless editorial work and support, and her husband, Donald Davis, for doing without her through the last very intense months; and Jacky Bateman for having done all the spelling corrections, and understanding my terrible grammar.

I also want to thank Diana and Bruno Costes Brook at La Puisaye, Auve, Normandy, for feeding and looking after me in great style, arranging for me to see chateaux and places of interest and making my time in France a complete pleasure; Mary Stewart for taking me around eighteenth-century Paris; Lauri Hornik for all her astute and helpful notes; my agent and dear friend Rosemary Sandberg; Dr. David Andress, reader in modern European History at the University of Portsmouth for taking the time and trouble to read the manuscript and correct historical inaccuracies; Thomas Acton, professor of Romani studies at the University of Greenwich for sharing his extensive knowledge with me.

Finally and not least I would like to thank Fiona Kennedy and all her team at Orion, as well as the sales and marketing departments, for all their hard work.

It seems to be a fashion among authors these days to thank absolutely everybody and everything; but I am truly grateful to all those mentioned. All have had an enormous input and impact on the writing of this book.

Please allow me one indulgence. Oscar, my dog, deserves a mention for all the hours he has sat beside me while I ticker-tacked away at my laptop, for his patience while I read the book aloud to him, for sacrificing walks when things were going well, and putting up with me when they were not. I am still waiting to hear what he thinks of *The Red Necklace*.

TURN THE PAGE FOR A PREVIEW
OF THE SEQUEL TO *THE RED NECKLACE*

the silver blade

Chapter One

Yann Margoza was dressed as a vagabond in an old greatcoat that had seen better days, with a muffler wrapped around his neck, and a hat that had equally lived life to the full. Only if you saw his dark eyes with their unmistakable intensity would you ever have recognized him. His companion, Didier, was a huge bear-like figure of a man. The two had one thing in common: They possessed the ability to merge almost unseen with their surroundings.

They had been on the road now for three days and, although it was March, they could still feel winter's bitter breath in the wind. By late afternoon, an eerie yellow light flooded the woodland path. Soon pitch-blackness descended, as if the sun had been snuffed out. Thunder trumpeted in the approaching storm, a furious call to arms. Lightning tore at the sky. Finally the heavens opened.

Didier once more had the feeling that had troubled him ever since leaving Paris three days previously: They were being followed.

"Listen," he said.

"It's the wind," replied Yann.

"It sounded more like the howl of a wolf to me."

Yann kept walking, not listening, not looking, thinking only of Sido. The thought of her weighed so heavily. He barely noticed how cold, footsore, and hungry he was. Or that Didier was right.

Sido, Sido. In his mind's eye he could see her oval face, her blue eyes, her mass of wavy dark hair. He knew there was no other road his heart would travel but the road that led to her.

His thoughts had been thus engaged ever since leaving Paris; a tangled knot of desires. His mind drifted again to their first meeting all those years ago, at the Marquis de Villeduval's château. A fateful night that had changed the course of both their lives. His employer, Topolain the magician, had been shot dead by Count Kalliovski, and in the space of a few hours he had not only met his greatest adversary, but a young girl destined to be his greatest love, the keeper of his soul.

Now Kalliovski was long dead and Sido free, safe in England. No harm could come to her there. Why then did he have this feeling of foreboding?

Keeping his distance, Balthazar looked for telltale signs that he was on the right track. Mere mortals can't see in the dark without the light of a full moon or a lantern to guide them, especially not on such a stormy night as this, but the young man in the vagabond coat was different. Like his master, he walked with an almost supernatural confidence, as if it were broad daylight. Balthazar watched his every move, could smell his blood, hear his heart beat, almost taste his flesh.

He longed to find his old voice. He had been robbed of it; the only sounds left to him were those of a wild beast. He gave a mournful howl as hunger for the young man overwhelmed him.

"I'm right, aren't I?" said Didier, water dripping miserably off the brim of his hat. "There is something out there."

"Let's just keep walking," Yann shouted above the scream of the wind.

Didier reassured himself with the sound of his footsteps. One-two, one-two, the rhythm comforted him. He thought back to the time when Yann, spiriting a prisoner out of La Force, had left a silver blade from a street peddler's toy guillotine suspended over the sleeping head of a corrupt corporal. The weasel-faced man, instead of keeping his foul mouth shut, had boasted to one and all that the next time the Silver Blade, as he called him, came into his prison he would have his guts for garters, so he would. Didier, even in this bitter wind and with a stomach like an empty larder, felt comforted thinking of it. The corporal's boasting had backfired. He was sent to fight and was never heard of again, while the Silver Blade became a legend, a name whispered on the lips of despairing men, a name that brought hope to a city where hope had been banished.

No one who had been lucky enough to see Yann Margoza perform as the Harlequin in Paris at the Circus of Follies would ever in a thousand years of Sundays have suspected that he led a double life. But that is exactly what he did. The theater was a smokescreen for an altogether more subversive operation, that of helping citizens escape from the guillotine. Every member of Monsieur Aulard's theater company played his or her part in this dangerous venture, all knowing that their lives depended on Yann's talent.

Their backers were two English bankers: Charles Cordell, who lived in Paris, and Henry Laxton, with whom Yann had spent three years in London when younger. It was due to Laxton that he had received the education of an English gentleman. Both men had immediately seen the potential in Yann, demonstrated by the near-impossible feat of snatching Sido de Villeduval from the carriage of Count Kalliovski. Neither doubted that Yann could save many more lives, for he possessed courage and an ability to hold his nerve, no matter the situation in which he found himself.

That on its own would not have been enough, but Yann was of Gypsy blood, and had unusual skills. He was able to read people's thoughts, and had a gift for making clients forget quite how they had ever come to be rescued in the first place. In this way, his identity had remained something of a mystery. Without Yann's talents, the whole enterprise would have amounted to nothing more than a barrelful of good intentions. But with him, it had proved to be one of the most efficient operations in Paris.

Têtu, the dwarf, and Citizen Aulard, the theater

manager, worked together behind the scenes. It was their job these days to make sure that Yann and Didier had everything they needed to make each assignment a success. And recently, with the rumors of impending massacres once more circulating in Paris, their workload had doubled, if not tripled.

Yann and Didier's business, this time in Normandy, was to arrange the escape of the Duc de Bourcy and his family. It had been Têtu's decision that they should not travel from Paris by coach or on horseback, for such things would be remembered and could prove fatal. Instead he had insisted for their own safety that they take a boat up the Seine into the heartland of Normandy and go the rest of the way on foot.

What Têtu hadn't reckoned on was the weather. Originally they were only meant to be gone for five days, three of which had already passed, and they were yet to arrive. The delay put their whole operation at risk, leaving poor Monsieur Aulard and the rest of the company to cover for the Harlequin's absence.

"Did you hear it? Did you?" asked Didier, desperate not to be the only one to have heard the low, menacing growl. "Wasn't it you who told me that a wolf at the beginning of a journey is bad luck?"

"No," said Yann. "Russian Gypsies believe it is a good omen."

"I hope to God they're right," said Didier.

Lightning flashed, illuminating everything with looking-glass sharpness. They were in an abandoned graveyard, filled with silver birch trees standing guardian over the crumbling tombstones and broken, wingless angels. In the middle were the skeletal remains of a church, its roof long gone, only three walls preventing it from total collapse.

Yann moved toward it, quickly followed by Didier. Both were glad at last to have some protection, feeble as it was, from the spiteful wind, which hissed and wheezed around the masonry.

Looking into the bleakness of that devil-dark night, Yann heard no wolf howl. He heard nothing but his own gallow's-bird thoughts.

Why hasn't Sido replied to my letter? Three weeks and not a word. Perhaps I misunderstood her. What did she write?

Oh Yann, I long for thee, she had written.

Come back to me.

No, I didn't misunderstand her. We have hidden nothing from each other. Nothing. Except I have never told her I'm a Gypsy. I will when the time is right. Now I have told her what I should have told her ages ago, that I love her.

In the dark of the forest, in the light of his imagination, he pictured Sido as they had stood alone in the garden two years before, the smell of sea and autumn in the air, that moment when he had kissed her and held her. Why hadn't he had the courage to tell her then he loved her? Instead he had given her his precious talisman to wear, an amulet, the *baro seroeske sharkuni*, the shell of the shells. She had held it in her hands and brought it to her lips as he turned and walked away. She had whispered into it and he heard her words, soft as the waves kissing the seashore. Even then he could have changed everything. Why hadn't he? It was simple: He had wanted to earn her love, to prove, despite his Gypsy blood, that he was worthy of her.

It was after they had parted that he had started writing to her, frightened he might have lost her altogether. Soon their letters, dangerous as they were, became their lifeline, each more poignant, yet still skimming over what they longed to say. The last one he had received three weeks ago.

Why do I torment myself? I am a tightrope walker

over the Valley of Death. If I lose my balance I am lost. Sido's feet are on the ground. She owns all her tomorrows, has all her years to be arranged. A suitable husband, children. She lives in another country. Her time is measured by another clock. Her life has longitude and latitude. Mine has only now. If I live to see the end of the Terror, I will be a fortunate man.

He hit his hand hard against the side of the building. Didier looked at him.

"Are you all right?"

"Yes," mumbled Yann.

I love her. What is wrong with that? Everything, and I know it. It will take more than a revolution before society smiles on a Gypsy marrying a marquis's daughter.

"Can you hear it now?" said Didier.

Hell, why haven't I been paying better attention? Didier is right. And a wolf at the beginning of a journey is not a good omen to French Gypsies.

"Yes," said Yann.

Didier had started shivering. "I don't like this place. It may sound daft, but my feet don't feel as though they're standing on solid ground."

Yann had the same feeling.

"Is it man or beast?" asked Didier, blowing into his mittened hands.

"I'm not sure."

Didier looked about nervously. "That's not like you," he whispered. "Can't you see none of those threads of light thingumajigs you always see?"

The threads of light, thought Yann. Of course. Why are there no threads of light? Even tables, chairs, have straight ones. Everything has threads of light . . . except the dead.

"Shh!" said Yann.

A twig snapped.

Didier stood stock-still, feeling the hairs prickle on the back of his neck. All around him was an endless, smothering, velvety blackness.

"It's something evil. I feel it," he whispered to Yann.

"It belongs to the darkness, not the light, that's all I know."

They walked through the graveyard, Didier clinging to Yann's coat, fearful of losing him. They passed the broken remains of a large dovecote and emerged in the formal gardens of a château. The rain turned to icy sleet as they made their way up the stone steps. On either side of the front door stood statues of roaring

lions, their mouths open, water dripping off their chiseled teeth.

Yann looked back the way they'd come. It was then
he heard her voice, caught on the wind's breath.

Run. The devil's own is on your trail.

He knew that voice, a ghost calling to him on a soulless night.

At that moment he saw it on the gravel drive—the
liquid black shape of a great dog or wolf. It stayed
watching him before finally moving into the shadow
of the gardens. Balthazar, thought Yann. Kalliovski's
dog. But that was impossible—for he, like his master,
was dead, killed by the mob on the Pont Neuf.

He shuddered, remembering what Têtu had told him:
That was the day the devil had gone walking, searching for one irredeemable soul to blow his fiery life into.
There could be no man more deserving of the devil's
attention than Count Kalliovski. If he was alive, then
no one was safe.

Sido was not safe.